just another meet CUTE

just another meet CUTE

JENN P. NGUYEN

Scholastic Inc.

Library of Congress Cataloging-in-Publication Data available

ISBN 978-1-339-01020-5

10 9 8 7 6 5 4 3 2 1 25 26 27 28 29

Printed in the U.S.A. 40

First printing 2025

Book design by Stephanie Yang

TO MY MOM,
THANK YOU FOR ALWAYS BEING THERE.
CON NHỚ MẸ.

1

Three hours and twenty-six minutes. That was exactly how long it took for this family reunion to make me go running into the woods like Bigfoot being chased off by the villagers. Although instead of running, I requested an Uber to Flint Rock Loop.

Squinting up at the beaming sun, I fumbled in my bag for my sunglasses. Luckily, it was still cool enough that I didn't instantly melt into a Nina puddle on the trail. Which was pretty rare for this time in the summer. Thank God for the freak cold front that blew through this past weekend.

Being a native Austinite, I knew that anything below ninety degrees was pretty much a miracle. This past year in Houston wasn't much different though. I pretty much traded in tangerines for mandarins when I moved.

Despite the nice weather, the park wasn't too crowded today. There were just a few lone hikers here and there—the hardcore ones with actual climbing boots and metal insulated water bottles hanging off their leather belts. They made my tiny cross-body purse and juice box look pathetic in comparison. At least I was wearing sneakers though. Thank goodness I left behind a pair in my aunt's hall coat closet before we moved from her house to Houston. They were a little dusty, but they still worked for my escape.

I felt kinda bad hiding out here. I mean, I love my family. I waited all year to see Aunt Sarah and my cousin, Linh, again. Being with them made me warm and happy. Finally, our family could be together again. The way it's supposed to be.

Too bad it never lasts. Once my aunt started complaining about David—I mean, Dad—she kept going. And going and going.

And going, like a bitter Energizer bunny.

Until finally, I had to leave before I accidentally blurted out something that would *really* get me grounded. Not to mention embarrassing the hell out of Mom.

So really, I was doing us both a favor for bolting. *You're welcome, Mom.*

I glanced at the map on my phone. A mile and a half in forty-five minutes with only another mile left in the trail. Not too bad. I could probably make it up there and back before grabbing a bubble tea at Tea Café before it closed. Maybe I'd even get the winter melon one for Mom so she wouldn't be too mad at me for ditching her.

With the extra boba and herbal jelly just in case she was *really* mad.

Resting one hand on the leaning tree, I took in a deep breath and soaked in the silence. All I could hear was the water rippling below me. An occasional bird chirping or squirrel rustling in the trees next to me, or at least what I hoped was just a squirrel and nothing bigger. Whatever it was, at least it was relatively quiet.

Finally.

My phone buzzed in my pocket interrupting my serene moment. I swallowed my groan. "Hey, Mom."

"Nina? Where are you?"

"Just—" I glanced around the empty trail. "Walking around. Getting some fresh air."

"Are you doing anything in an hour and a half?"

"Not really." Digging into my shorts pocket, a tube of Chapstick fell onto the ground and I had to stop it with my foot before it rolled down the path into the bushes. "Do you need something from the store?"

"Uh . . ." Mom cleared her throat loudly for so long that I instantly tensed up. "Your dad finished his seminar at Ole Miss, and he caught an early flight. Do you think you can pick him up from the airport in two hours?"

"Uh . . ." When I needed it the most, my brain drew a blank as I scrambled for an excuse *not* to pick Dad up.

"Nina . . ." Her warning tone was low but effective. "If you don't pick up your dad, then I'm going to tell your aunt the mysterious 'stomachache' you had that made you miss her murder mystery dinner last year was really binge-watching *Game of Thrones* for the fifth time."

Betrayal from my own flesh and blood.

"Fine, I'll get him. Text me his flight info."

"Thank you," she said brightly, like she didn't just blackmail me. "Love you."

"Love you, too."

And then there were a few more seconds of silence before she hung up. Like she wanted to say something else. Or maybe I wanted her to say she was joking and that *she* could pick him up herself after all. That this was a test and I passed with flying colors.

My relationship with Dad has always been . . . rocky. Like the steep cliffs on Rocky Mountain. Rocky like the old rocking chair in Bá's room that always felt like it's about to collapse beneath you. Rocky like . . . well, Rocky Balboa in the *Rocky* movies. Like he says, *The world ain't all sunshine and rainbows.*

Bá had been a huge fan of ol' Sly. I spent every Sunday watching his movie marathons with her. I could pretty much recite all his movies by heart from the time I was thirteen. Sometimes I turned on one of his movies in the background just to feel like my grandma was still around.

In a lot of ways, Stallone was considered family more than Dad was. Then again, Dad's only been around the last two years or so. And Mom and I may have moved to Houston a year ago to be closer to him, but that didn't mean I was any *closer to him*.

Which was why the *last* thing I wanted to do right now was to pick him up from the airport and spend the next twenty-five excruciating minutes making small talk about my summer reading or what movies were in theaters. I mean, it's not like we ever talked about anything important—like why he ditched Mom before I was born. Or why the hell he decided *now* to come back into our lives instead of staying with his other family. And, most importantly, whether he was planning to do that to us.

After all, he already left his other kids once. What made me special enough to keep him around when it's just me?

Sometimes I wondered if Lucy and Adam even saw it coming. Or maybe he disappeared from their lives just as quickly as he appeared in ours. One second he's with them and *poof* he's with us now. Like a bad magic act. The Vanishing Dad.

Gah. I could already feel a throbbing headache popping up. Rubbing my head between both hands, I sat down on a nearby rock. Hard.

And immediately felt something cold and wet beneath my butt. I sprang upright, but the back of my shorts was already completely soaked. Trickles of something sticky ran down the back of my thighs and into my socks.

"What the hell?!"

The light fruity scent was a dead giveaway. I flipped open my purse. The half-empty juice box was busted on one end. There was a strange yellowish stain on the white satin lining of the bag that matched the back of my drenched shorts. Basically, it looked like I peed myself.

Definitely a bad day to wear white.

"God, could this day get any worse?" I half expected to hear thunder or something in response.

At least there wasn't anyone around. Thank goodness for small miracles. Tiny as it was. Hopefully I could get down the trail without bumping into anyone or twisting an ankle.

After dumping the rest of the juice out, I wiped my legs to get the extra liquid off and rubbed my sticky palms on the end of my T-shirt. My wet socks rubbed uncomfortably against my ankles, but there was nothing I could do about it now. Unless I could fashion a pair of shorts or something out of leaves. Even if I was that handy, I'm not sure I could pull off the Tarzan look.

Suddenly—and because apparently God thought today would be the perfect Screw with Nina Day—I saw someone coming up the narrow path, blocking my way. A guy with a backpack, maybe around my age, but I couldn't exactly be sure.

At first, I thought he was a mirage, since the sun in the background made his frame sort of glow like a Greek god. But sadly, no mirage. Just a full-fledged guy who became hotter the closer he got to me. Tall and lean, but I could tell by his fitted T-shirt that he had muscles on his arms. Not too many, just enough.

His baseball cap was pulled a little low over his face as he clutched at the straps of his black book bag. His dark hair was cut short around his ears, which stuck out a bit beneath his simple black-and-white baseball cap. A perfectly straight nose. His lower lip was a bit fuller than his top lip. When he was about five feet away, he glanced over at me and smiled. A cute, almost boyish, shy smile that was the tiniest bit lopsided. And he had a dimple in his right cheek. A freakin' dimple.

Yep, *definitely* hot and *definitely* my type. Double damn it. Why did I have to bump into him now?

Flustered, I stumbled backward into a huge rock jutting out in front of a couple of trees. My hands immediately sprang to my hair and smoothed the damp strands off my face. I didn't need a mirror to know that my face was probably super red though; the only trait I inherited from Mom. Instead of sweating like normal people, our faces got so red that we resembled an overripe tomato about to pop. But somehow, even with the lack of sweat, I still *smelled* sweaty.

Needless to say, guys always stayed away from me in gym class.

Oh God. Did I even remember to put on deodorant this morning?

I resisted the urge to sniff myself, but I had a feeling the answer was no, since I ran out of the house earlier. Yeah, probably not.

On second thought, now probably wasn't the best time to meet the love of my life. I adjusted the frames on my face and ducked my head a bit so my bangs fell over my eyes. I hunched over and froze like that would help me disappear into the trees.

Please let him pass me right up. Please . . .

At first, I thought that he really was going to walk right by, but at the very last second, he suddenly stopped in front of me.

Damn. Time for plan B.

I straightened my back and tried to look nonchalant, but flirty. Cool, but approachable. Sounds impossible, but I swear Linh perfected this look in middle school. I, however, could barely pull any looks.

Would it be too obvious if I leaned casually against the rock? Maybe even crossed my legs to make them look longer? Probably.

The Cute Guy cocked his head to the left and he pointed down at my knee. His dark brown eyes were wide with concern. "Are you okay? You're bleeding."

"I—what?" I glanced down at the blood dripping down my leg. A steady, straight ruby-red line from the top of my knee down to my ankle, staining my sock. The cut itself wasn't too bad or deep. Barely bigger than an inch or two. And it was the exact height of the rock beside me.

As soon as I spotted the blood though, the pain hit me like a bolt of lightning and I stumbled backward. "Damn it! Jeez, that—Owww . . ."

He reached out and grasped my elbow, so lightly that I barely felt his touch through my pain. "Why don't you sit down? I have a first aid kit in my bag that you can use."

"No, it's . . . it's okay." I shifted my weight to my other leg and sucked in my breath at the movement. I've never been able to deal with blood well. My gaze skimmed around as I looked everywhere—anywhere—but at the cut. "I don't want to bother you."

With a half smile, he clasped his hands together like he was praying. "Please? You'd be doing me a huge favor. The path is pretty long and this book bag will be *so* much lighter if you took a couple of Band-Aids off my hands."

Cute with a sense of humor. I guess it wouldn't hurt to hang out for another few minutes. And looking at him actually made the pain hurt less.

"Well, okay. Only because it would help *you* out," I said with an exaggerated sigh as I slowly sat on the rock. Wincing, I stretched out my leg toward him.

"You're a lifesaver." A full-on smile crossed his face as he pulled a small white first aid kit from the side pocket of his book bag. "My name's Ian, by the way."

"Nina."

He knelt down beside my bleeding leg and dug around in the box. "That's a pretty name."

"Thanks. It's short for Nina." After the words popped out of my mouth, I wanted to smack myself on the forehead for sounding so stupid.

Thankfully, Ian mistook my word vomit for humor or charm or something and laughed. He pulled a couple of wet wipes from a pack and cleaned my leg and cut as best as he could before shoving them into a small plastic bag. Then he spread some white ointment on the cut and unwrapped a couple of Band-Aids. His fingers were long and moved quickly, like this wasn't his first time. After he put two Band-Aids on my cut, he pressed the edges down to make sure it was firm.

This time I felt the warmth of his fingertips on my skin, and the goose bumps that rose on my arms in response.

Rubbing my arms to make them go away before he noticed, I gently stood up. "I'm okay now. Thanks."

"Are you sure? Your face still looks kind of red."

Embarrassed, I adjusted the sunglasses until they fell lower on my face, like a shield. "No, it's just—the sun. It's hot today."

He glanced up at the overcast sky. It was so thick with clouds that you could barely see the sun anywhere.

"It was sunny earlier," I said quickly. "Like scorching sunny."

"Yeah, Texas's weather is pretty unpredictable." Still crouched down, Ian leaned to the left to pack everything up. When he was done though, he still didn't immediately get up. Instead, Ian stared at something on the rock behind me. I followed his gaze and groaned out loud in horror. There was a dark butt-shaped smudge right where I had been sitting a few seconds ago.

With a puzzled expression, his eyes slid up and down my legs—which sounded way dirtier than it was. I almost wished it *was* dirty so at least I'd know he was thinking of me in a cute-girl-I'm-attracted-to way instead of a weirdo-girl-he-regretted-bumping-into way.

I knew the exact moment when my embarrassing situation clicked in his head. It was almost like his brown eyes cleared—as impossible as it was. My first instinct was to bury my face in my arms and flee, but my feet were frozen in one spot.

To my surprise, Ian didn't immediately run away. Instead, he stood up, still digging in his bag. His head ducked down until I couldn't see his face anymore. Especially as one hand messed with his hat, tugging it side to side. I could see that his ears were flaming red though. "Well, I think I have something else in here to help you with . . . that. If you—you need it."

"What do you—" I glanced down at my legs and his pink face. Until my eyes finally landed on the tampon and pad he held out in his hand.

Oh. My. God.

I didn't know how this could get even worse, but somehow it did.

My red cheeks nearly exploded with embarrassment as I shoved his hand away. "No. NO! I didn't—this isn't what you think it is. I just sat on my juice box."

"Your. Juice. Box."

Even though he only paused a second or two between each word, it felt like an hour. An eternity. Time had frozen. Melted into nothingness. And I never wanted to escape *so* badly. Like make a *Mission Impossible*–style roll off the cliff and dive into the stream below. It didn't even matter that I didn't know how to swim, my survival instinct could kick in.

Hopefully.

Since escape wasn't possible, again, I tried to play it cool.

With a loud cough, I swept my hair over my shoulders. "Band-Aids, pads, and tampons? You're like a walking pharmacy."

"Oh, yeah." Looking sheepish, Ian glanced down at his shoes. "My family likes to go hiking, and I have a bunch of older sisters who always make me hold their stuff for them. I also have some hair clips and Midol in here somewhere if you need them."

"I'm good. You're basically like their pack mule. That must be super embarrassing for you." At this point, I was so desperate to change the subject that random words were basically pouring out. Apparently random insulting words.

Not seeming to mind, he snorted. "Pack mule and errand boy. I have to go to the dry cleaners on Fifth Street this weekend to pick up a bunch of dresses for some Vegas bachelorette trip they're going to next month. And one really weird-colored bed sheet. I didn't really want to ask for details."

My lips pursed together in sympathy. "Well, at least you had a lot of siblings growing up. I'm an only child, so it was pretty boring sometimes. Actually, all the time."

"Really? Just you?"

"Well, I have a half sister and a half brother. Sort of. It's complicated." I shook my head. Why did I have to tell him that? "You don't want to know. But I do have a cousin who's like a sister to me."

"Well, sisters aren't too bad. But sometimes I wish I *could* be bored. You don't want to know about all the times they made me play dress-up with them growing up." His face was scrunched up like he was in pain from trying not to smile. "It's too traumatizing. I try to block it from my memory whenever I can."

Momentarily forgetting about my own embarrassment, I laughed. Probably harder than I should have. "Your secret's safe with me."

"Thanks." Ian unzipped his navy jacket and shrugged out of it. "Here, why don't you use this to cover yourself up?"

"Oh, no, I couldn't—"

His right dimple flashed at me and my stomach did a backflip. "Come on. I doubt you'll ever make it home if you have to walk backward the entire time. Plus, I don't have anything better than Band-Aids and gauze to patch you up if you *did* fall again."

"How do you know? I could be pretty awesome at backward walking," I said, wagging my finger at him. "I certainly can't be less graceful than walking normally."

"You do look like a girl with many talents." He leaned over and wrapped his jacket around my waist before tying the sleeves into a knot so it wouldn't fall off. This pulled me a little bit closer to him and our faces were barely a foot apart when he looked up.

Without realizing what I was doing, I reached out to fix his crooked cap. My hands lingered on the sides of his head and froze when I noticed him staring back at me.

With a nervous laugh, Ian rubbed the side of his neck with one hand and stepped back. "Maybe you could tell me about your other talents some—" A loud buzzing rang through the air before he could finish his sentence. With a sigh, he dug his phone out of the side pocket of his book bag. "Sorry, it's one of my sisters. You know, the bullies."

"Oh, go ahead."

He walked over to the trees and turned around. "Hello? What are you . . ."

This would be the perfect time to escape. I could just run like hell down the path and never look back. Pretend that this horrible hike was just another nightmare. I mean, this pretty much ranked right up there with the zombies and that freaky Chucky doll.

Before I could even take a step, this overwhelming reluctance to leave swept over me like a tidal wave. Despite the fact that I pretty much made the worst first impression ever and had a thousand and one reasons to get the heck out of here, I couldn't. Because there was one major reason to stay that overshadowed everything else. And just then he looked right at me and smiled. A slow smile that started at the corners of his lips and sparkled in his eyes. I swear, even my goose bumps had goose bumps by now.

Maybe the blood loss was finally making me loopy.

I had just sat down when Ian hung up and came back. He chewed on his lower lip and gave me an apologetic look. "Sorry, I have to go. An emergency came up with my family." Ian glanced back and forth between the phone in his hand and me. "Do—"

Before I could say anything, his phone rang again. Somehow it seemed louder and more urgent than before.

With an annoyed sigh, Ian gave me a small wave before racing down the path. His phone was already pressed against his ear as he disappeared around the corner. Gone almost as quickly as he had appeared.

"Bye, I guess." With a sigh, I kicked a rock and it ricocheted off a nearby tree. Guess there was nothing left for me to do but start my own slow trek back to the parking lot. Alone.

Funny how I came all the way out here to be by myself and now it just felt . . . lonely.

My phone buzzed in my back pocket. Probably Mom texting me with Dad's flight information. I fumbled with the oversized jacket around my waist before it suddenly hit me, and I stared at the jacket I was still wearing. Ian's jacket.

"Oh crap."

Racing down the path that he took as fast as I could, the cut on my leg stung with each step. I scanned the area around me, but it was too late. He was gone. Man, he was fast. He had left only a few minutes before me. How did he disappear so quickly? It's like he had a magical pumpkin carriage that whisked him away.

My fingers played with the soft sleeves, swinging the ends back and forth against each other, as I tried to figure out what to do. Of course, the nice—honest—thing to do was to return his jacket. But how? I should have gotten his number or something. Maybe he would come back once he realized he had left his jacket. Should I wait? But for how long?

He did say that his family hiked a lot. Maybe he would be back tomorrow. Or the day after that. I mean, technically, I was free all vacation anyway. If we bumped into each other again, then it would be fate. And this time, I'd be sure to be a little more glamorous and a lot less sticky.

Although was I really going to hang around the trail all day hoping to catch a glimpse of Ian again? Would that be considered low-level stalking? I wasn't sure I wanted to be *that* girl. No matter how cute he was. Or funny. Or—

My phone vibrated again like a wake-up call. I carefully draped the jacket over one arm as I read my messages and groaned. Apparently, the nice Texas weather also helped the pilot fly their planes faster because Dad had landed early. And now I was late picking him up, which would only make the car ride even more awkward.

Great.

Back to reality and life, I guess. No time for daydreaming about cute dimply boys who I was probably never going to see again.

2

"Rosemary or thyme?"

"Whatever you want." Barely listening to Linh, I hummed to myself as I scrolled through Instagram. My finger automatically clicked on Lucy's name in the search bar. Huh, she went skiing with her family a few weeks ago. The swirling, lush snow made her pictures look like a scenic postcard. Especially the one of her and Adam having a snowball fight. It was *almost* as adorable as the one where the entire family posed by the rocky fireplace.

The familiar pit in my stomach grew. Was it weird to be jealous of someone you've never met? Probably. I don't even know exactly what I was jealous of. Their picturesque family. The carefree joy on their faces. How gorgeous Lucy looked. I mean, we both had the same shade of dark brown hair like Dad, but why was hers in perfect curls while mine was wavy and slightly flat on the top like wilted lettuce?

And seriously, where did they even find snow in the summer?

My head jerked back when Linh shoved a spoonful of something thick and creamy at me. "What is this?"

"Mushroom and kale risotto." Her hand followed me back and forth as I dodged her attempts to force-feed me. "Something is missing, but I can't figure it out. Just try it for me. I need your golden tongue."

"You know it sort of sounds dirty when you call it that."

"Only if you have a dirty mind. What are you doing anyway?"

Snap! I quickly shut the laptop. "Nothing."

Pursing her lips, she eyed me suspiciously. In case she decided to lunge for it, I gave her a wide smile as my right hand subtly pushed the laptop away.

Linh and I never really had secrets growing up. She was more like a sister than a cousin. Before Dad came back into our lives, we shared a room for over fourteen years, so it's not like we were able to keep anything from each other anyway. We even got our first periods around the same time, even though she was nearly a year younger than me.

But I couldn't tell her the truth now. I mean, what was I going to say? "Oh, I'm cyberstalking my half sister who doesn't even know that I exist. No biggie. Want some chips?"

Even I knew that made me sound . . . a bit loony. Like Batman Joker loony.

"Give me that spoon again." I sniffed the risotto a few times before I stuck it in my mouth, chewing slowly. "It's not bad. Could probably use a few more minutes on the stove. And maybe a different type of mushroom? Something that doesn't blend in as much . . ."

"I used regular mushrooms, but I could get some portobello or porcini mushrooms next time." With one hand on the counter, she leaned in to stare at me intently. "What else?"

"I don't know." I scratched the top of my head. "Maybe lemon or something?"

Linh clapped her hands together. Her eyes were so wide in excitement that they dwarfed her face, like an anime character. "Lemon! Yes! So it could have some freshness to it. That's exactly what it needs to break up the heaviness. Brilliant."

With a wry grin, I handed her back the spoon. "Glad to be of help."

"I'm so glad that you're here. Mom can't help with any of my recipes. She always tells me to add fish sauce. For someone who doesn't know how to cook Vietnamese food, she sure puts fish sauce in everything."

"Sometimes it does work. I mean, the spaghetti with fish sauce the other night wasn't *that* bad," I teased.

"Don't remind me." Shuddering to herself, Linh waved the creamy ladle in my direction. "You're seriously going to have to move to New York with me someday. I need you as my muse if I'm going to work at a Michelin-starred restaurant. Think of all the Broadway shows we could see and bagels we could eat. Think of the dim sum and ramen."

"Yeah, moving across the country to be your taste tester isn't exactly my career goal."

"Well, it's not like you have an actual career goal anyway."

Ouch.

I would have been annoyed if anyone else had said that, but I knew that Linh wasn't being intentionally mean. She was just being her brutally honest self, and sadly it *was* the truth. I didn't have a career goal. I didn't even have an interest in *anything*. There were plenty of things that I liked or was semi-good at, but nothing that I was *great* at. And definitely nothing that I wanted to do for the rest of my life.

To be honest, I was a little jealous that Linh had a passion that consumed her. All I had were a bunch of interests that fizzled out. While Linh spent her allowance on cookware and ingredients, I splurged on all kinds of books and beginner class fees for random stuff. Countless hours were wasted on YouTube tutorials and reading articles on everything and anything, but nothing sparked me.

If only I could major in random facts in college, then all my problems would be solved. Useless Information 101. I'd probably make the dean's list.

The funny thing was that it wasn't such a problem before. One minute I was a junior and too young to understand "adult stuff." Then suddenly this summer—the summer before senior year—careers and college majors were all anyone ever seemed to talk about. It even trumped prom. And the question of what to do next hovered over me like an invisible gloomy cloud.

"You're going to have to learn how to survive without me." I smirked. "Besides, what if you get on *Top Chef*? I can't go on the show with you and be your crutch. What will Tom think?"

She let out a sigh. "That's true. I can't disappoint him."

Linh fangirled about the host on *Top Chef*, Tom Colicchio, like I fangirled about any of the Chrises from the *Avengers*. (And seriously, I mean, *any* of them.)

But she didn't have the "golden tongue" like she claimed I did. I couldn't cook at all, but for some reason I had a really strong sense of taste. I could figure out the different ingredients for dishes when we went out to eat and always knew what was missing. I was like the rat in *Ratatouille*, minus the actual cooking talent.

Maybe that could be a career choice. Didn't royalty need taste testers anymore?

Humming one of the theme songs from the latest Korean drama we watched together last week, Mom popped into the kitchen. She wandered over to the stove and peered into the pot. "That smells delicious, Linh."

"Thanks, Dí, it should be ready in a few minutes."

"Your mom is so lucky that you can cook. Especially since she can't cook at all."

"Aunt Sarah can cook a little bit," I pointed out.

Technically, I should have called her Bác, since Aunt Sarah was Mom's older sister, but she forbade me to call her that. She said it made her feel too old. And I couldn't call her Dí, since that was reserved for younger siblings. So Aunt Sarah it was.

"Reheating stuff isn't considered cooking." Mom leaned onto Linh's shoulder and wiggled her eyebrows. "You forget that I grew up with her. She may be older than me, but I did most of the cooking with your Bá. Thankfully she's good at washing dishes."

"You forget that I *still* live with her, so I can't really agree with you if I want to survive," Linh quipped with a grin. "But we all know who really cooks around here."

As they both laughed, I was struck by how alike they looked. For some reason, Linh looked more like Mom than Aunt Sarah. Growing up, everyone thought that Mom and Linh were mother and daughter, and that I was just the neighbor's kid who came over to play every day.

Not that I could blame them. Their dark brown eyes were the same color and round shape. They were both tall with dark hair and fair skin. Although now Linh's hair had medium caramel highlights running through it from the salon.

I had dark eyes and hair, too, but my hair was wavy rather than straight, like theirs was. And my eyes were a tad lighter. Once I found a paint color that was my exact eye color, called Magnolia Elemental. Not sure what any of those words has to do with an *actual* color shade, but it made me feel better about having boring brown eyes.

I always knew I looked different from everyone in the family. In fact, I barely looked Asian at all. I just looked . . . average? Like me. It wasn't until I met Dad that I realized that I didn't look like me, I looked like *him*. This total stranger and me. My face was narrow with a pointed chin like his. I tanned easily like he did. I even suspected that I had wide feet like him, although I never really checked out his feet so I wasn't 100 percent positive about that.

With one last pat on Linh's head, Mom straightened up. "Well, I'll go set the table then so you won't get into trouble. Nina, can you help me?"

"Sure." Sliding my laptop back into my bag, I jumped off my seat.

Mom grabbed some plates from the lower cabinet and handed them to me. "I've been wondering . . . does that trail you went hiking at have a camping site?"

"I don't think so. Why?"

"I thought it would be nice if we could all go camping this weekend." Avoiding my eyes, she concentrated on gathering her dark hair into a perfect bun like her life depended on it. "It'll be fun."

I stared at her. "Fun. Our entire family. Camping."

She had to be joking. The only thing worse than being stuck at home with my family was being stuck with them in the *woods*. Even now, I could barely hear Mom over Aunt Sarah and Dad fighting in the living room next to us. I don't even know what they were arguing about this time: the weather, what to watch on TV, what water to drink. It didn't matter. She always found something to complain about with Dad. Always.

From the way they were going at it right now, you would have thought that Dad had knocked up and abandoned her instead of Mom.

Thank God for earphones.

"I don't know, Mom. I don't think we—it's just I—"

Clunk! Suddenly, Linh dropped a plate of breadsticks between us. "Nina has a date this weekend."

Wait, what?

Mom and I both turned to stare at her.

"She does?" Mom asked with a frown. "With who?"

"Uh . . ."

Before I could say anything else, Linh nudged my arm. Hard. "With that guy she met during her hike yesterday. Ian? Remember? You were telling me about how he told you all about his sisters." Turning to fully face me, she wiggled her eyebrows and mouthed something.

"Right. Ian. I met him on the hike." Great, now I sounded like a parrot. My mind scrambled to find something else to say. "He's nice. Really nice."

Mom laughed. "Well, I'd hope so if you're going out with him. I guess this means that we can't go on a camping trip after all then."

Squealing inside, I let out a disappointing sigh that I was proud to say was halfway convincing. "Yeah, too bad."

"Oh, well. Some other time." She took the bread plate and headed toward the dining room. "But maybe you can bring Ian home. I'd like to meet this guy."

"Uh . . ." Shooting an alarmed look at Linh, I shook my head. "I don't know about that. It's just a casual date. Don't want to scare him off or anything."

"I promise we'll be on our best behavior. Invite him over next week. I'll tell your dad. I'll even try to cook something half as delicious as Linh's food."

"No, Mom, seriously, I couldn't—" I stopped short when she turned around and gave me The Look. I could only count a handful of times when she had given it to me before. Mostly since she and Dad started dating again. "I'll try."

Waiting until Mom left the kitchen, Linh gave me a half salute and a cheeky grin. "You're welcome, by the way."

Blinking rapidly, I gaped at her. "You're wel—why did you tell her that I had a date with Ian? I don't have a date. I don't even know the guy. And now they want to *meet* him."

She chewed on her lower lip. "Yeah, that is kind of a problem."

"It's a HUGE problem! A titanic, astronomical, gigantic problem." My palm hit my forehead with each word.

Linh's hand shot out and caught my wrist before I gave myself an even bigger headache. "All right, Ms. Thesaurus, maybe instead of showing off your vocabulary words from English class, you should focus on a solution."

"Like?"

"Like, didn't you say that you still had his jacket?"

"Yeah . . ." It took a couple seconds for it to sink in.

With a smirk, Linh switched off the stove and rubbed her hands against the side of her jeans. "I think that if you want your solution, you need to find Ian. And you better do it fast."

3

After Linh and I escaped the Dinner from Hell with our parents, we retreated back to her room. I grabbed Ian's jacket from the laundry heap in the corner while she flopped on bed. Her head was bent down as she fiddled with something on her phone.

There wasn't anything in the side pockets, but I could hear some jiggling when I shook the jacket. *Jackpot!* Pulling out a pair of keys in the inside pocket, I let out a happy sigh. "Thank God I didn't do the laundry this morning like I was planning to."

Without looking up, Linh raised a fist in the air. "Procrastination for the win. What did you find?"

"A couple keys with a dog key chain. A library card. A flash drive. And a card to . . . something." I squinted at the tiny, faded words on the tiny gray key fob. "At least we know he's a dog person."

"See? We're finding stuff out already." Finally done with whatever she was doing on her phone, Linh clapped and held her hands out. "I'll take the passes and you check out the flash drive. Maybe you'll find something useful on there."

"Like a phone number?"

"Right now, I'd settle for a whole name. But a phone number would be nice, too."

I unhooked the flash drive from the silver ring and tossed the keys to her. "Okay, so let's say this actually works. What's the plan? We track him down and drag him back to our house for dinner? 'Cause that's just weird."

"I think we'll figure it out once we find Mr. Unicorn. Minus the dragging."

"Mr. Unicorn?"

"A guy who carries around tampons and *isn't* grossed out by the thought of us having our periods every month?" Linh wrinkled her nose. "Sounds pretty mythical to me. I'm still not positive that he's *real*. I mean, if it wasn't for the jacket, I'd think you had a heat stroke and imagined him."

I couldn't help laughing even as I rolled my eyes. "Okay, that nickname is pretty perfect. Mostly because, like an actual unicorn, I'm positively certain it will be impossible for us to find him."

"Challenge accepted," she murmured, always having to have the last word in.

If I didn't love her so much . . .

Digging out my laptop, I stuck the flash drive into the USB slot. As I waited for it to load, I curled on the bench in Linh's reading nook. It used to be my closet growing up, but after I moved out, she took the door off, built a little bench, and put shelves on the wall. She even sewed a couple of velvet pillows to hide the fact that the bench was pretty crooked.

After we left, Linh could have taken over both closets or even moved into

Bá's old room, but she claimed that it was too much trouble to move. And it was easier to get dressed with her clothes all over the place. She was obviously lying, but I didn't call her out. For the same reason that I slept in her room instead of in Bá's empty room. It felt nice to have things back to normal. Even if it was just for a few weeks.

Linh flopped backward until her head was halfway off the bed. "By the way, how's it going with your dad? Are things any better?"

My eyes were glued to the colorful spinning circle on the screen. "Depends on what you mean by 'better.'"

"Guess that's a no then."

It's no secret that Dad and I weren't exactly pals. Not even pen pals who emailed once every couple of months to "check in." I mean, I just recently started calling him *Dad,* mainly because Mom's been nagging me about it since they got engaged.

It wasn't even that hard since that word literally didn't mean anything to me in the first place. It was just a word. One I've barely used my entire life. So I called him Dad, instead of David like Mom did. It didn't *mean* anything. Like *lollygag* or *malarkey.*

To be honest, part of the reason I didn't talk to Dad was because of how he completely abandoned his other family. One minute he was with them and now he was with us. Switched families as easily as switching to a different phone plan. And if he did it once, then he could easily do it again.

Wise ol' Sylvester Stallone once said that love is absolute loyalty. Everything can fade except loyalty. You can depend on loyal people. And I'm not sure Dad was one of them. So why should I bother trying to fit him into my life if he may be a temporary piece?

Plus, my life was fine the way it was without him. I wasn't missing out on anything. I had everything I needed. Everyone I needed. But he's here now, and Mom kept trying. And I do want to make her happy . . .

"I mean, it's not *better*, but it's also not worse? It's . . . complicated." My fingers drummed against the side of my laptop. "Like really complicated."

"Maybe things will get better later on, " Linh said with a hopeful grin.

"Like when your mom and my dad stop making snide comments to each other?" My face scrunched up for a minute and I shrugged. "Or, you know, when we get world peace."

"So, basically, never." She shook her head and turned back to her phone. "You make me glad that my deadbeat dad never tried to come back."

My eyebrow rose. "You act like your mom would ever *let* him come back."

"That's true. He is pretty much the source of her man hatred after all. The origin story." Linh shook her head. "Oh well, back to business."

When the flash drive finally loaded, I was surprised to see only a few files on it. A history paper on the Civil War. A PDF comic of *The Amazing Spider-Man*, Vol 1. And a folder that was labeled *Essays*. Only one file was on in it though and it was barely a page.

What are your strengths and weaknesses?

Family is something that I've always considered to be one of my biggest strengths. It's the one thing that makes me feel special. Different. They're the reason I'm able to strive to do my best. To push myself to go the extra mile. Coming from a huge family, they've been my identity for my entire life. They're my past and my present.

- homework nights at the kitchen table
- weekly hiking trips
- family vacations (specifically the road trip to Minnesota and Pennsylvania)

But are they my future?

If I'm completely honest, I feel like my family can also be considered my weakness. They can be my biggest cheerleaders, but they're also my crutch. I don't know how to be on my own. I mean, who am I without my family? What could I—How could I do anything on my own?

Yet somehow lately, even when I'm with them, I feel like I'm by myself. Alone. Like I don't belong anymore and now I'm forced to figure out who I am. Sometimes I'm afraid that—

I stopped reading mid-sentence. There were still a couple of paragraphs left, but I—I had to stop. This wasn't just an innocent college essay; it was something else. It was raw and personal. And *definitely* private. I felt like I was snooping in Ian's diary or something. Me. A complete stranger. I didn't even know his last name. I didn't have a right to know about his strengths and weaknesses and especially *not* his fears.

Yet somehow, his words felt so familiar to me. Having a family but feeling lost. Not knowing who you were and not belonging. I could understand that on so many levels.

Even when we moved to Houston to be near Dad, I couldn't jump into this little family that Mom wanted us to be in. No matter how much time passed or how hard she wanted for us to get along. It had been almost two years, and Dad and I still tiptoed around each other like we were strangers. Sometimes it could be so exhausting. All I wanted to do was go back home to Bá, Aunt Sarah, and Linh.

Yet now that I was finally here, things were different. And not in a good way. It wasn't just because Bá was gone or because everything in the house was still exactly the same. I knew every inch of this house, every creaking floorboard and scratch on the walls, but it didn't feel like *my* house anymore. It didn't feel the same. And I didn't know what I could do to fix it.

"Did you find anything?"

My eyes snapped back and forth between Linh's expectant face and the laptop. The essay was still open on the glowing screen, beckoning me to take another peek. I closed the screen and tugged the flash drive out of my laptop before I could be tempted to read anymore. "No, not really. Just a history paper and a Spider-Man comic."

"No name on the history paper?"

"Nope."

She let out a sigh. "Mr. Unicorn isn't making this very easy, is he?"

Letting out an identical sigh, but for altogether different reasons, I crossed my arms. "If it were easy to find people, private investigators would probably be out of a job, Sherlock."

"That's true. Okay, Nancy Drew, next step. I *could* ask my friend who works at the library to look up his information for us. See what books he checked out. When they would need to be returned. Maybe get his contact information." She tapped her chin with her index finger and frowned. "Although on second thought, maybe she won't tell me. Library privacy laws and all that."

"Well, getting arrested sure takes the fun out of everything."

"Yeah." Letting out a groan, she flopped onto her stomach and pressed her face into the bed sheet. Her words were muffled. "I love you, but I *think* I might have to draw the line at going to jail with you."

Grabbing my heart, I let out an exaggerated gasp. "I thought you wanted me to live with you. We could probably get bunk beds and be roomies for life! Think of all the quality time we'd be spending together. We could learn how to knit."

"Yeah, I'm going to pass." She tossed the keys at me. "But don't worry. I'm not just a pretty face. I already figured out that the key fob is for The Fitness Pack gym. I bet that's where Mr. Unicorn works out."

What? How did she—I gaped at her in surprise. "How did you figure that out?"

"Because I'm brilliant and awesome."

With a scoff, I let her preen for another minute or two before tossing a pillow at her face. "And . . . ?"

"And I know how to read." Dramatically tossing her hair back, she pointed at the key chain in my hand. "The key fob has the letters *TFP* on the bottom and the faded squiggles on the side? They're not squiggles. They're muscles."

Turning my head from side to side, I squinted at the little key fob. I *guess* it kind of looked like an arm flexing. Although I never in a million years would have figured that out on my own. I snapped the flash drive back onto the key chain. “Okay, so now we have to figure out which one.”

“Way ahead of you. There are only two Fitness Pack gyms in Austin. I bet he goes to the one by the mall on Century Oaks ’cause the other one is way across town.” Linh dropped her cell on her nightstand and crossed her arms. “So, what do you want to do now? Your call.”

What did I want to do?

An hour ago, I wasn’t even sure about finding Ian. I mean, he was super cute and I felt like we had a connection, but he was still just another guy.

But now . . . now I had so many more questions. I wanted to know more about him. More than what he wrote in the essay. If he had such a huge family, why did he feel so alone? What was he searching for? Who was he?

The curiosity to find out these answers was overwhelming. His words hit me deep in the gut. Now I felt like I *had* to find him again. Had to *see* him. And most importantly, I wanted to see if he found the answers to all his questions, because maybe that would help me find the answers to mine.

Plus, seeing his right dimple again wouldn’t hurt either.

I let out a deep breath and glanced down at the key chain in my hand. Specifically, the flash drive. My fist slowly closed around the flash drive, squeezing it tightly. “I think it’s time for us to hit the gym.”

4

Linh pressed a hand against the mall door when I tried to open it. "Okay, before we go in, I have to ask you a serious question." She squinted at me. "Are you wearing mascara?"

Cheeks flushing, I quickly turned away. I rubbed a finger against my lower lip in case she'd noticed the lip gloss I had on, too. "I don't know what you're talking about. So, are you coming in the gym with me or not?"

Narrowing her eyes, she finally released the door. "Of course I am! I came this far with you. I don't mind going into full-on stalker mode, too."

It took every ounce of willpower I had *not* to roll my eyes again. Despite her sarcasm, I knew she would come with me; she always did. Whether it was to get my ears pierced, my driver's license, or even to get my wisdom teeth pulled. Unfortunately, her undying loyalty came at a price, usually an unlimited supply of grumbling and sarcasm. With some free food thrown in.

Good thing we were already at the mall.

The sugary cinnamon smell swirled around us as soon as we walked in. My mouth automatically watered and I could already taste the pillowy goodness.

I wrapped my arm around her shoulders, which was pretty tough since she was 5′6″ and I was barely 5′1″ or 5′2″ if I teased my hair just right. I used to be the taller one, but Linh shot up over four inches in the past year and a half. "Good. But first we need to get a Cinnabon, because I've been craving one all week."

She snorted. "Only you would eat a huge snack before going to the gym."

"Not a whole one. You're splitting it with me." I gave her a big cheesy grin. "We're in this together."

"I was afraid of that," Linh said, shaking her head. "Fine, but you're buying and we're getting the caramel pecan one. With a taro bubble tea on the side. Extra egg pudding and no boba."

"Deal."

After our satisfying snack, we walked over to the gym and peeked in. It was pretty crowded for a Thursday afternoon. Or maybe this was the usual crowd for a weekday. I didn't really know. My idea of a fun afternoon was eating pizza or going go-kart racing. Certainly not sweating buckets on some machine.

One quick glance around and I could already see that Ian wasn't here. Unless he was in the locker room, but I was pretty sure I wasn't allowed to check in there. Images of a shirtless Ian popped in my mind, and my face immediately burned. I physically had to shake my head to focus.

"Okay, so what's the plan?" Linh whispered as she looked around, ducking her head a bit to hide behind me. Like that was even possible.

"Ummm . . ."

She rapped her knuckles against the side of my head. "You don't have a plan, do you?"

I really didn't. Up until this point, I was pretty much winging everything.

I cleared my throat. "I'm improvising. Unless you have something in mind?"

"I don't—"

"Hi, can I help you with something?"

We both squealed and jumped upright. Our heads smacked together like the Three Stooges. My hand grasped the doorframe so I wouldn't fall on my face.

"Are you all right?" A really tall guy in a blue polo shirt peered over at us from behind the counter. He looked about eighteen or so. A little bit on the nerdy side, with his black wire-rimmed glasses and tucked-in shirt. But a cool, chic type of nerd, like he didn't care what people thought.

"Hi!" Startled, I automatically waved aimlessly for a few seconds before realizing how stupid I looked. "We were—We were . . ."

My mind drew a blank until finally Linh stepped out from behind me. With a flirty grin, she swept her dark hair over her shoulder. "Hi, I'm Linh. And this is my cousin, Nina."

"I'm Todd." He barely took his eyes off her as he reached out to shake my hand. "So, what can I do for you, ladies?"

"I, uh, found this key fob outside. Some guy dropped it. Maybe you know him? His name is Ian. Dark hair. Asian. Probably a couple of inches shorter than you." *Incredibly good looking, with a smile that could melt you like a rocky road ice cream cone on a summer day*, I internally added.

"Uh, no, sorry. I don't think I know Ian. If you want, I could hold the gym fob if he comes looking for it." His hand reached out toward my hand, and I jerked away.

"Oh." I glanced down at the computer in front of Todd. "Do you want to check the computer first? To make sure that he belongs to *this* gym? I don't want to leave it here if he doesn't."

"I'm sure he does. That looks like one of our—"

"Could you check anyway?" My voice came out a little louder than I intended. I cleared my throat and smiled. "Please?"

Giving me a funny look, he let out a heavy sigh under his breath and held out his hand again. This time I surrendered the key fob and he shoved it under the computer scanner thingy before giving it back to me. I held my breath until it beeped. It took ages, like time had slowed down. Finally, a profile flashed on the screen. Tiptoeing forward, I peered over Todd's shoulder.

There he was. Ryan Nguyen.

Wait a second . . .

I leaned in closer to squint at the blurry ID picture on the screen to check again. His hair was a little bit longer, but the smile and the eyes were exactly the same. And the dimple.

My mind raced through our short conversation from the other day, but I was certain that he said his name was Ian. Almost certain. 'Course, looking at his gym profile now, I couldn't be 100 percent positive . . .

"Excuse me?"

"Hmm?" I glanced up at Todd's frowning face. He waved both hands at me to back up and I realized that I was practically draped over his shoulder.

Cheeks flushing, I jumped back behind the counter and grabbed Linh's arm. "Oh, sorry. I was—Uh, Linh, didn't you need something?"

"What?"

"Remember?" My eyes flitted back and forth between Todd and the computer so many times I could feel my contacts sliding out of focus. "You wanted to check out the gym while we were here . . ."

Following my gaze, her face brightened and she nodded. "Yeah, I've been meaning to join one for a while. Do you think you could show me around?"

Todd rubbed the back of his neck. "I don't know. I'm supposed to watch the front. But if you want, I can get one of the trainers for you."

"Oh, I assumed that you were a trainer because you're so . . ." Linh trailed off and leaned against the side of the counter toward him. Her fingertips tapped against the surface as she pouted. If anyone else did this, it would have looked totally obvious. But Linh's wide eyes and slightly rounded cheeks made her look sweet and innocent. Gorgeous, but still innocent. "Are you sure *you* can't show me around? I think I'd be more comfortable checking out the place . . . with you."

I almost laughed and blew our cover, but thankfully I hid it with a loud cough. It didn't matter though. I'm pretty sure I could have done a backflip and Todd wouldn't have noticed.

Looking flattered, he cleared his throat and adjusted his glasses with one hand before glancing around. Finally, he came out from around the counter. "I guess I could. Most of the people who come here on the weekdays are regulars. They know what to do. Did you want to join us, Nina?"

"Oh, no. I'm good." Trying not to be too offended at the relief on his face that I wasn't joining them, I pushed Linh toward him like an offering. "Go ahead and have fun. I'll stay here and wait for you to finish. Check my email or something."

She beamed. "Should we get started?"

As Todd walked toward her, I cheered silently to myself and got ready to pounce on the computer to get a better look at Ian—no, Ryan's—profile. But at the very last second—as though he knew what I was plotting—Todd leaned back and logged out. The screen instantly disappeared and was replaced with a screen saver of dogs playing in the park.

Crap.

I waited until they left before leaning across the counter to poke the computer mouse. The user login screen popped up. *Double crap.*

Now what?

Before I could figure out plan B on how to hack into the computer, a bell rang out over my head and a group of overly buffed guys came in. They were so busy nudging each other and laughing that they almost ran right into me, still draped over the counter.

The tallest one gave me an odd look. "Are you okay?"

My mind raced. "Of course. There was just a smudge or something here." Smiling awkwardly at them, I dusted off the edge of the counter with my hand before backing away from the front desk. "Oh, darn, I'm already late for my workout with . . ."

Before any of them could say anything, I raced across the room and turned around the first corner I saw. In one swift movement, I plopped myself down on the first machine I could reach and tried to blend in. Thank God, leggings were usually part of my everyday outfit, so I didn't stand out *too* much.

Heart racing a mile a minute, my arms gripped the handles of the machine. Even though I wasn't exactly sure what the machine I was sitting at was for, I knew it had something to do with legs. I attempted to push it forward with my feet, but it only moved up a few inches before slamming back down with a loud clang.

People turned to stare. I ducked my head to avoid their eyes.

"Uh, excuse me, are you using this machine?"

My head whipped around so quickly that I swear my neck made a loud crack. It instantly began to throb. "Sorry, what?"

A guy around my age leaned over from the machine next to me. His honey blond hair was cut close to his head, and I could almost see the beads of sweat on his scalp. He motioned at me again. "The machine. Are you still using it?"

"Oh. Oh!" I jumped up and wiped my hands against the side of my leggings. When did they get so sweaty? "Yeah, I'm done with . . . that. Be careful, it's heavy."

He flashed a half smile at me and sat down. "Thanks."

To my surprise, the guy began pushing the bar with one leg. Back and forth. Back and forth.

Realizing that I had been staring at him for at least a full minute like I was hypnotized, I coughed and turned away as my eyes scanned the gym. Where the was heck was Linh? Maybe I should escape without her. She's a big girl; she could probably find her way to the exit.

"I'm Mike, by the way," he said between huffs and puffs. "Did you just join this gym?"

I shifted my weight back and forth on my heels. "I'm checking it out. This is my first time here."

He dropped the weights with a loud clack. "Ah, I figured. I've been here for years and I've never seen you before."

"Hmm . . ." I started to inch away when suddenly it hit me. "Hey, do you know someone named Ia—I mean Ryan? Ryan Nguyen?"

"Ryan? Yeah, why?"

My eyes widened and I zoomed back next to him. "Is he here today? Or do you know if he's coming? I, uh, found his keys by the door and I wanted to return them." I even took out the keys from my bag to show him.

"Let me see." Kevin stood on the bench and scanned the gym.

I subtly wiped underneath my eyes in case my makeup smeared. Was it too obvious to check myself out on the wall of mirrors? *Screw it, I'm going to do it anyway*. That's what mirrors were for.

"No, I don't see him anywhere. Why don't you give me the keys and I'll return them to him the next time I see him?" Kevin suggested with an outstretched hand.

"Uh . . ." Unwilling to give up the only link I had, I clenched the key chain in my hand as my mind raced. "I'd rather give it to him myself. I mean, no offense, you look nice, but I don't really *know* you, so how do I know if you'll actually give Ryan back his keys?"

Kevin looked surprised as he hopped off the bench. "I guess that's true.

How about we give it to one of the trainers? You could trust them, right?" Without waiting for me to answer, he cupped both hands around his mouth. "Hey, Tim!"

A muscular blond guy in a dark green T-shirt about ten feet away looked up at him. He wasn't overly tall, but he had a chiseled face and a friendly, easygoing smile. "Hey, man, what's up?"

"Ryan left his keys at the gym. Do you mind giving them to him the next time he's here? Or maybe you could even call him to let him know you have them."

"Oh, no problem."

They both turned to look at me expectantly, and I groaned to myself. What was I supposed to do now? I didn't want to give him the keys, but it's not like I could run away with them. I mean, I *could*, but I probably wouldn't get very far with all these cute trainers and buff guys surrounding me.

Why did everyone here have to be so darn helpful?

With no other choice, I surrendered the keys to Tim. Or rather, I threw them at him.

Catching them with one hand, Tim shook the keys at us with a grin. "I'll let Ryan know that you guys found these for him."

"She's the one who found them . . ." Kevin turned back to look at me. "What did you say your name was?"

I froze. Uh-oh. I couldn't tell him my name. What if Ryan remembered me? Then he'd know that I didn't *really* find the keys at the gym. And that I lied. And that I tracked him down here. What—

Filled with panic, I backed into a bench with weights and banged my knee against the metal side.

With his forehead crinkled with concern, Tim took a step toward me. "Are you okay?"

Laughing a little too loudly, I waved him off as I continued to back away. "Yeah, I'm totally fine. It's . . . leg day. I guess the machines turned my legs into jelly. You know how it is. So, I forgot I have something to do and I'm late. Uh, bye!"

Turning around, I shot Linh a quick text that I was leaving and raced toward the exit. Painful needle pricks shot up and down my leg. I could already tell that I was going to get a major bruise.

Great. A giant bruise on one leg to go with the cut on my other leg. I've never been very graceful, but jeez, what was wrong with me these days?

A few minutes later, Linh caught up with me at the Starbucks kiosk.

Smiling from ear to ear, she whipped out her phone and waved it around. "Lucky for you, I got Todd's number. You know, in case we need to go back to the gym for something later on."

"For me, huh? How selfless of you."

"I know. Just call me Mother Teresa."

Shaking my head, I crossed my arms and leaned back in the armchair. "Well, that was all for nothing anyway. All I got was a name. Plus, I lost the keys."

She gaped at me. "How did you—"

"Don't ask."

"Well, okay. A name is all we need! A full one at least. So, what is it?"

Staring up at the ceiling, I let out a sigh. "Ryan Nguyen."

"But . . . I thought you said his name was Ian," she said slowly with a frown.

"Yeah, I thought so, too. I guess I was wrong."

"It's okay. We can do this. We have to look for his social media. He has to have something. Twitter. Instagram. Nguyen . . . Ryan Nguyen." Her tongue stuck out the corner of her mouth a bit as she typed on her cell phone. "God, why did he have to be a Nguyen though? There are literally thousands of them out there. I had four Nguyens in my sophomore class alone last year."

"You beat me. I had three." I held up three fingers like she was a kid who didn't know her numbers. "Besides, you never know. We could have been Nguyens, too, if Bá didn't get adopted when she was small."

"No, we would have been Trans. Bá told me herself a while back."

I rolled my eyes. "Like that would have been any better."

"It would have been. There were only two Trans in my class last year." She flopped back in her chair. The side of her shoe kicked against the leg of my chair. "I'll keep looking, but this might take a while."

As I watched Linh continue searching on her phone, her brows furrowed together. Something that she always swore would give her premature wrinkles someday. A pang of guilt hit me for stressing her out with my problems. Although this was kind of her fault, it still wasn't her mess to fix.

It was mine. And even though it seemed hopeless, there was still one thing that I haven't tried yet.

One last resort.

5

As the barista grabbed the different spices from the shelf overhead, she glanced over her shoulder and smiled. Her red ponytail bounced as she bobbed her head in time to the music in the background. "So, did you get a lot of writing done?"

"What?"

She shook something into the blender and pointed at the table I was sitting at. "I've noticed you sitting at the same spot with your laptop for the past couple of days, so I figured that you were a writer on a deadline or something. We get a lot of those in here."

"Oh, right." I glanced over my shoulder at the booth by the window and coughed nervously. "Yeah, I was writing . . . a novel. A romance novel."

"Nice. What's it about?"

My fingers twisted around the straps of my bag. "Hmm, a girl and a guy. Obviously. Who just met and fell in love within a day, but then they lose contact with each other, so she goes to find him in his hometown. You know, check out all the places he likes to go. That kind of stuff."

"Sounds interesting. Hope she finds him."

I forced myself to smile. "Yeah, I hope so."

After we hit a dead end at the gym, I knew I had one last resort to find Ryan, and that was the Golden Cleaners on Fifth Street. The one that he said he needed to pick up his sisters' stuff at this weekend.

So I basically camped out all day at the Coffee Bean across the street from the dry cleaners. Even got a nice cushy booth by the windows with a perfect view of the street. Basically, go full-on stalker mode, like Linh said. The only thing I was missing was my night vision goggles.

Finally, the barista slid the cup toward me. "I think there's a writer's group or something that meets at the library on Thursdays. If you want, I could ask around and pass them your email address or phone number."

"NO! No, I'm writing for fun. Nothing serious. It's not something I—" I cleared my throat and glanced down at my phone. "Oh, I have to go. Thanks for the drink. I mean, making the drink."

Before she could ask any more questions, I grabbed the cup, even though it was scorching hot, and rushed out of the coffee shop. A couple of burned fingers were a small, although painful, price to pay to avoid answering more uncomfortable questions.

If only I could avoid Mom and Dad just as easily.

"So, uh, how was your day, Nina?" Mom asked as she passed me the bread plate.

"It was okay."

"Just okay? What did you do?"

That was a hard question to answer. I stuffed a giant hunk of bread into my mouth so I wouldn't have to respond to her right away.

Two days. For the past two whole days, I'd been at the coffee shop, and all I had to show for it were a dozen solved sudoku puzzles, an impressively high score on Candy Crush, and enough coffee to last me a month. But no Ryan. So basically, it was all for nothing. At least I was able to rewatch my favorite movies on Netflix, otherwise, this whole weekend would have all been a total waste.

Finally, I swallowed. "Oh, I hung out in town. Walked around the mall. That kind of thing."

"By yourself?" Dad looked startled like even he was surprised by what he just said. He scratched at the stubble on his chin and looked away. "Not that there's anything wrong with hanging out alone. It's not . . . weird. You do whatever you want to do."

"Thanks, Dad."

The table got quiet again. So quiet that I almost wished that Aunt Sarah were here. She always knew how to steer the conversation. Or drop a bomb to completely change the subject. She and Linh had that in common.

Clearing my throat, I passed Dad the bread plate. "I know Linh had to work late today, but where's Aunt Sarah?"

"Oh, she had a meeting with the homeowners association tonight." Mom reached out to clasp each of our hands. Her fingers tightly held on. "I thought it would be nice to have dinner together. Just the three of us. Isn't it nice?"

What was she talking about? We always ate together. Even though Dad had his own place, he slept over practically every night and hung out on weekends. His other apartment was basically a giant storage unit that he left his stuff at.

As usual, Dad nodded. "Sure, honey."

She turned her expectant gaze toward me, so I offered her a weak smile that was *my* usual. "Sure. Nice." I struggled to tug my hand out of her tight grasp. "Uh, Mom? Could I have my hand back? I still need to finish eating."

"Sorry!" She dropped my hand like a heavy weight. "I am surprised that you're home for dinner, Nina. Didn't you have a date today?"

Oh, crap. I forgot that I told Mom that the date was today. After spending so much time at the coffee shop, I barely knew what day it was.

"Uh, we decided to go out next week instead. Ryan had a family thing." I jabbed at the carrots on my plate until they turned into mush. "It's not a big deal."

Mom nodded, but Dad leaned against the table with a frown. "I thought his name was Ian?" he asked. "I mean, that's what your mom told me."

Ducking my head, I shifted uncomfortably in my seat. "Uh, no. His name is Ryan. Maybe Mom heard me wrong. Or she didn't remember."

Dad still looked confused, but Mom waved her hand and laughed. "Ian. Ryan. It doesn't matter what his name is as long as your date goes well. And remember, you promised to bring him home sometime."

"Uh, right." My appetite was definitely gone now. I picked up my plate and stood up. "Can I go? I need to . . . call Ryan back."

Thankfully, she nodded. "Go ahead and leave the plates. Your dad and I will clean up."

Once I was safely in Linh's room, I let out a heavy sigh and sat down on the edge of her bed. My fingers poked at the lacy holes in her cream quilt.

To be honest, I hated lying to Mom. We used to be really close before Dad came back into our lives. Sometimes she would even sign me out of school early so that we could hang out. Whether it was spending the afternoon at the bookstore or going to the movies and staying for two or three of them. Sometimes we just went home to bake cookies and talk.

And she was so easy to talk to. She *understood* me, almost better than I understood myself, without any judgment. Back then Mom would have easily been the first person I told about Ryan. Heck, she would have been on her laptop next to Linh helping me track him down. Before Dad, we had each other.

Before Dad . . .

Sometimes I still couldn't understand how she adapted so quickly from our life with Aunt Sarah, Bá, and Linh to a life with Dad and me. How she could forget everything he did to her. To us. She just rewrote history and was happy. Because she was *really* happy.

Somehow.

And that was the only reason I went along with everything. Why I kept my mouth shut and smiled as, day by day, the two of us became the two of them. And I was left on the side like a forgotten, wilted side salad.

Maybe it was better this way. I'd be going to college soon (hopefully), and it'd be Mom and Dad together anyway. They'll retire to some beach condo where Mom can do yoga on the balcony during the sunrise. And they'll continue their traditional Friday date nights when they're not hanging out with their new neighbors.

And I'll be . . . well, I had no clue where I'd be or what I'd be doing. As usual. The uncertainty seemed extra heavy tonight. My stomach churned, and I didn't know if it was the usual nerves again or if I was hungry. Probably a bit of both. I didn't really eat much dinner.

Letting out a tired sigh as I pushed the doubts out of my mind, I shoved my laptop, charger, and noise-canceling earphones into my bag and set my alarm for seven a.m. The laundromat opened at eight, and I didn't want to risk missing Ryan tomorrow. He looked like the type of person who woke up early.

Honestly, I didn't really feel like going back to the coffee shop. I'd had so much coffee the past couple of days that it was practically seeping out of my pores by now. I could sweat caffeine instead of, well, sweat.

Just one more day left. Ryan was bound to be there tomorrow.

Hopefully.

6

As I watched the sun set over the trees behind the laundromat, I finally accepted defeat and shoved my laptop into my bag. I wasn't even sure what I was thinking. This was a horrible plan from the start. Like super senseless. Rash. Moronic. A half-baked plan.

I had time to work on a couple of crossword puzzles while I waited.

Even though this wasn't exactly a date, I felt like I had been stood up. Now all I wanted to do was drown my disappointment in a tub of red velvet ice cream.

Glancing around the partially empty street, I waited for the light to turn before I went to my parked car. Well, Linh's parked car.

Maybe I should tell Mom that Ryan stood me up. That was better than telling her the truth, and embarrassing enough that she and Dad probably won't ask any questions. Almost as embarrassing as the truth itself.

Why did I think this was going to work? I mean, it's not like my life was a plot in a cheesy romantic movie. Not even a Lifetime movie that premiered at eleven o'clock at night on a Wednesday or something. And believe me, I've seen a *lot* of those growing up. Mom and Aunt Sarah had traditional movie nights at least twice a month. Some weekends it was binging cop shows like *Law & Order*. Other days it was Lifetime movies. In November, it was always Hallmark Christmas movies. Those had an extra dose of cheesiness.

But movies were definitely not real life. I mean, just because Ryan said he was *planning* to come by didn't mean that he would. Maybe he was busy. Or maybe one of his other sisters came already. I didn't think to keep a lookout for them.

Digging into my bag for the keys, my arm bumped into someone standing next to me. "I'm so sorry, I—" My mouth flopped open and I blinked once. Twice. And then all I could do was gape because suddenly *there* he was right in front of me. Barely a foot away.

Ryan.

My hand flew to my mouth. "Oh my God, it's you!"

He glanced over at me, gave me a polite smile, and then . . . turned away.

Okay . . .

Over the past few days, I'd imagined a hundred scenarios of how we'd meet again. I'd look great, thanks to the additional hour of primping in the bathroom. Especially since Linh lent me her fancy makeup that she usually reserved for special occasions. And Ryan would look handsome and surprised, but extra excited to see me.

But now . . . okay, he was still handsome, but the excitement was a bit lacking. In fact, he barely seemed to notice me at all. Which was weird.

Tucking a strand of hair behind my ear, I glanced over at him out of the corner of my eye again. He bobbed his head and adjusted one of the earphones he was wearing. And he still. Didn't. Look. At. Me.

Should I say hi? Reintroduce myself again? Give up entirely? It seemed like such a waste of an entire week of searching only to give up with him a few feet away.

But I didn't have a plan for this. It's just . . . *how* could he not remember me? I thought we had a connection. Had *something*, at least. Did I imagine it? Maybe I wasn't as memorable as I hoped, but he still should have remembered *how* we met. At least that was pretty memorable, humiliating as it was.

Unless he was used to handing out tampons to girls every weekend.

My fingers slowly reached out to touch his sleeve. Inch by inch. A little shaky. Just when he was within reach, Ryan suddenly moved away.

For a split second, my heart stopped. I automatically backed up a few steps before realizing that Ryan had only moved because the light decided to turn green at the worst possible moment.

Seriously bad timing.

Still debating whether or not to follow him, I looked up at a loud honk. Followed by two shorter but equally loud honks. A navy car barreled down the street and weaved between two cars in front of it. It swerved a little into the left lane and didn't slow down, even though the light was red. Instead it shot straight at Ryan.

And he kept walking.

Oh my God.

OH. MY. GOD.

"Look out! Ryan!" I yelled out so loud that it felt like my lungs were about to burst, but he kept moving forward. What kind of song could he be listening to?

In a moment of panic, I lunged forward and shoved him out of the way. As I plunged to the ground, it almost felt like I was falling in slow motion. I didn't even have time to brace myself for the fall. Yet somehow, like in the movies, Ryan immediately turned in the air midway and caught me in his arms. There was a surprised look on his face as we both tumbled to the ground together. His hands and forearms cradled my head, but my elbow still scraped against the pavement and instantly stung.

Thankfully, the car swerved in the opposite direction and narrowly missed us. It barely slowed down before barreling down the next street. Tires squealed as it turned the corner.

My heart was pounding so loudly that it was practically ringing in my ears. It took a minute or two for me to realize that Ryan was talking and snapping his fingers in my face.

"Hey, are you okay?"

"Yeah . . . yeah, I'm fine." I pushed myself upright. My carefully styled hair flopped to the side. I shoved it off my face. "Wait, are *you* okay?"

He looked relieved and a little in awe. "I'm good, thanks to you."

We sat there for a few seconds or so awkwardly looking at each other before a car honked. Ryan coughed. "Uh, we should probably get out of the street."

"Oh crap." I jumped to my feet just as he held out his hands to me. It didn't hit me until I was already standing that I missed the opportunity to hold his hands and let him help me up.

Nice going, Nina.

He handed me my bag and held up the slightly smashed coffee cup. "Sorry I made you spill your drink. I could get you a new one if you want."

"Don't worry about it. I was done anyway." I slid the bag onto my shoulder. "So that car was crazy, huh? Should we call 911 or something about him?"

Ryan jabbed his thumb over his shoulder as we walked across the street. "Someone at the coffee shop saw what happened and called the cops already. You were kind of dazed, so you probably didn't hear them. But I think we should probably wait until the police come before we leave. In case they want to ask any questions or something."

I stopped in front of a bench. "So, we just wait here . . . together?"

"Unless you want to go inside the coffee shop?"

"No!" I cleared my throat and sat down. "No, I think I'd rather stay out here. Get some fresh air and clear my head. Calm down a little bit. I'm still a little shaky."

He nodded and sat down beside me. "Sounds like a good plan."

Things got quiet for the next few minutes as we sat on the bench together. Cars occasionally drove by, but all you could really hear were some birds and music from the coffee shop whenever someone opened the door.

Now that the adrenaline had died down and our lives were no longer in danger, I couldn't believe that I was finally sitting next to Ryan. I could reach out and poke him if I wanted to. (But I wouldn't because that would be so weird.) After being the only thing on my mind for days, I finally found him.

And he *still* didn't seem to recognize me.

Like he knew I was thinking about him, Ryan turned his head and gave me that adorable dimply smile that I'd been thinking about for days. "So, uh, before I forget, thanks for pushing me out of the way. And saving my life."

"That was just luck."

"No, it was super brave of you. The way you shoved me out of the way was like a superhero. Like Spider-Man or something. And not the flashy Spider-Man in the movies, but the ones in the comics like—"

I laughed. "You mean like in *The Amazing Spider-Man #334*, where he fights against the Sinister Six?"

Ryan's mouth dropped and he stared at me. "You—you read comics?"

Oops, I didn't mean to say that out loud. It slipped out.

Before I had surrendered the key chain to Tim, I had ended up giving in and reading and rereading Ryan's personal essay—short as it was—so many times that I practically had it memorized. But I also skimmed his report and the Spider-Man comic that was on the flash drive. Definitely not enough to carry on a conversation now though.

"I just know a few things." Rubbing the back of my neck, I finally noticed the scrape on my elbow. "Oww . . ."

Ryan blinked rapidly and dug in his pockets. "Oh no. Here I have some tissues."

"It's okay. It's not really bleeding or anything."

"Still, it probably hurts." He snapped his fingers and jumped to his feet. "I know, let me get you some ice. I'll be right back."

"Thanks."

The small thoughtful gesture reminded me so much of him taking care of me during the hike that I couldn't help but smile. He really was such a nice guy. One of the main reasons I wanted to see him again. I mean, yeah, he was still super cute, but it was his personality and kindness that drew me in.

When he got back with a bag of ice, I held it against my elbow. "Thanks."

"No problem."

"So, I have to ask." I leaned back against the bench and frowned at him. "What the hell were you listening to that you didn't notice the car? Or hear the yelling and car horns?"

"Oh." He blushed until practically the tips of his ears were pink. "It's stupid . . ."

"Come on. I'm dying to know." I put down the ice and made the X sign in front of my heart. "I promise I won't tell anyone."

Ryan grimaced and let out a sigh. "Okay, I was listening to this audiobook mystery. It's by E. Hahn, and it was almost at the end and . . . I guess I was so into it that I wasn't paying attention to anything else. Like I said, it's dumb."

I tried not to laugh since he looked so embarrassed. It was super hard though. "I get it. Mysteries are addicting. At least the good ones are. And it pulls you along until you're so invested that there's no choice but to get to the ending."

Ryan nodded eagerly. His dark hair flopped across his forehead. "Don't tell me that you're a mystery lover, too."

I tried to think of something witty but my mind was blank. So I just played it cool instead. "I like all sorts of books. But next time you should probably cross the street before you listen. To be on the safe side."

He let out a booming laugh. "Yeah. Just in case you're not around to save me again."

"That's a good idea." Enough with the small talk. I shifted my weight back and forth on the bench and let out a deep breath before I took the plunge. "Are you sure we've never met before? Because you look very familiar."

"No, I don't think so." His eyes flickered down to my empty coffee cup still on the seat between us. "Nina. That's a pretty name. Now I'm sure I would have remembered you."

Except he didn't.

Narrowing my eyes, I searched his face for something—anything—but he continued to give me a small polite smile.

Then two things hit me at once.

First, maybe he didn't recognize me because of my makeup. I mean, I was wearing more than I usually did. A lot more. I barely recognized myself when I looked in the mirror this morning. Plus, on my hike, I wore those huge sunglasses that covered half my face. And my hair was in a ponytail

Second, if he didn't remember me . . . then maybe this was my chance to make another first impression. A better one. Like WAY better. It wouldn't even be hard. I was already off to a pretty good start. This was practically the definition of a rom-com meet cute, one that would make it into the theaters.

I mean, sure, I planned the whole thing, but a meet cute was still a meet cute, right? And it's not like I planned the crazy car. That was a happy coincidence.

"So . . ."

I straightened on the bench. "Yes?"

Kicking his left foot at the sidewalk, Ryan jabbed a thumb over his shoulder. "I was thinking, after we talk to the police do you—do you want to get some ice cream with me? I know this place nearby that makes awesome homemade waffle cones. It's the least I could do, since you saved my life."

For a split second, as he gazed down at me with such an earnest expression on his face, a pang of guilt seeped into my gut. He was such a nice guy, both now and on the hike. He probably wouldn't mind if I told him the truth. After all, the more I lied to him now, the worse it was going to get.

But when I opened my mouth, nothing came out.

The thing is, it wasn't every day that I got a chance to rewrite history. Instead of being the weird girl he met on the hike who got injured and wet her pants, I could be the cool girl from the coffee shop. The one who knew about Spider-Man comics and liked mystery novels. The one who went around saving people and probably had her entire life planned out. And definitely didn't have any family issues. The girl I always wished I could be, at least for a little bit.

And this was something I was definitely going to take advantage of.

Plus, technically, I wasn't doing anything *wrong*. Not really. I was just tweaking our meet cute story a *teensy* bit. If *he* didn't remember me, then it wasn't really *my* fault.

I gave him a bright smile. "Make it a double scoop and you've got yourself a date."

7

"Nina, are you ready?"

"Yeah, pretty much. Thanks for dropping me—" I stopped short at the front door and let out an involuntary gasp. All I could do was blink at Linh and the huge brown dog next to her on the front step. A dog that was so fluffy that it resembled a giant teddy bear more than an actual dog. "What's that?"

She stooped down to scratch between its ears. The dog cocked its head to the side and nuzzled against her arm. "Nina, I want you to meet Chrissy. Chrissy, this is Nina."

I still didn't move. "Uh, hi. So, why—why exactly are you introducing me to Chrissy?"

"Well, you need to get to know each other before you go on your walk. Don't worry. I borrowed her from my neighbor for the entire day so you can take your time."

With a cough, I automatically took a few steps back. My fingers reached behind me to grasp the doorknob. "Excuse me? Who is taking what for a walk?"

Linh let out a heavy sigh. "Come on! We know that Ryan is a dog person because of the key chain he had. So, you can bring Chrissy along when you meet him at the park. Bond over your mutual love for canines. He'll fall in love with both her *and* you. Boom. You're dating by dinner time." She jumped to her feet and shoved the navy leash at me, or at least tried to. "It's the perfect plan."

"There's only one tiny problem that you left out." I held both hands up when she tried to hand me the leash again. "I'm allergic to dogs, and I'm pretty sure one whiff of that particular furball will make my face swell up in five seconds flat. And I doubt Ryan has any interest in dating a blowfish."

"Oh." She frowned. "I didn't know that."

"It was a recent revelation." *Thanks to Dad*, I quietly said to myself.

In one of his dozen ploys to win me over six months ago, he brought home an adorable corgi named Melanie. I'll admit, it actually started to work. Dad and I took her on walks and had a few conversations that weren't totally awkward. That was until we realized that my burning eyes and itchy face weren't because of the pollen outside or my new contacts. It was little Melanie.

The next day, she went straight to Mom's coworker, Heather, and our conversations disappeared right along with her.

Linh's disappointed face was so long that I stopped trying to get away for a second. "Well, maybe I could take some Benadryl or something. That might help."

"Won't it make you sleepy though?" Before I could answer, she snapped her fingers together. "Maybe some coffee will cancel out the effects of the medicine. Come on. We can pick some up from Starbucks on the way to the park."

"I'm not sure that's how it works, but we could try." Even though the thought of drinking coffee again made my stomach turn, I made one last ditch effort to get out of the plan. "Wait, do we even have any allergy medicine? Maybe *you* should take Chrissy—"

"Don't worry, we should have some Benadryl in the kitchen. Along with a box of Salonpas and a dozen tiny bottles of dầu xanh. You know, the green Eagle Brand oil that Bá loved."

With that decided, Linh tugged the dog down the porch steps, or at least tried to. It was pretty difficult, since Chrissy was gigantic—her head was practically at Linh's waist—and she clearly didn't feel like moving yet. "By the way, Chrissy called shotgun so you'll have to sit in the back. Don't worry, I cleared out the back seat for you already."

"Gee, thanks. Are you going to roll down the window for me, too?"

She winked. "Only if you're good."

This time I didn't even try to suppress my groan as I trekked back into the house to search through the medicine cabinet. As I rummaged through the stacks of various bottles, one thought kept looping over and over through my mind.

Ryan better be worth all this trouble.

Out of all the dogs in the world, Linh had to get me the happiest, fluffiest dog that *everyone* wanted to pet. On the *one* day I did not have time to be friendly.

It took nearly fifteen minutes for me to drag Chrissy across the park to meet Ryan. Not only did she stop to sniff every freaking flower along the way, but also people kept fawning and stopping to play with her. Kids, teens, adults. It didn't matter. Everyone loved this dog. Plus, they kept asking me questions about her breed and her age. And they wouldn't take "I don't know" for an answer.

At least the Benadryl seemed to be working. Twenty minutes in the car with her and I hadn't gotten itchy or puffed up yet. Thankfully, Linh wasn't joking about cracking a window for me, so the fresh air helped.

Finally, after saying goodbye to what felt like the hundredth person that afternoon, I spotted Ryan by the hot dog stand next to the fountain.

"Come on, Chrissy. Time to make him fall in love with us." I tugged on her leash until we were both practically running. Skidding to a stop about ten feet behind Ryan, I walked the rest of the way and tried not to look too eager.

Chrissy, on the other hand, didn't care about playing hard to get. I barely said hi before she nuzzled his leg and leaped up until her paws were all over his chest. To my horror, she left a couple of big ol' brown paw prints on his clean blue polo shirt.

"Oh my God! I'm so sorry!" I tugged on her leash. "Down, girl. Come on, down!"

Thankfully, Ryan just laughed, which only encouraged her. Woofing excitedly, she stretched up and licked his face a few more times before finally jumping down.

After I was sure that she wasn't going to pounce on him again, I rushed to his side. "I'm so, so sorry. Here, let me . . ."

My hands swept up and down the front of his shirt to get the dirt off. Even though I felt terrible, I couldn't help noticing how firm his chest was. I pressed down a little bit with my fingertips. Yep, definitely all muscle through the thin shirt. Those gym sessions must be REALLY worth it. Damn . . .

The hot dog guy coughed, and I realized that it looked like I was standing there stroking Ryan's chest like some kind of perv. I swear, even Chrissy was giving me The Look now. Like she hadn't been doing the same thing a minute ago.

And yet . . . I was still feeling him up.

My cheeks exploded with heat, and I yanked my hands back. "So, uh, what do you want to do?"

"We could walk around the park for a bit. There's a dog park not too far from here." Chuckling, Ryan nodded at Chrissy. "It looks like she has some pent-up energy to work off."

"She definitely does."

"You're a pretty girl." He reached down and scratched behind her left ear. She cocked her head to the side for him to get better access. "Although I usually like to get to know someone's name before I let them go to second base with me, but I think I'll let her be an exception."

I laughed. "Her name is Chrissy."

"Chrissy." Ryan nodded with satisfaction. "Now I feel better about being so easy."

Shaking with laughter now, I fell into step beside him and we started down one of the walking paths. It was a little narrow, like it was made for only one person. Every once in a while, the back of our arms or our hands would brush against each other—just for a second or so. And then again. And again.

Whenever this happened in the movies, the guy would always end up catching the girl's hand and holding it. In anticipation, I'd tense up every time Ryan brushed against me, but he still didn't make a move.

Maybe he wasn't a big movie person.

"So, it's obvious that you like dogs. Do you have any?" I asked to fill the silence.

Shaking his head, Ryan gave me a wistful half smile. "Not right now. I had a dog, Chance, for five years, but he died two years ago. It still makes me sad to think about him sometimes."

So much for bonding over our mutual love for dogs. I grimaced. "I'm sorry for bringing it up."

"It's okay. You didn't know. The funny thing is, he wasn't even mine at first. My mom brought him home for one of my siblings."

"One of your sisters?"

He stopped short. "How did you know I have sisters?"

Crap. "Uh, you mentioned them to me. The other night when we were waiting for the police. Remember?" I crossed my fingers, praying that he didn't.

"Oh, I guess that night is still a blur for me." His hand rubbed against the back of his neck. "But no. Chance was for my brother."

I tugged on the leash to get Chrissy to stop sniffing the flower. "I didn't know you had a brother."

"I didn't mention him? That's funny. We're pretty close—"

Before he could tell me exactly how close they actually were, Chrissy let out a low growl and sprinted off toward the trees. The leash flew out of my hand as she chased down a squirrel in the distance.

Ryan and I exchanged alarmed looks and raced after her. "Stop, Chrissy!"

"Come here, girl!"

Completely ignoring us, the sweet-tempered fluff ball became a fierce wolf as she charged at the poor squirrel like it was her mortal enemy. They both ran in circles as we got close to them.

Panting slightly, Ryan lunged forward to grab her leash. And missed. "Does she do this often?"

I tried to block her off on the other side, but she easily ran around me. Man, she was super fast. I whirled around and attempted to slow her down. "No clue. This is the first time I've ever walked her."

"Wait, what? Isn't she yours?"

"Not really. She's my cousin's neighbor's dog. I'm walking her as a favor." Something I was definitely never going to do again, I noted to myself with a heavy sigh.

Finally, the squirrel sprinted up a nearby tree and out of danger. All Chrissy could do was stand at the bottom of the tree trunk and bark furiously up at her.

Still breathless, I reached her side and grabbed the leash off the ground. "Bad dog!"

Within a blink of an eye, Chrissy transformed back into the sweet teddy bear. She wandered over to my side and let out a soft whine. Her nose rubbed against my leg. Despite the fact that I was super annoyed, I couldn't help petting the top of her head.

Ryan came up behind us. "Well, now she's sad. Poor girl. Luckily, the dog park is right up ahead. Maybe that will cheer her up."

"Okay."

Not sure if it was because of my impromptu chase or that the meds were finally kicking in, but I was suddenly exhausted. My head felt fuzzy and my legs were like Jell-O. It took all the energy I had just to shuffle my feet along the path to follow Ryan. I turned my head and hid a yawn with my hand. Twice.

Apparently, I wasn't very subtle, because he turned and gave me a concerned look. "You look a little tired. Do you need me to take you home?"

Fat chance. It took so much for this date to happen that I definitely wasn't letting it end now. I squared my shoulders and gave him a bright smile. "No, I'm fine. I'm a little tired from chasing Chrissy around. I'll be better after we sit down."

Once we were inside the gated dog park, Chrissy was practically bouncing with anticipation. Ryan stooped down to let her off her leash. Rubbing my eyes, I stumbled forward and sat on the bench nearby. When Chrissy was finally free, she ran off and he came over to sit next to me.

"So, do you have any sisters or brothers?" Ryan asked, angling his head in my direction.

"Well, I do have a half brother and half sister. Remember?"

"No, I don't think you've ever told me about them."

"Really? I could have sworn I did when we were—" I suddenly broke off as it hit me. I did tell him on the *hike.* Which he didn't remember. "Hmm, I do have a sister and brother, but I've never met them." I shook my head, not wanting to get into all my family drama on our first date. Didn't want to chase him away already. "It's a long story."

He laughed. "You seem to have a lot of those."

"You have no idea." Summoning up all the willpower I had, I tried to stifle another yawn. And failed again. "Sorry."

"It's fine. Are you sure you're okay?"

"I'm good." Or at least I hoped I was. Everything was starting to look a little blurry now.

This was definitely the last time I was ever going to listen to Linh again. Or take Benadryl. I didn't care how bad my allergies got.

My eyes fluttered heavily against my will. I leaned my back on the bench and slouched down an inch or two to get comfortable. "The sun's in my eyes. But I'm okay. It might help to close my eyes for a little bit though."

He sat back, too. "Okay, if you really think so."

I assured Ryan again that I was fine. Or at least I think I did. To be honest, I had no idea when or how it happened, but I passed out. Like one second I was looking at his handsome face, and the next I was conked out. Practically dead to the world. I don't even know how long I slept, but when I finally woke up, the sun was already behind the trees.

It took a little while for my head to clear. Like the pieces were still catching up in my mind. Slowly in small doses. Bit by bit. Dogs were barking in the distance. People were talking behind us. There was a fresh minty scent that surrounded my nose. Not like the trees or flowers. Just . . . fresh and clean. And my head was on something soft but slightly hard at the same time.

I finally opened my eyes only to realize my face was nestled against Ryan's shoulder.

Embarrassed, I pushed myself upright. "Sorry. How long was I asleep?"

He rubbed the arm I was laying on seconds ago. "Just a little over two hours."

No way. Two hours? I buried my face in my hands. "I can't believe I did that. I'm *so* sorry."

"It's okay. Really." He stretched his arms over his head and continued massaging his upper arm with his other hand.

I peeked up at him through my fingers. "Are *you* okay?"

Stopping, he grimaced. "Uh, yeah. My arm's kind of numb from being used as a pillow for so long. You seemed really tired, so I didn't want to move and wake you up."

I started to apologize again when my eyes zeroed in on something else on his shirt. Right where I was a few minutes ago. Oh. My. God. Was that a huge wet spot on his sleeve? My hand flew to my mouth, and I inwardly groaned at the drool I still felt on my chin. I swiped at it with the back of my hand.

That's it. This was officially going on record as the Worst Date Ever.

"I'm sorry about your shirt. And your arm. And . . . falling asleep on you." I winced. "Basically, everything that happened today."

He gave me the sweetest smile in response. "It's okay. My arm will survive. And I'm just hoping I'll be able to keep you awake next time."

My heart jumped. "Next time?"

Now it was his turn to look embarrassed. "Uh, unless you don't want to go out with me again. I didn't want to assume—"

Before Ryan could continue, I leaned against his shoulder—the same one that I drooled on—and gave him a quick kiss on the cheek. "Next time would be great. Although—"

Lacing his fingers through mine, he lightly kissed the top of my hand like he was a prince at a ball. His breath tickled my sensitive skin, and I swear I could feel the tingles straight down to my toes.

No wonder Cinderella fell for Prince Charming after only one dance.

"Sorry, you were saying?" he asked.

I let out my breath slowly to clear my head. "I was just saying that I probably won't bring Chrissy next time. She's kind of an attention-hogger."

Chuckling, Ryan gave me a wide dimply smile and tucked a strand of hair behind my right ear. "Deal."

8

Whistling under my breath, I browsed the aisles at T.J. Maxx with Linh as she debated over the practicality of spending sixty-five dollars on a bottle of luxury white truffle oil. On one hand, that could be a whole lot of mochi waffles or even a pair of cute sandals. On the other hand, she could use the truffle oil to experiment on brand-new recipes. Plus, it was 50 percent off. On and on she went about the pros and cons.

I knew what her decision would be before she even made it. I mean, this was the same girl who spent half her summer babysitting so she could buy the newest fancy Vitamix blender. And I swear, it was exactly the same as the old one except for a new button on the side.

"I could use it with my flatbread recipe. Or maybe the mushroom pizza with thyme . . ."

Barely listening to her rambling, I picked up a round little jar with a pearl sheen and a teal edge. It fit in the palm of my hand and would be perfect to hold Mom's scrunchies. They were all over the house, yet she always complained about never finding one. I could surprise her with it while we made dinner. It was our turn to cook tonight.

After I added it to the basket, my finger poked at a saltshaker in the shape of a turtle and giggled to myself.

Linh glanced over at me with a raised eyebrow. "Either that turtle told you the funniest joke or you're thinking about that hottie Ryan again."

"Maybe a little bit of both," I admitted with a sheepish smile. "He told me a joke about a turtle the other day. You should hear it from him."

"Don't know if I'll think it's as funny as you do. After all, I'm not in love with the guy."

After the Worst Date Ever ended up not being *too* bad, Ryan and I went on our second date to the movies a few days later. And that one was way better. This time, I actually stayed awake. Plus, he stopped by the house to meet everyone first. Not only did they not scare him off, but everyone *loved* him. Even Aunt Sarah and Dad were able to swallow their animosity for each other and be on their best behavior. Mom was already talking about how cute our prom pictures would look.

Everything was perfect. HE was perfect.

The only thing that *wasn't* perfect was the nagging guilt I felt for lying to him. It would be easier if I didn't like him so much. And if he wasn't so sweet. The nicer he was, the more the guilt grew and grew. Like Pinocchio's nose, and it poked at me all day long.

Stupid conscience.

But what were my choices? I could either tell the truth and possibly scare

Ryan away or keep everything to myself and hope my guilt wouldn't turn me into a nervous wreck.

Neither seemed very appealing to me.

"And now you're frowning again." Linh shook her head and put the bottle back onto the shelf. "I told you. Everything's fine. You're happy. Ryan's happy. Just let it go."

"I know, but—"

With a sigh, she covered my mouth with her hand to shut me up. "Look, you're not even doing anything wrong. He doesn't remember how you met, so you're not going to remind him. Technically that barely counts as a little fib."

I yanked her fingers away. "But he keeps talking about our meet cute and he thinks I'm this amazing person who saved his life and—"

"Uh, you *did* save his life. And you *are* amazing. Even if the way you met was staged, saving his life wasn't. So give yourself a break." Linh wiggled her eyebrows. "And next time he brings it up again, make out with him. I'm sure that will make him stop talking."

"Ha, you're full of great ideas."

"I know. It's a curse." She picked up the truffle oil bottle again and stuck it into the shopping cart. "Now I'm going to ring this up, and then we have to go straight home because I can't afford to shop for the rest of the week."

As Linh disappeared between the aisles, my phone buzzed in my pocket. "Hello?"

"Hey, what are you doing?" Ryan's warm voice over the phone already sounded like he was smiling.

My fingers traced the pastel porcelain plates and bowls on the shelf in front of me. "Just shopping with Linh. How about you?"

"I'm at home waiting to have lunch with my family. It's kind of a family tradition to eat phở together every Sunday."

"Aw, that sounds like a lot of fun."

He sighed loudly. "It's not. At least not with my family. But it's the price I have to pay to get my weekly dose of phở. Otherwise, my entire week is screwed up."

I laughed. "Well, we wouldn't want that to happen, would we?"

"Definitely not."

A low and muffled girl's voice called out over on his end. "Ryan, what are you—wait, are you on the phone with *her*?"

"Yes . . ."

"Let me—"

"No, you can't—"

There was a loud *thud* noise and then silence. "Hello? Ryan?"

"Hi, Nina!" The girl's voice was loud now and slightly high-pitched. "I'm Ryan's sister, Kathy."

"Uh, hi."

"I'm so glad to finally talk to you. Ryan's been going on and on about you since you two met." There was a distinct low groan in the background. "And I seriously mean on and on. The dude won't shut up about how awesome you are."

My cheeks instantly flushed from her gushing. "Thanks, I guess."

Kathy let out a gasp. "Why don't you come over to the house now? I have to meet the heroine who saved my dear Anh. I'll repay you with a homemade bowl of life-changing phở. It's only fair."

"I don't know if I should—"

"You know what? You're right. Our phở is better than saving Ryan's measly life. Oh well, you should still come over anyway. I'll text you our address!"

Before I could say no again, Ryan's voice came back on the phone. "I'm sorry about her. She can be so annoying sometimes. No, wait, all the time."

"Hey!"

I couldn't help laughing. "It's okay. She seems nice. I like her."

Ryan let out a heavy sigh. "You may change your mind once you meet her later . . . or another day. You really don't have to come over if you don't want to."

"Yes, you do!" Kathy piped up in the background.

"Would you shut—" There was some scuffling and muffled voices before his phone hung up on me.

Okay . . .

I waited another minute or two to see if Ryan would call me back, but he didn't. He did send me a text with a sad face and a tear though. Two seconds later, my phone buzzed again as I received another text. This time it was from an unknown number with an address with a ton of smiley emojis and exclamation points.

My finger fiddled with my phone as I debated what to do. Somehow, this felt like a sign. Like this was the perfect opportunity to come clean. I could go over to his house to return his jacket. Just be like, "This phở is delicious; by the way, remember this jacket? It's a funny story. It's yours, and I'm the girl from the hike. Surprise!"

Okay, maybe not *exactly* like that.

Still, maybe everything would turn out okay. I mean, Ryan would probably understand. After all, the fact that we had met before wasn't *that* big of a deal. Maybe he would even think it's funny.

As long as I didn't tell him *everything*, just enough to ease my guilt. The entire truth might be pushing it. Especially the gym stuff and three-day laundromat stakeout. Besides, like Linh said, stalking or not, I *did* save his life. I think I deserved to keep that little bit to myself as a reward.

Making my decision, I quickly texted Ryan that I'd be at his house in half an hour. "It should be okay. No, it *will* be okay," I muttered to myself.

Hopefully if I said that enough times, then it would end up being true.

No turning back now.

Letting out a deep breath to calm my jittery nerves, I carefully draped the navy jacket over one arm. Then I quickly rang the doorbell to Ryan's house before I could lose my nerve and bolt.

A pretty girl opened the door and beamed at me. "Hi! Are you Nina?"

"Yes . . ."

"I'm Kathy!" Reaching out, she grabbed my arm and tugged me to her side and into the house. "I'm so glad you came over!"

She was oozing with so much enthusiasm that I felt like I was obligated to show some excitement, too. I plastered a giant smile on my face. "I'm so excited to be here!"

"Come on. Everyone's in the kitchen."

As I followed a few steps behind her, I couldn't help thinking how amazing it was that Kathy looked exactly how I imagined her. She was a bit shorter than me—which was pretty unbelievable—and skinnier. She had Ryan's round eyes and broad smile, although she didn't have his left dimple. Her hair was a bit lighter than his, too, with honey-brown highlights. And she was so full of energy that she practically bounced with each step she took, like an overeager puppy that you wanted to cuddle even if you didn't like dogs. I couldn't help thinking that she and Chrissy would get along great together.

Ryan came down the stairs as I got to the living room. He leaned forward and gave me an awkward one-armed hug. "Sorry my little sister dragged you over here."

"It's okay. I wanted to come." I cleared my throat and fumbled with his jacket still in my arms. "Do—do you think we could talk for a bit? Alone?"

Kathy poked her head between us, breaking us apart. She looped her arm through mine and shoved Ryan behind her. "You can talk after phở. Come on. It's getting cold!"

Looking over my shoulder, I shot Ryan a look for help. He gave me a sheepish smile as Kathy dragged me through the living room. For such a petite girl, she had a really tight grip.

I guess it didn't hurt to push the conversation off a little longer.

Kathy finally let go of me as soon as we entered the kitchen. "Here we are!"

I stopped so suddenly that Ryan bumped into my back. He immediately apologized as his arm wrapped around my shoulders to steady me. I barely heard him, I was too busy staring at the twenty or so people who were crowded in the giant kitchen. And who were all currently staring right back at me.

"Uh, Ryan . . . ?"

"Yeah?"

With wide eyes, I pressed back against his side like he could hide me from all the curious glances. "Who are all these people?"

"I told you my family always has phở together on Sundays."

"Yeah, but I thought you just meant your *family*. Not like your *entire* family."

Looking confused, he glanced around the room before smacking his forehead with the palm of his hand. "I'm sorry, I'm so used to all of this being normal that I completely forgot to explain. My grandma usually cooks phở every Sunday, and all my uncles and aunts come over to eat it at our house because we have the biggest kitchen." He leaned down until his lips were inches from my ear. "You can still run off if you want," he muttered the last sentence under his breath. "I'll cover you."

Fat chance. Not with everyone's eyes glued on my every move.

Letting out a deep breath, I squared my shoulders. "No, I'm fine."

Ryan grinned down at me and squeezed my arm. "That's my girl."

Even though I was still fighting the urge to escape, my stomach fluttered at his words and they gave me the courage to take a couple of steps forward.

The kitchen was huge, but it felt smaller with all the people and tables squished in it. There were a total of three tables and a whole bunch of folding chairs. And they looked like they were sorted out according to age group. A nearly full table of adults was right by the stove. Behind it was a table of older teens and maybe a couple of women in their twenties. And the last table by the door was full of preteens and kids.

Kathy immediately grabbed two bowls by the stove and started scooping noodles into them with a pair of chopsticks. Behind her, I could see an assembly line of bowls and plates of veggies and meat all laid out on the counter.

"I would introduce you to everyone, but I'm sure you won't remember their names anyway. I'll take you to the most important person first." His hand slid down from my shoulders to lace his fingers through mine. Ryan nudged me toward the farthest table, where an old woman in a purple sweater and long skirt was sitting. "Nina, this beautiful lady right here is my grandma. Bá, this is Nina; she's my friend."

I shyly tucked a strand of hair behind my ear and kind of bobbed my head. "Chào Bá."

Her head jerked up to look at Ryan in surprise. "You teach her that?"

"Nope, she did that herself."

Before I could explain, she waved me forward with a smile, and I could see that she had the exact same dimple in her left cheek that Ryan had. "Come. You can sit here and eat with me."

My eyes flickered from the table full of prying adult eyes to the other tables full of teens and kids by the door. I inched a step toward the safer table. "Oh, it's okay. I can sit over there."

"No, you're a guest. You *have* to sit here," she said, patting the wooden seat right next to her. Her words were soft, but I could hear the steel command beneath it.

Trapped, I shot a pleading look at Ryan, but he laughed and picked up his bowl of phở from the other table. "It's true. Guests get to sit at the fancy table. But don't worry, I'll come over and keep you company. Since I'm such a gentleman."

Still at the stove, Kathy crossed her arms and scowled. "Don't be fooled. He's just using you as an excuse to sit at this table."

His grin stretched from ear to ear. "It's true. This is the only time I'll ever get promoted to sit at the adult table. It's mostly for my grandma, uncles, and aunts. I'm usually tossed in the back to fight for a bowl and chopsticks. And even then, I still have to stand in the corner to eat."

One of his younger cousins from the other table snorted. "Next time bring your own utensils if you want to eat. Or better yet, go somewhere else. There are plenty of seats at a restaurant. More food for the rest of us."

"Ha, I'm sure you would love that, Thi. Kicking me out of my own house." Ryan nudged my arm. "Stay away from her. She makes Kathy seem nice in comparison."

"I am nice!" Kathy complained as she put a steaming bowl right in front of me.

"Nice like a mountain lion," a boy cousin said with a booming laugh.

"Don't you start—"

Ignoring their fighting, Ryan's Bá waved me over. "Sit next to me, Liv."

Liv? I glanced behind me, but there was no one there.

Ryan coughed and gently touched her arm. "Bá, she's Nina, remember? Not Liv."

"Oh, sorry."

Wondering who Liv was, I sat in the chair next to his grandma. Ryan pointed at various people around the room to introduce them. It was a blur of names. A few of them stuck out to me though. An uncle named Tuan who was married to a Julie sat across from us. Ryan's two other sisters besides Kathy. Anh and someone else. A cousin named Kevin. Or was that his uncle?

And to make things even more confusing, there were a couple of people who looked exactly the same. Evidently twins ran in his family. There were at least three pairs, including twin aunts. One of them was named Riley, but I wasn't sure which one.

After Ryan went through everyone in the room, he immediately dug into his bowl. Everyone did, like there was some kind of silent signal to start. There was still some talking here and there, but it was mainly slurping noises all around the room.

Everyone except for an aunt (either Aunt Lily or Lila) who handed me a napkin with a gentle smile. "Have you eaten phở before?"

I picked up the hoisin and sriracha bottles on the side and squirted a bit into my bowl. "I love it, but I only get to eat it at the restaurants. Never at home like this. My family doesn't really know how to cook Vietnamese food."

She laughed. "Not many people do. I barely cook it at home, and we ARE Vietnamese."

"So is Nina," Ryan commented when he took a break from his food to breathe.

His aunt immediately looked confused, and I hurried to explain. "Well, my mom is. My dad isn't. And I look like him, so it can be confusing."

This was a conversation I had a lot growing up. How I was Asian but didn't actually look it. I don't know why it was so hard for some people to understand. It seemed simple enough to me. Once I even had a little grandma at a restaurant insist on speaking to me in broken English even though I ordered the food in Vietnamese.

Ryan's Bá looked interested. "Chaú biết tiếng việt?"

"Dạ vâng." I wish I could have continued the conversation, but I knew that my limited vocabulary wouldn't be able to keep up. Sheepishly, I held up two fingers an inch apart. "A little. I understand it pretty well, but not enough to talk a lot."

"You're still better than most of those kids over there," one of his uncles said with a pointed glance.

I thought Bá would be disappointed, but she laughed. "It's okay. Some is better than nothing."

This was the first time that anyone accepted it so easily. Accepted me.

My smile grew as I looked around. Sure, I was still super overwhelmed by everyone, but it felt . . . nice. Like, *really* nice. Almost like our old dinners back when we still lived with Bá, Aunt Sarah, and Linh. Not that we ever ate with this many people, but the arguments and the teasing. Everyone said and did whatever they wanted. The closeness. It was comfortable. Free.

Dinner with Mom and Dad was totally different. We talked. Or rather they did. Most of the time I didn't really have anything to say. Mom tried to include me, but it felt awkward and forced. Sometimes I stuffed myself as soon as I came home just to escape from dinner.

Ryan's Bá shook her head and tapped my bowl with the tip of her chopsticks. "How is it?"

"It's delicious! This isn't like the phở at the restaurants though," I said, pointing at the giant plate of bones and meat at the center of the table. "What do I do with that?"

"It's like *The Hunger Games*. Just grab whatever piece you can before someone else does," Kathy said as she bent over Aunt Lily/Lila and piled pieces of meat into her own bowl.

Ryan smacked his chopsticks against hers. "Hey, stick to the plate on your table."

"But you know there's nothing left over there once Ollie and Nathan get through with it."

"Too bad for you."

Narrowing her eyes, she stuck her tongue out at him and slumped back to her table. "Wait until you get demoted back to this table next week. I'm not leaving you anything."

"That's why I'm soaking it all in now," Ryan said with a laugh.

Ignoring her grandkids, Bá nodded at me. "Why is it different?"

"Well, the broth is definitely different," I added with a slurp.

Another aunt cocked her head in my direction. "How?"

"It's not as clear. But the taste is also richer and thicker . . ." I sipped another spoonful and racked my brain to figure out what was different. "And it tastes kind of smoky for some reason? I don't know. Maybe it's just me."

"Smoky?" Uncle Tuan let out a booming laugh. "I think you've been eating too much Texas barbecue."

I gave him a sheepish smile. "Maybe."

To my surprise, Bá shook her head and laughed. "She's better than all of you. How did you guess my secret?"

"Secret?"

She leaned toward me and placed her small hand on my arm. "I roast all the vegetables and herbs over an open flame until they're charred, to bring out the flavor before I simmer the broth overnight and all morning."

In awe, I blinked at her. "Oh, wow. And you do this *every* week?"

"It's a lot of work. But my family's worth it." Her eyes sparkled as she gave me a wink. "Sometimes."

A wave of nostalgia washed over me as she patted my arm and, for a split second, it was like I was sitting with my own Bá again. Not that they looked anything alike. My Bá was into bright colors and flashy jewelry, while Ryan's Bá was dressed in simple muted colors. But she had the same soothing grandma aura. Maybe it's a requirement to be a Bá. It was like biting into a warm donut: soft and pillowy with the right amount of sugar glaze to make you happy.

And I hadn't felt this way since my grandma died.

Resisting the urge to give her a huge hug, I flashed her a bright smile instead.

"I guess you are pretty good. Just for that, you deserve a prize." One of his other uncles stole a chunk of meat from the center plate—right out from under Ryan's chopsticks—and put it in my bowl. "Here."

Giggling at Ryan's indignant "Hey!" I broke off a piece of the tender meat and popped it into my mouth. "Thanks."

"At this rate, I might as well go sit in the corner again," Ryan complained with a mock scowl.

I shrugged innocently. "If you want. You'll definitely be missed though."

"Ouch. That's harsh." Uncle Tuan laughed and gave me a high five. "I like you. You get a permanent seat at this table from now on."

"I better leave before I get kicked out. I'm done anyway." With a deep sigh, Ryan stood up and walked behind my chair. "By the way, where did you get that jacket from?" he asked, pointing his chopsticks at the jacket draped on the back of my seat.

I almost choked on the mouthful of noodles I had just put in my mouth. It took a few minutes and a full glass of water to clear my throat enough to speak. My fingers played with the soft fabric for a second or two before picking it up. "Actually, I wanted to tell you—"

"It's funny. It looks exactly like the jacket that Ian lost last week," his sister, Anh, interrupted from the other table. "Remember when my car broke down on the highway and he had to come get me? Afterward, he rushed back to the hiking path to find the jacket."

Ryan laughed. "I don't know why. It's a plain navy jacket. I bet . . ."

I couldn't hear the rest of their conversation because there was a loud ringing in my ears when his sister said the name *Ian*. Surely, I heard her wrong. There was no way—it couldn't be, because there was no Ian. There was just Ryan.

I cleared my throat. "Who's Ian?"

"Ian, my twin brother."

. . .

Twin brother. Twin brother. TWIN BROTHER.

The words echoed over and over in my head but it took a while for them to sink in. Like I had downed a mango slushie way too fast and my brain was still fighting the cold to work properly.

But if Ian wasn't Ryan and Ryan was just Ryan, then that meant Ian actually existed. And if Ian existed then he was . . . he was . . .

Here.

As if I had conjured him by thinking his name too many times, a guy suddenly appeared at the doorway. Again, with the light behind him, like he was glowing. Still tall and lean like Ryan was, although now I could see that he was skinnier than his brother. He wasn't wearing a cap this time. His hair was obviously shorter than Ryan's and a bit darker. But the same eyes. The same perfectly straight nose. And even though he wasn't smiling, I had a feeling that his dimple would be on the right side of his cheek. Not on the left like Ryan's was.

Judging by the shocked look on Ian's face, there was no doubt that this was *my* Ian.

And that he definitely remembered me, too.

9

The urge to flee swept over my body, practically overwhelming me. I slumped down into my chair like my entire body was made of Jell-O—the cheap cafeteria brand that dissolved into liquid at the slightest touch. If I could, I would have slid underneath the table, too, but Ryan was still standing behind my chair, blocking my escape.

Thankfully, everyone else went back to eating their phở like everything was completely normal. Even though my heart was pounding in my chest a mile a minute, and my palms were sweaty. And it only got worse the longer Ian stared at me from across the room. My palms, not my heart. I'm pretty sure at this point my heart couldn't beat any faster without collapsing on me.

Why was it suddenly so hard to breathe? Like the air had gotten too thick. Was seventeen too young to have a panic attack?

"Ian!" Ryan's voice was so loud behind me that I visibly jumped in my chair. My fingers clenched the arms of the chair, pressing into the wooden grooves. "Come here, I want you to meet Nina."

Ian blinked once, twice, before tearing his gaze away from me to look at his twin. "Who?"

"You know, the girl who saved my life outside Golden Cleaners last week." Ryan's hands lightly touched both my shoulders. "Nina, this is my brother, Ian."

Oh God. I was wrong about my heart.

With each step that Ian took toward us, I could feel my heart beating louder and louder until it was ringing in my ears. Even though I knew it was pointless to hide now, I couldn't help trying anyway. I ducked my head a bit and tried to avoid looking straight at Ian's face. My gaze focused on his left ear instead. Specifically, his earlobe. "Hi."

"So, it's great to finally meet the girl who saved my brother's life." His low voice was a little hesitant. Like he could feel how awkward I was feeling. Maybe he was feeling it, too. ". . . Nina."

Pulled by an invisible string, I glanced up when he said my name. Low and slow. His dark eyebrows furrowed together, making his face scrunch up with unspoken questions. Ones that I couldn't answer without giving myself away. I quickly looked away again. "It really wasn't a big deal . . ."

One of Ryan's hands tightened on my shoulder as he scoffed. "Are you kidding me? I was crossing the street like a stupid idiot before you appeared out of nowhere to shove me out of the way. If it weren't for you, I'd probably be squished roadkill right now. Flat like a pancake."

Cheeks flushing, my left hand rose to rub at the back of my neck as I studied the lace tablecloth. The tiny rip at the corner of my hand. A hole beside it that was big enough to poke my finger through. I didn't test it though. Instead my fingers tugged at the jacket on my lap, stretching out the fabric on the sleeve. "I didn't appear out of nowhere. I happened to be standing right next to you when the accident happened. Total coincidence."

"Yeah, but that still makes him a stupid idiot for blindly crossing the street," Kathy said with a giggle. "But what else is new?"

Ignoring his sister, Ryan continued gushing. "Seriously, it's like fate knew that Nina *needed* to be there at that *exact* moment to save me. I mean, what if you weren't there? What if I didn't stop by to pick up Grace's stuff that Sunday? I wasn't supposed to. Ian was going to pick it up, but he was too busy. Like I said, fate."

"I didn't know the accident was in front of Golden Cleaners," Ian slowly commented. Each word rolled off his tongue, hitting me like arrows on a target. "You're right. *I* was the one who was supposed to be there. Me."

It wasn't what he said, but the way he said it that made warning bells ring in my mind. Something in his voice. Even as my brain was telling me to keep my head down—to not meet his gaze—I couldn't resist looking up at him.

To my surprise, Ian wasn't even looking at me. Not at first. He was staring at my hands—no, my lap. Specifically, the navy jacket on my lap.

His jacket.

My breath got caught in my throat as everyone stopped talking. Or maybe I stopped listening. Within seconds, I could practically see everything clicking into place like a puzzle. His forehead suddenly smoothed out and the frown lines disappeared. When Ian finally looked up at me, one of his eyebrows rose and he gave me a tiny smirk. There was a twinkle in his eyes that made my stomach leap into somersaults before dropping into a pit.

"I guess it is a *really* lucky coincidence that Nina was there at the right place. At *exactly* the right time."

Crap. He figured out everything.

The creamy sweet chè that Ryan's Bá offered me after phở felt like a lump of glue in my mouth. Crazy Gorilla Glue that wouldn't dissolve. And it didn't help that I could feel Ian's gaze on me from across the room the entire time.

But somehow—by some miracle—I was able to force half the bowl down my throat. Any other day and I would have inhaled the whole thing and asked for seconds.

Any day but today.

Finally, I made a bathroom escape before my nerves exploded into a thousand pieces all over the kitchen like a grenade. I ran out of there so quickly that I didn't realize I was still holding the navy jacket in my hands until I collapsed against the bathroom door.

I tossed it on the counter and dug my phone out of my pocket. I quickly sent Linh a 911 text to come get me as soon as possible with a dozen exclamation points. She promised to be nearby in case Ryan didn't take my confession well, but I wasn't sure where her idea of "nearby" was. For all I knew, she could be at home testing out her new truffle oil.

As I waited for her answer, I turned on the water faucet. I wanted to splash water on my face to calm down, but that would wash all my makeup off. All of

Linh's hard work. Although by now my face was so flushed that it didn't even make a difference. Still, I dabbed my cheeks lightly with a damp towel and fanned my face to cool down.

Breathing slowly and evenly, like Mom did during her yoga sessions, I tried to concentrate only on the flow of air between my lips. In and out. Deep breaths. One. Two.

Two. Like a set of twins.

My stomach churned, and I frantically fanned myself harder with both hands as I paced back and forth around the small bathroom. Ten steps to the right and back again.

Yeah, this wasn't working. I would have attempted the downward dog or sphinx pose to calm down, but now my wrist was starting to cramp up. Plus, I had a feeling that I had been in the bathroom way too long. I didn't need all the Nguyens to think I was weird.

One of them was enough.

Opening the door, I had taken only a step or two into the hall when I heard a low voice behind me.

"So, it's nice to see you again, Nina. Short for Nina."

I bumped into the doorway when I jumped backward. Pressing a hand against my slamming heart, I whirled around. "Oh my God! Why are you sneaking around like that?"

Ian snorted and pulled away from the wall he was leaning against. He made a big show about looking around. "Uh, I'm standing in the hall at my own house. I don't think that counts as 'sneaking around.'"

My eyes narrowed. "You just *happen* to be in the hall at the same time that I'm coming *out* of the bathroom?"

"Yeah." With both hands shoved in his jeans pocket, he cocked his head to the side and gave me a lopsided wide smile. "Call it a *coincidence*. Kind of like how you saved my identical twin brother."

Damn, he got me there. "Uh, about that. I was—"

Ian let out a low whistle. "Actually, there's been a whole lot of coincidences lately. I mean, Ryan was only picking up the dry cleaning for me because I had to go to the gym that day. Turns out they found his keys that I lost last week on a hike. Not sure how those keys ended up at the gym though, since I lost them *with* the jacket. The one you're holding now. Isn't that interesting?"

That shut me up.

The right corner of his mouth twitched like he knew I was trapped. And that darn right dimple popped out. Again. Taunting me.

Earlier it was obvious that Ian figured out that I deliberately went to the laundromat to find *him*. But I didn't think that he knew about the gym thing, too. Or that he would piece everything together so quickly.

Good God, was he Sherlock Holmes in his past life?

"Why did you have Ryan's keys with you?" I asked with lack of anything else to say.

"Because I left my keys at home. Well, at my other house with—"

"Other house? What other house?"

"At my dad's." He shook his head. "Wait, why are you asking me all these questions? I should be the one asking you the questions."

Damn. I thought I distracted him enough to make a quick getaway.

It was a tiny bit ironic that I spent days searching for Ian only to be running away from him now.

Okay, *really* ironic.

"Or . . . we could go back to the kitchen and hang out with everyone." Quickly I turned and tried to move away. "In fact, I think I should eat another bowl of your grandma's banana chè. She'll be sad if I don't."

Freedom was just a few steps from the end of the hall when Ian's arm shot out and hit the wall in front of me, blocking my escape. With one swift movement, I ducked under his arm—or at least tried to—but Ian grabbed the edge of the jacket that I was still holding to pull me back toward him. For a few seconds, we played tug-of-war before I realized what I was doing and released the jacket. He stumbled backward a few steps like it was a rubber band.

"You should take that back. It is yours after all."

To my surprise, Ian shook his head and handed the jacket back to me. "I can't. If I take it now then everyone will wonder why you had my jacket in the first place, and then your secret's out."

At his words, I stopped trying to escape and stared at him. My heart swelled with hope. "So does this mean you're not going to tell Ryan about . . . well, anything?"

He slowly shook his head, dousing my glimmer of hope with a bucket of ice water. "For now. I haven't decided how long I'm going to keep my mouth shut though. I think I might need a little more convincing before I decide." He turned away slightly, like he was about to walk away.

Gaping at his back with wide eyes, this time my hand shot out to block him. In desperation, I grabbed his wrist. "Wait, what do you mean by *convincing*?"

"I'm not sure yet." Ian leaned down until our noses were barely inches apart. His face was dead serious, but I could see the humor dancing in his dark brown eyes. "I'll let you know when I figure it out."

"But—you can't—I—" Why couldn't I get any words out? Frustrated with myself (but mainly at Ian), I pursed my lips together to keep myself from shouting at him. "God, you were so much nicer on the hiking trail."

To my surprise instead of giving me a sarcastic taunt, Ian looked down at our hands and shrugged. "Yeah, well, a lot of things are different now."

With an indrawn breath, I realized I was still tightly holding on to him. My fingertips wrapped around his wrist. And if he moved his hand slightly, he could touch me, too. But he didn't. I could feel his warm skin under my fingertips. The steady beating of his pulse. Each heartbeat like a tiny drum beneath my palm.

Dancing. Throbbing. Pounding.

I'm not sure how long we stood that way. It could have been a few seconds. It could have been forever. But for some reason, I didn't let go, and Ian didn't move away.

And that was how Ryan found us. His eyebrows crinkled together. "I was wondering what you were—what's going on?"

Just like that, we jumped apart. Ian swept his hand through his hair and coughed. For some reason, he looked extremely guilty. I'm sure both of us did. For a dozen different reasons.

But I was saved from having to say anything, because just then Linh texted me to say that she was down the street. "Oh, my ride's here. I should go tell everyone goodbye," I said a little too brightly as I moved toward the living room. *And now I can finally get the heck out of here.*

Ryan gave both of us another funny look. "I'll walk you outside."

Everyone was still sitting around or eating fruit when we got back to the kitchen. That is, when Ryan and I got back. Ian disappeared somewhere along the way. I gave their Bá a brief hug as she shoved a to-go box into my hands. Backing out of the room, I didn't remember everyone else's names, so my voice trailed off awkwardly at the end of my goodbyes.

Linh was pulling into the driveway when we got outside. I started down the walkway, but Ryan stopped me with a light touch on my elbow. "Sorry about my family. I know they can be a bit—well, they're a lot to take in."

"Oh, no, it's okay. I liked them. They're fun." With the exception of an annoying twin brother, that is.

He rolled his eyes. "You don't have to be nice. They can't hear you from out here."

"You're right. They're crazy," I joked. "But your grandma's phở was so life-changing that it almost made everything worth it. I can see why you're all addicted."

"Oh, definitely. It's the only way she keeps us in line." Ryan leaned in for a kiss on the lips. It was quick. Soft. Tender. But the best part was afterward, when his hand lingered on my face. Longer than the actual kiss was. He ran his thumb from the top of my cheek down to my chin very slowly. All the while looking straight into my eyes, before pulling away.

And I basically melted.

He grinned boyishly. "I'd give you an actual kiss, but knowing my family, I'm sure at least two people are spying on us right now."

With a laugh, I glanced behind him to see if there really were faces peering out at us from between the blinds. For some reason, the image of Ian lurking behind curtains popped in the back of my mind, and I stiffened. "Well, if they are, they're doing a really good job of hiding."

"It's not their first time." He gave me another smile and squeezed my arm before letting go. "I'll call you later."

"Okay."

Feeling warm, I almost skipped down the walkway. I didn't though, since Ryan was still standing there watching me. Well, him and maybe a few relatives in the house. Instead, I concentrated on not falling on my face in front of my unseen audience.

Once I got into the car, I slumped forward and banged my head on the dashboard. Not enough to actually hurt, but enough to get my frustrations out.

"So I guess the confession part didn't go well?" Linh let out a low whistle as she pulled out of the driveway. She reached out to pat the back of my head, smoothing my hair a bit. "It couldn't have been that bad since he gave you a kiss goodbye. Or was it a *goodbye* goodbye kiss?"

"It's even worse." My voice was muffled against the leather dashboard, but I didn't even lift my head. "You have no idea."

10

Desperate to escape Linh's thousands of questions (with a bit of cursing tossed in once I told her about Ian), I slipped into Bá's old bedroom in the corner of the house to panic in peace.

The door creaked when I came in, like it hadn't been opened in a while, but I knew that wasn't the case since there wasn't a speck of dust on any of the furniture. Even all the picture frames crowding the dresser were polished until they sparkled. It was probably Aunt Sarah's doing, since Linh was pretty much blind to dust and hair on the ground. I doubt she even knew where the broom was in the house. The only room she cleaned religiously was the kitchen.

Despite the fact that Bá had been gone for almost a year, her room was still exactly the same. From the pearl-green cardigan draped on the foot of her bed to her gray-and-white star slippers tucked neatly next to her desk. Strangely enough, there was even a strong smell of dầu xanh swirling in the air.

The knot in my stomach instantly eased, like I had rubbed some of the medicated oil on. For the first time since we came back to Austin, I finally felt like I was home again. Which was strange, since this room was missing the most important person. Maybe it was because I had met Ryan's grandma today, but I suddenly wished that I could hug Bá.

I sat down on her bed and looked around, almost expecting her to come in to turn on one of her Sylvester Stallone movies. Right on cue, the door creaked again, and I swung around.

Instead of Bá though, Mom stood at the doorway with a surprised look on her face. "I thought I heard someone in here, but I figured it was your aunt tidying up. Why are you hiding?"

So I was right about Aunt Sarah cleaning in here. "I wanted to get some peace and quiet to think."

"About?"

I shrugged. "Life?"

"That's pretty vague." She came in and sat down in front of me. Her hand smoothed out invisible wrinkles on the thick comforter. "It's kind of weird to be back here, huh?"

"You mean in this room?"

"I mean in this house. I can't put my finger on exactly what it is. Like everything's the same. Your aunt hates change, so even the salt and sugar are in the same spot your Bá used to keep it. But something in this house is off to me."

My eyes widened a bit at her words. How did she—I would have thought she had read my diary or something, except I didn't have one since I was eight. But I never even told Linh, or anyone, how I felt, and I especially never thought that Mom would feel the same.

"Maybe it's not the house," I said carefully, testing out the thought that had been lurking in my mind for the past week. "Maybe it's you who's changed."

Leaning back on her palms, she laughed. "You're probably right. A lot did happen these past two years. I guess we can't go back to the way things were, no matter how much we try. I wish I could take back a couple of these wrinkles though. Those Korean face masks aren't strong enough for me."

I knew that Mom expected me to laugh at her joke, but I was too distracted with what she said about not being able to go back. My brief moment of relief evaporated with Mom's words. All year, all I wanted was to go back to the way things were *before* Dad. That was the main thing that kept me moving forward. But now, the thought of that being impossible was scary and paralyzing.

Mom was quiet. I didn't know if she was lost in her own thoughts or if she was just letting me figure mine out. Not that there was ever a chance of that happening. If anything, I was more lost than before.

The essay from the flash drive popped in my head, and I couldn't help wondering if Ryan or Ian wrote it. Logically, it was probably Ryan's, since it was his key chain. But a part of me felt like it was Ian's words.

"Do you have any plans tomorrow?" I asked to fill the silence, even though I already knew the answer. Mom and Dad had been disappearing for hours each day so I assumed that they'd be doing that again.

To my surprise, she shook her head. "No. Your dad has to do some paperwork for most of the day. I was thinking of walking around the mall a bit. Do you need anything? You can come with me. We could grab some lunch, too."

"Sounds like fun. I'm free."

"So it's a date!" With a beaming grin, Mom bent over to study my nails.

"Maybe we could fit in a manicure, too. It's been so long since it was just the two of us."

She was right. It had been a while.

It's funny, but I never realized until this exact moment how much I missed her. We're together all the time, but like she said, it wasn't the same. Ever since Dad came back, I felt like I took a back seat in her life. Not that I expected her whole life to revolve around me forever. I wasn't *that* selfish. But it would be nice to feel important in her life again.

We may not be able to go back to exactly how things were before Dad, but we could still pretend for a bit. Like when you covered up a zit with concealer and foundation. You knew it was still there, could feel it, but you pretended that it wasn't.

As I listened to her make plans, my phone buzzed in my pocket. Pulling it out, I saw that I had a text message from an unknown number.

It's Ian. Meet me tomorrow at 7:00 at Shamrock Patio if you still want to convince me.

My good mood instantly vanished. Like someone had dumped a bucket of ice water over my head.

I chewed on my lower lip as I mulled over what to do. I didn't particularly want to see Ian again, especially alone. But I *did* want to see Ryan again. And his family. I wasn't lying when I told him that I liked them.

Why did Ryan and Ian have to be twins? Or better yet, why did I confuse them in the first place? Their names were *barely* similar. Okay, a little more than barely, but I still should have figured out that something was wrong.

But twins? Really? What were the odds!?

"What's wrong, honey?" Mom pressed against my furrowed forehead with her fingertip. "You have more wrinkles than I do right now."

"It's—it's nothing."

She swept my hair off my forehead like I was five again. "Are you sure? Because the last time you looked like this, it was because they suddenly ended that drama with Park Bo Gum."

"That's because I invested three months into that show and it ended on a cliff-hanger. The train got derailed before he could talk to Susie!" My sigh was so heavy that I slumped backward from the force. Grateful for the distraction, I leaned my head against the wooden headboard. "Not to mention, he's your future son-in-law. I would think that you'd want his dramas to end well."

"Of course, I'd want him to have a successful career. How else are you going to gift me with a château in Singapore when I retire? Not that I don't have faith that you can afford it yourself in the future." Her nose crinkled. "But then you still don't know what you want to do in the future, right?"

My shoulders slumped and I cleared my throat. "I still have time. Maybe I'll win the lottery instead."

"If Bá never won anything in the thirty years of weekly lotto tickets, I sincerely doubt you will. Now are you going to tell me what's really bothering you or do you want to keep changing the subject?"

Damn. One of the sucky things about your mom being one of your best friends growing up was that it was almost impossible to lie to her. Not that I did it very often. I barely needed to. She was that cool.

I was so tempted to confide in her like I used to. She had all the answers and would probably be awesome at dealing with this Ian/Ryan problem. It would be so easy to have her tell me what to do.

But the distance between us that grew over the past year and a half made me freeze. It was a giant blinking hazard roadblock that stopped me in my tracks. Like she said before, we couldn't go back to the way things were before, no matter how much I wished we could. One conversation couldn't change that.

I gave her a bright smile before leaning on her shoulder. "Keep changing the subject. Do you want to get pizza tomorrow or some Korean BBQ before our manicure?"

Something else that was great about Mom was that if I really didn't want to talk about something, ultimately, she wouldn't push me. "Or we could get both if you want. We have all day. How does that sound?"

She played with my hand on my lap, pressing at the tip of my ring finger like she always had ever since I was a kid. "It sounds perfect."

11

The day dragged on like it was stuck in honey. Ice cubes melting on the sidewalk. Linh getting ready on a Tuesday. The mall date with Mom was fun, but I was still pretty much a jittery mess by the time I left to meet Ian the next night.

Luckily, I had to circle the block three times before I was able to find Shamrock Patio and another two rounds to actually find parking. By the time I was finally able to squish Linh's car between a Jeep and SUV on the next block, I was too annoyed to be nervous.

The restaurant was on the corner of a regular neighborhood street, but cars were parked everywhere. It was a tiny little building with a huge covered patio surrounding the three sides. There were at least a dozen old picnic tables spread out. In the back corner, there were a few green metal tables with three or four chairs around them. And almost all the chairs were filled with people eating and drinking.

I dodged a couple sitting in the front with their two kids. The little boy was playing on an iPad while his little sister leaned backward in her chair. She giggled as the fan behind her whipped her black hair around her face.

As I squeezed past her and the fan, my hands dropped to my thighs so I could hold down the front of my skirt before I accidentally flashed someone. It definitely wouldn't be the first time.

A bead of sweat ran down my back, and I was tempted to take off my chunky maroon cardigan. It was a bit warm tonight, and I knew I was a little overdressed. *Okay, a lot.* But I couldn't take any chances today. I needed the Lucky Outfit to work its magic.

Usually I wasn't the superstitious type, but something good *always* happened when I wore this outfit. It was luckier than a leprechaun wearing a four-leaf clover shirt and a horseshoe necklace.

First time it worked its charm was in my calculus class last year. I completely forgot to study for the test, which would have dragged my average from a B– to a C. Luckily, Mr. Barnes had a flat tire that morning, so class was canceled. Not so lucky for Mr. Barnes though.

Next time I wore this outfit, Mom and I were out at dinner at our favorite Thai restaurant, when I spotted Darren Criss—my all-time celebrity crush—a few tables over. He was munching on some drunken noodles and sipping Thai tea. I left the restaurant with a hug and selfie with him. And I didn't make a *complete* fool of myself over my gushing, or at least that's what Mom told me.

Finally, the last time I wore this outfit, I left my wallet at home and was running on a nearly empty gas tank when I miraculously found a ten-dollar bill on the pavement right next to my car. From then on, this outfit was forever dubbed as the Lucky Outfit, and I never went anywhere important without it.

But it had to be *exactly* the same. Right down to the star necklace and worn cowboy ankle boots. Once I wore sandals because it was hot, and Dad came to pick me up from school instead of Mom. And then our car broke down on the way home.

Longest. Afternoon. Ever.

I didn't want Ian to think all this effort was for him. If I had dressed with only him in mind, I would have worn my rattiest sweats and T-shirt. Instead, I put on the high-waisted flowered cream skirt and black tank with the thick straps. Add the cardigan, along with the necklace and boots, and I was dressed and ready to do battle.

Now if only I knew where my opponent was.

My eyes skimmed all the tables, but I still didn't see Ian anywhere. *Was I early?* It was already past seven. Maybe I got the time wrong or he changed his mind. Maybe the outfit was working already.

I started to text him, when I heard someone in the back of the crowd call out, "Two steaks and a pork chop coming up!"

That voice sounded familiar. I edged around the crowd and found Ian standing behind the grill with an empty plate in each hand. The front of his hair was a little damp and stuck to his forehead. He rubbed his right forearm against his face, but all he did was make the ends stick up in funny angles.

"Uh, Ian?"

He flickered a glance over his shoulder at me. "Hey."

Then Ian visibly froze and turned to look at me again. Longer this time. His gaze went from the top of my head down to the tips of my cowboy boots before going back up again. I noticed that he lingered a few additional seconds on my legs, and I fought the urge to shift back and forth.

When he finally glanced back up at my face, Ian turned red, realizing that I was watching him. With an embarrassed cough, his head snapped away. I couldn't help blushing a bit, too. He annoyed me, but it was still nice to be admired.

The power of the Lucky Outfit was strong today.

Clearing my throat, I took a couple of steps closer to him. There were big containers of steaming corn and mashed potatoes along with a basket of small biscuits. "What are you doing?"

He grabbed a ladle and plopped a scoop of corn onto each of the plates. Then a scoop of mashed potatoes for each, before topping it with a biscuit. "Sorry, I thought I'd be done by now, but the crowd today is crazy. Must be because of the nice weather."

"Done?"

Grabbing the plates, Ian brought them over to a picnic table nearby and handed it to them. He came back and grabbed another empty plate from the side. "Yeah, I help out Mr. Alan a couple nights a week for Steak Night. We stop taking orders at seven though, so we're catching up now."

I nodded even though his explanation still made no sense to me. "Should I wait for you to finish or—"

A tall man with a nice smile came over and dropped a steak on a plate. "Ian, you didn't tell me that you had a date today."

"This isn't a date," we both said in unison.

I frowned at how quickly he agreed with me. I mean, it's true that we weren't on a date, but did he have to be so adamant about it? Maybe the Lucky Outfit was losing its powers.

Looking thoughtful, Ian chewed on his lower lip. "Actually, Mr. Alan, Nina's here to help."

"I am?"

As he grinned at me, I could practically see the devil horns sticking up from his dark hair. Especially as he held up the fork like a pitchfork and pointed it at me. "Remember I told you I needed some convincing? Well, helping us out would get you a ton of points for that."

I narrowed my eyes at him as Mr. Alan watched us curiously. "Yeah . . . I don't mind helping. Do you need me to take orders? Wash dishes?"

Mr. Alan laughed. "No, sweetie, the customers order inside and clean up after themselves. All you have to do is help Ian fill these plates with the sides and bring them to the tables."

"Okay, that doesn't seem too bad." Sweeping my hair over one shoulder, I leaned over the picnic table toward Ian. "Why don't you fill the plates and I'll serve it to the tables?"

He scooped up the corn and dropped it on one of the plates. "Are you sure you can run around in that skirt?"

"Excuse you." I waited until he finished loading up the plate before grabbing it from him. "I could run laps in this skirt."

His eyebrow rose, but he nodded. "Ah, another one of your many talents? Well, that goes to the third picnic table on the right corner. For the lady in blue."

I resisted the urge to stick my tongue out at him. "Okay."

We worked as a team for the next half an hour. It wasn't that bad. Like Mr. Alan said, all I was really doing was delivering the food to the right tables. Everyone got their own drinks and utensils from inside and cleaned up after themselves. And I'd slip the tips they handed me in the tip jar by the rusty keyboard in the corner.

When the last order went out, Ian shut the empty containers with a loud snap and wiped at the sweat on his brow. "And we're done." With a sigh, he sat down in the seat across from me. His foot propped up on the chair in front of him.

"Not yet." Mr. Alan suddenly appeared at our table and dropped two plates with a sizzling steak in front of us. "You can't *not* feed your lady."

"I'm not his lady."

"She's not my lady," Ian said at the exact time.

"Either way, a girl's still got to eat. Especially when she's been working so hard." He gave me a quick wink and held up the half-full tip jar. "Consider it my treat since I got extra tips because of you. The customers barely give us anything when it's just ol' Ian here helping me."

I laughed as Ian glared at the older man. When he turned his glare on me, I pretended to be absorbed in my steak. Which wasn't that hard. It was medium rare with a crisp blackened edge, exactly the way I liked it.

I didn't realize how starved I was until I took my first bite. *Oh God.* I forgot how delicious steak could be. So soft and almost buttery. We didn't eat much beef anymore because of Dad's high cholesterol. Mom even tried to make us vegetarians at one point, but I had to draw the line somewhere.

Closing my eyes from the delicious bliss, I let out a heavy sigh and dug in. Within minutes, I was almost done with my piece while Ian barely ate a third of his. "So how do you know Mr. Alan?"

Ian took a long sip of water before answering me. "He was my piano teacher for two years. And he grills here for Shamrock. They buy all the food, and he cooks it for them in exchange for the tips. Last year, I started helping each week for some extra cash until I moved, but now I help him for fun whenever I'm in town."

"So you don't get any money?"

"Nah, I don't need it." He glanced over his shoulder and leaned toward me. "At least not as much as Mr. Alan does. His mom is in a fancy nursing home in Florida that he pays for."

My hand paused for a second. "Oh, that's . . . nice of you."

"I *can* be nice, you know. Sometimes." Ian gave me a mock insulted look. "But it's my turn to ask questions. How did you and Ryan start dating?"

"Uhh . . ."

Instead of answering, I shoved the last bite of steak in my mouth and occupied myself with chewing. With a raised brow, Ian leaned back against his seat and crossed his arms. The chair squeaked a bit with his rocking.

A full three minutes went by. I was reluctant to swallow the steak, but I had no choice. By now it was practically liquefied in my mouth. And he was still watching me with a tiny grin and thoughtful eyes. "I thought you already figured it all out."

"Kind of. But I wouldn't mind hearing the whole story from you."

I let out a sigh. "It's not that special. Linh figured out what gym you went to from the key fob, so we went there. Found out Ryan's name but nothing else. Then I staked out the coffee shop next to the laundromat until he showed up. That's it."

"That's it, huh? And how many days did you stake out the coffee shop?"

Wincing, I turned my head to look away. "Just one or two days."

"Was it one or two?"

"Actually, it was closer to three days."

I have no idea why I was telling him the truth. I could have lied and said one day. Anything I told him now would just be more information that he could use against me later on.

To my surprise, Ian let out a low whistle. "Three days. Wow, I guess I should be honored that you spent so much time and effort looking for me. Plus, I should be lucky that you didn't hack into my library card or something."

"Oh, I would have. But that's kind of against the law."

"So that's where you draw the line? Committing a crime?"

Despite the fact that I was still dying of embarrassment, I couldn't help breaking into a small smile. "Pretty much. Going to jail is where most lines are drawn, or at least it should be."

He tossed his head back and laughed. "Good to know. Those guys, Kevin and Todd, asked about you and Linh when I picked up the keys."

"Who . . . oh, the gym guys."

Wait, did that mean—

I grabbed his arm that was resting on the table. "Did they ask Ryan?"

"Oh, no. I told them not to." Ian lifted his arm and pulled away until only our hands were touching. "Trust me. Your secret's safe with me."

Somehow, I believed him. Even though his voice still had that lingering teasing note, his eyes were serious. And his thumb was rubbing tiny circles on my palm. So soft that it didn't even look like he knew what he was doing. But I did. My heart lightly fluttered at the touch.

But my heart shouldn't be fluttering for Ian. It can't. Not anymore.

I immediately pulled my hand away. "So, you know how to play the piano?"

"Yes—"

"Ian is my favorite student," Mr. Alan called out from the grill he was scraping. "Why don't you play her something?"

The smile immediately wiped off Ian's face. And he looked a little sick. "Oh, I don't think Nina wants to hear me play."

"But I do."

"No, you seriously don't."

Enjoying the nervous look on his face, I beamed at him. "Yes, I seriously do."

Groaning under his breath, he stood up. "Don't say I didn't try to warn you."

I turned completely in my seat to watch as he made his way over to the keyboard. His right hand brushed at the dust on the plastic keys before he sat down. His face was downturned as he examined the board, adjusting a few buttons here and there.

Now that he was distracted, I couldn't help studying his features. The sun had already set, so the porch only had some can lights and lanterns flickering from the corners. The dim light cast his face in the shadows. But I could see the concentration on his forehead. How he scrunched his face up and bit his lower lip. His dark eyes were bright as he glanced over at me and smiled.

I've always had a thing for musicians. It's a particular weakness of mine. Some girls liked the jocks and others liked preppy guys. One instrument was enough to make my stomach jump. And there was no denying how handsome Ian looked right now. No matter how much he annoyed me.

Which actually wasn't that much at this exact moment.

Goose bumps rose on my arms as Ian finally let out a deep breath and lightly pressed down on the keys. It started off slowly at first, then became faster and faster as he played.

Really, really badly.

His playing sounded like he was alternating between playing a song and banging his hands on the keyboard. My ears started to hurt from the noise, and I leaned back in my seat as though the slight distance would help.

Ian smirked at the frozen look on my face. "I told you that you wouldn't want to hear me play. He said I was his favorite student. Not his best one."

With a chuckle, Mr. Alan shrugged. "Not even close. Ian's lucky I like him so much or I would have failed him after the first semester. He is the most improved though."

"You mean, he used to be even worse than this?" I blurt out in shock.

"Yep. There's a reason why he serves the food rather than providing entertainment." With a laugh, Mr. Alan moved back toward the grill. "I don't know why he bothered trying. He's practically tone deaf."

"I didn't have a choice. My parents made me take a music class. It was either the piano or the violin. And I thought the piano was cooler." Shrugging, Ian turned off the keyboard. "Girls love musicians, and I need all the help I can get."

"I don't think you need any help," I automatically said before my jaw dropped. *Oh my God. Did I just say that?* "I mean, you did look pretty cool at first. Until you made me want to plug up my ears with this leftover steak."

Instead of being snarky, Ian rubbed the back of his head and turned to stare at a couple of flyers on the wall next to him. His ears were bright pink against his dark hair.

Brushing invisible crumbs onto the floor, I piled the dirty plates and utensils on the edge of the table. "Well, it's getting late. My parents are probably waiting for me."

He stood and came over to grab everything to dump in the dirty tub on the other table. When he was done, he wiped his palms against the sides of his jeans and fell into step beside me. "Sorry we didn't get a chance to talk much."

"Yeah, that's too bad. Next time. But I am *super* busy the rest of this week. And most of next week."

That annoying smirk reappeared. "That's fine. We don't even need to talk." Ian dug his phone out of his pocket.

"We don't?" I should be relieved, but for some reason, I could imagine the devil horns on top of his head again. And it made my nerves vibrate with dread.

"Nope. I've got a better idea." He nodded at my phone as it buzzed. "Why don't you check it out and let me know what you think?"

Still totally confused, I checked my phone. Ian had sent me a picture of something. It was words. A poem or a . . .

A list. Fourteen questions, all ranging from my family and hobbies to even my grades. When did he even—"Are you kidding me?"

"Well, since you are *super* busy," he mimicked my voice. He crossed his arms across his chest. I tried not to notice how the movement tightened the shirt around his shoulders. And how tempting it was to touch him. "I figure this way, you could fill it out whenever you're free, and I could still get my answers. Unless you change your mind and want to meet up after all."

He was delusional. Mad. Batty. Like that crazy tunnel scene in *Willy Wonka & the Chocolate Factory*. Just when I thought he was starting to be nice.

"So, if I answer this"—I waved my phone in his face—"this essay packet, are you going to keep my secret?"

He uncrossed his arms and tapped his chin with his right index finger. "I don't know. It depends."

"On what now?"

"On your answers. And whether you can pick up my dry cleaning at Golden Cleaners tomorrow." Grinning, Ian winked at me. Nice and slow. "Don't worry, I already paid for it, so all you have to do is pick it up."

"But why should I be the one to—"

His grin turned into a broad smirk and he patted my head like I was a puppy. I resisted the urge to bite him. "I assume it would be easy for you since you know exactly where it is anyway."

12

TO: Ian.The.Nguyen1@gmail.com

FROM: Nina_Riley456@gmail.com

SUBJECT: Stupid Questionnaire from Hell

1. **What would your last meal be?**

Green eggs and ham.

2. **Favorite place in the world?**

The top of Mount Everest so I could scream my frustration at having to fill out this questionnaire.

3. **What are your hobbies?**

Making a fool of myself to strangers who end up blackmailing me about it.

4. **Biggest fear/worst nightmare?**

That I might have to be your butler for life.

5. **What's the first thing you would do if you won the lottery?**

Hire someone else to be your butler.

6. **What do you wish your superpower would be?**

I don't wish. I do have superpowers. I'm Batman.

7. What's your kryptonite?

Being in the same room with you for another second.

8. What's your GPA?

12.0

9. Do you have siblings? (Specifically, about your sort of half brother and half sister)

N/A

10. You murdered someone and need to hide the body. Who do you call?

Ghostbusters. Because I assume I killed you and now you're haunting me.

11. Do you believe in love at first sight?

No.

12. How many guys (or girls 😌) have you dated?

None of your business.

13. Have you ever been in love?

Every time I walk past an ice cream shop.

14. Had your heart broken?

Only when the ice cream shop is closed.

TO: Nina_Riley456@gmail.com
FROM: Ian.The.Nguyen1@gmail.com
SUBJECT: Incredibly Creative Questionnaire from Super Brilliant Guy

Nice try. I think you'll have to do better than that. Btw Batman doesn't have any superpowers. He's just rich with a ton of technology at his fingertips.

-Sent from my iPhone as I sit next to a particular twin brother.

P.S. My hand is slipping. I hope he doesn't catch sight of my phone . . .

TO: Ian.The.Nguyen1@gmail.com
FROM: Nina_Riley456@gmail.com
SUBJECT: Completed Questionnaire that better be enough to keep your mouth shut.

1. **What would your last meal be?**

Pizza. Any kind as long as it doesn't have black olives.

2. **Favorite place in the world?**

Here in Austin with my family.

3. **What are your hobbies?**

I don't know. I do normal things like everyone else. Read. Watch too much TV. Not cooking though. I can't cook.

4. **Biggest fear/worst nightmare?**

Heights. And planes.

5. **What's the first thing you would do if you won the lottery?**

How big of a lottery is this? I'm assuming smaller instead of buying an island type of lottery. So . . . I'd buy a car.

6. **What do you wish your superpower would be?**

Teleporting so I wouldn't have to get on planes anymore.

7. **What's your kryptonite?**

Durian. One whiff of it and I'll pass out.

8. **What's your GPA?**

Last I checked it was 3.2. I'm awesome at English but fail at calculus.

9. Do you have siblings? (Specifically, about your sort of half brother and sister)

Obviously, you *know* that I have a half brother and half sister, so this question is a bit of a waste.

10. You murdered someone and need to hide the body. Who do you call?

My cousin, Linh. She'd be the first one there with a shovel and a list of top-five places to hide a body.

11. Do you believe in love at first sight?

No.

12. How many guys (or girls 😌) have you dated?

Three guys.

13. Have you ever been in love?

Yes.

14. Had your heart broken?

Yes. Once.

TO: Nina_Riley456@gmail.com
FROM: Ian.The.Nguyen1@gmail.com
SUBJECT: Satisfied Questionnaire

You passed the first test. Now, about my dry cleaning . . .

13

"So that's one taro milk slush with half sugar, extra boba—the small ones not regular—and egg pudding?"

Biting my lower lip, I skimmed Ian's text for the tenth time to make sure it was right. "Yes, thanks."

Despite the fact that I answered his stupid questionnaire honestly, Ian still ordered me around left and right at all times of the day. It's only been three days since his last email, and he's texted me with an errand every single day. And I couldn't be positive, but I swear his smirk got bigger and bigger each time I saw him. I wouldn't be surprised if it were permanently plastered to his annoyingly handsome face by now.

Annoying face. Not handsome. Just annoying.

The cashier girl gave me a bright smile. "That will be $8.35."

As instructed, I punched in Ian's phone number so he could get the reward points and handed over the gift card he gave me. At least he wasn't making me pay for his drink. That was something.

Although he was probably worried that if I paid for it, then I'd be tempted to spit in it. Normally, I would never do anything like that, but it did sound tempting . . .

A familiar voice called out my name behind me. "Nina?"

I whirled around, and my eyes widened at the handsome face in front of me. "Ryan! What are you—how—uh, hi!" My stomach dropped and I nervously looked over my shoulder. Darn it, did he see Ian's name on the screen? What if he saw me put his brother's number in?

Leaning back against the counter, I shifted my shoulders to the right to block the register. I plastered a tight smile on my face.

"What are you—"

He knew. My mind raced ahead a million miles for a believable excuse.

"—doing here? I thought you were hanging out with your mom today?"

Oh.

"I am. I mean, I will. I'm about to meet her in a bit. But I was thirsty, so I just had to grab a milk tea for myself," I said with a nod. "Me and no one else. What are you doing here?"

"Just like you, except I'm grabbing milk tea for everyone in my family *but* me." He swept his dark hair off his forehead and shook his head. "I'm not really a big fan of it."

"It's still sweet of you to get it for everyone else." My head snapped up in panic. "Wait, what do you mean by everybody?"

I held my breath as my mind raced. Did Ian set this up? Was this all just a grand scheme for me to bump into Ryan and get caught? Maybe this was a way around his promise to keep my secret. But if that was the case, why make the promise in the first place? To torture me?

This didn't sound like something Ian would do. Then again, I barely knew him. Deep down, he could be an evil, diabolic, conniving schemer.

Not noticing my inner turmoil, Ryan continued talking. "Everyone but Ian. I ordered one for him anyway, just in case he wants it later."

"That's nice," I said absentmindedly. Okay, so not a schemer. Lost in my thoughts, I didn't realize that Ryan was still talking. "Sorry, what?"

With a little half grin, he motioned to the register behind me. "Do you mind if I . . ."

Flushing, I leaped out of the way and watched as Ryan punched Ian's number on the screen. Did everyone use the same number? It made sense with their big family, but then who gets the free drink? Maybe whoever was lucky at the time.

Apparently, Ryan ordered ahead because his drinks were already done. Ten various milk teas in different colors and toppings were carefully packed into two bags.

He grabbed the handles just as another girl behind the counter held out a cup to me. "Number 12. Taro slushie with small boba, egg pudding, and less sugar."

"Thanks." I looked up to see Ryan staring at me. "What?"

"That's Ian's exact order." He shook his head and laughed. "How weird is that?"

My eyes widened a bit and I tried to laugh it off. "Not—not really. I'm sure lots of people drink taro like this. It's on the menu after all. It wouldn't *be* on the menu if people didn't like it." Worried that he would hear the lie in my voice if I continued babbling, I jabbed a straw in the drink and took a deep swig.

Immediately, I tried not to gag.

The thing is, I *hated* taro with a passion. It's pretty much potatoes, and I'm sorry, I don't care what anyone says, but potatoes are *not* meant to be a drink. Roast them, fry them, heck, even potato soup is okay. What's not okay is blending it with ice and milk and having it masquerade as a *slushie.*

The lack of sugar only made the starchy taro flavor more prominent in my mouth. Somehow, I was able to swallow the disgusting, stomach-churning, unappetizing drink and give Ryan a smile. "Yum, my favorite."

Thankfully, his watch buzzed and he sighed. "Sorry, I have to go. My sister's waiting for me outside, and she's threatening to ditch me." Shifting one of the bags to his other hand, he reached out to catch my hand. His fingertips softly brushed against my knuckles. "I'll call you later?"

"'Course."

Once Ryan was safely outside, my smile dropped. Immediately abandoning the nearly full cup into the trash can on my left, I gagged as the taro flavor lingered in my mouth. A guy next to me shuffled a few feet away. Wise choice.

Digging into my purse for some coins, I moved toward the candy machine in the corner. It was filled with a bunch of random small treats and toys. Four cranks of the lever and I got my prize. Three Hershey's Kisses, a small package of Twizzlers, and a toy ring. Perfect!

I popped the chocolates into my mouth and let out a happy sigh as the smooth, sweet candy melted in my mouth, washing away all traces of the taro. If only all problems could be solved as easily.

As the threat of vomiting passed, I came back to the counter. "Can I get another drink? Same taro as before."

Even though she obviously saw me dump the drink just a minute ago, the cashier girl didn't ask questions as I pulled up Ian's number again.

I gnawed on a piece of Twizzler as I figured out what to do. This was getting complicated. Not only did I have to worry about letting something slip, now I had to worry about Ian slipping up, too. Whether intentionally or unintentionally.

The thing is, I knew that the more I dragged things on, the worse it would be when Ryan finally *did* find out. And the longer I lied to him, the more I was afraid that he wouldn't forgive me anymore. No matter how nice he was.

Plus, now that Ian was involved, I didn't even know how to start explaining.

The cashier girl spoke up, interrupting my thoughts. "Good news, with all the points you just earned, you have a free drink! Do you want to use it on this one or get something else?"

Finally, something good, even if it was just a free drink.

I should use it on Ian's new drink. After all, I did toss his perfectly good—although using the word *good* may not be correct—drink away. The right thing to do would be to give him the free one. It was the nice thing to do.

I dug the gift card out of my pocket. "I'll get another one. Regular milk green tea with herbal jelly. You can charge the taro on this card."

I'll be nice tomorrow.

14

Arrogant.

Wham!

Irritating.

Wham!

Conceited. Ass.

Linh's eyebrows rose higher and higher as she watched me pound at the dough on the counter. Finally, she pushed my hands away with a heavy sigh. "I asked you to help me knead the dough. Not murder it."

I brushed my bangs off my forehead with my arm since my hands were covered with flour. "What do you mean?"

"I mean—" She poked at the dough with her finger and it didn't budge. "Unless you want my customers to break their teeth biting into this, I think you should have stopped ten minutes ago."

With a frown, I glanced over at her perfectly bouncy, pillowy dough. In comparison, my dough looked like a dry pile of Play-Doh that had been left out a few hours. "Sorry, I guess I got a little carried away."

"Really carried away. Hopefully I can still revive it later. If not, then half the lunch boxes will get plain toast tomorrow. Hopefully no one complains, because I don't have extra money for refunds this week." She carefully wrapped both of the mounds of dough up and placed them in separate bowls before stowing them away in the fridge.

Three times a week, Linh made boxed lunches to sell. At first, she just made a box or two for Aunt Sarah and her friends from work, but soon it grew into a full-fledged side business as she cooked for the entire accounting department and a couple of neighbors.

Sometimes it felt like all she did was cook or work to buy fancy gadgets and groceries. But Linh never seemed to mind, since it all brought her one step closer to her dream.

I wish I had her focus and drive, but there was no point if there was nowhere to drive to. I felt like I was on a road trip with no road signs or GPS. And my empty gas light just turned on.

"They wouldn't dare complain. Everyone loves your cooking."

"I hope so, because I don't exactly have a plan B." Her voice was a little high-pitched and was missing that overconfident smugness that she usually had seventy-five percent of the day.

That was weird. With concern, I leaned against the counter toward her. "What do you mean?"

She paused with one hand still on the fridge. "Everyone knows that cooking is my thing and I love it. But half the time, I feel like I don't really know how to *do* anything else. And if for some reason this doesn't work out, or if

I don't get that internship next year . . . I honestly don't know what I would do next."

This was the first time that I ever heard Linh sound so vulnerable. She always complained that she couldn't cook without me, but I never thought that she ever actually doubted her own talent. Or what it meant to fail at something you want. Maybe having a passion in life wasn't always so great after all.

"You don't have anything to worry about. Your cooking is awesome." My smile widened as I crossed my arms. "There's a reason I'm never hungry whenever you're around. Your food is too irresistible."

"Thanks. Live for nothing or die for something, right?" After quoting one of our favorite Stallone lines, she let out an airy laugh and straightened. "Don't worry about it. I'm just anxious about my biscuits." With her arms crossed, she leaned one shoulder against the refrigerator. "Which reminds me, do you want to tell me why you're treating my poor dough like your own personal punching bag?"

Even though I knew she was deliberately changing the subject, I let out a deep sigh. "Do you even need to ask?"

"Does it start with an *I* and rhyme with *bein'*?"

I gave her a skeptic look as I headed over to the sink. "Bein'?"

"Yep. Like you're *bein'* crazy," she said before sticking her tongue out. "I dare you to find another word that rhymes with his name."

Challenge accepted. "European. Korean. Demon."

She tossed a bit of flour in my direction. "*Demon* doesn't rhyme."

"Close enough." My face scrunched as the powder tickled my nose, and I waved at the air in front of me. Flecks of water flew off my hands. "Or how about *điên* or *phiền*?"

Crazy and *annoying* actually described Ian perfectly.

"Okay, if we're going into Vietnamese, how about that boy is so hiền?"

"If Bá was still here, she'd knock you on your head for talking in half Vietnamese like that. And Ian is not *hiền*. A *nice* guy would not order me to pick up his dry cleaning, the 'super important book' from Barnes & Noble, and ship his clothes back to H&M at the post office like I'm his personal butler."

"You forgot about making you pick up burgers for him like you're an Uber Eats driver, too." Linh stopped cleaning the counter and frowned. "Although, I guess butlers can pick up lunch for their bosses, so maybe you're right."

I rolled my eyes but didn't respond to her technicality.

Buzz. Buzz.

Right on cue, my phone shook, and I could see a message flash from Ian. Here we go again. I wiped my damp hands on a dish towel and grabbed the phone. Instead of reading it though, I flipped it over to cover the screen.

"Yeah, 'cause that will make him go away," Linh said with a snort.

I glared at her. "Since we're family, you're supposed to be frustrated on my behalf."

"You would think that, but I think it's entertaining."

My hand balled up the dish towel to throw at her as my phone rang. We both glanced down at the phone. "I wonder who that would be?"

Without looking up, I hurled the towel in her direction and snatched up my phone. My finger punched in the speaker button so Linh could hear for herself how rude Ian was. "Seriously, what do you want now?!"

"Uh, sorry, is this a bad time?"

What?

The voice on the other end *sounded* like Ian, but it was hesitant and way too polite to be him. I quickly glanced at the screen and groaned inwardly. Linh's eyes widened, and she had to shove the dish towel against her mouth to muffle her laughter.

Cheeks flushing, I turned my back to her and turned off the speaker. "Oh, hey, Ryan. Sorry, I thought you were . . ." My mind drew a blank and I let my voice trail off. "What's up?"

He laughed lightly. "I wanted to see if you wanted to go to the movies with me this afternoon. There's an early viewing of the new Spider-Man movie, and I have a few tickets. Thought you'd want to see a fellow superhero on the big screen."

Sigh. I kind of wished that Ryan would stop bringing that up. "Sure, that sounds like fun. Are you going to pick me up?"

"Do you think you can meet me there in two hours instead? I'm still running some errands, and with the crazy traffic right now, I don't know if I could swing back to pick you up in time."

"I guess Linh could drop me off . . ."

"Why doesn't she come, too? I have an extra ticket that she could use."

"Let me ask." I peered over my shoulder and jumped a bit when I found Linh's face inches from mine. She didn't even bother pretending that she wasn't eavesdropping. "Do you want to come to the movies with us?"

"Well, I do love me some Tom Holland. But I don't want to butt in on your date or anything either. Especially if you guys start to . . . you know." Her hands motioned at her lips.

Oh God. If she wasn't my only cousin and I didn't love her so much, then I would definitely kill her.

My blush that just faded instantly came roaring back as Ryan snickered on the other end. "We're not going to—do you want to go or not?"

"I guess it would be okay. Maybe we'll think of some kind of signal you guys can use to get me to leave you alone." Her face scrunched up as she thought it over. "I would have to leave right after the movie anyway. The Haynes wanted me to watch their kid tonight, so you guys can make out after I leave."

Now there was choking laughter on the other end of the phone.

Never mind. I was going to kill her anyway. Cousins were overrated.

I put my hand on her forehead and pushed her away before turning my back to her again. "She said she'll come."

"Great, then I'll meet you guys there."

"Okay."

I started to hang up when Ryan called out my name.

"Hey, Nina?"

"Yeah?"

"Let me know what signal you guys figure out." I could hear the smile in his voice. "Just in case."

My stomach fluttered, and I knew there was a stupid grin on my face, but I couldn't help it. "Uh, okay."

Once we hung up, I glanced over at Linh, expecting her to tease me some more about Ryan. But to my surprise, she was already across the kitchen washing her hands. Her foot tapped against the cabinet door like she was figuring out a recipe or something important. "You know, I've been thinking . . ."

Uh-oh. That was *never* a good sign. "What?"

Linh wiped her wet hands on her leggings before turning around. Looking thoughtful, she leaned forward on the counter toward me. "Maybe Mr. Unicorn's annoying you so much because he likes you."

The grin instantly wiped from my face and all I could do was blink at her. The fluttery feelings from Ryan disappeared. "Why would you think that?"

"I think he's messing with you so much because he wants your attention. Like how Tuan would toss the ball at me for weeks during dodgeball before he got up the nerve to ask me out?"

Now it was my turn to snort. Loudly because she was ridiculous. "That's when you were both ten. I think things are a *little* bit different for us now."

"Throwing a ball at someone's head and ordering them to get you lunch aren't that different." Her index finger tapped against her lower lip. "Didn't his sister say that he rushed back to the hiking trail? He wouldn't do that if he didn't at least like you a little bit."

I regretted admitting that fact to her now. Especially because the Ian from the hike seemed like the complete opposite from the Ian now. "He probably just wanted to get his jacket back."

"I doubt he expected to just find his jacket on a rock." Linh delicately shrugged. "I'm just saying that it's a possibility."

"Uh, sure. An impossible possibility." I knocked my two knuckles on the top of her head like Bá used to do, making her yip. "And don't call him Mr. Unicorn."

"Why not?"

"That was his nickname when he was nice. Not a total ass like he is now."

She grimaced. "Ouch. Okay, but back to *Ian* liking you—"

I rolled my eyes. "And if you actually believe that, then it looks like Ian's not the only one who's điên around here."

Arriving at the theater before Ryan, we went into the bathroom to freshen up. Well, Linh did. I wanted to grab some tissues to scrub off the red lipstick she coerced me into putting on. It looked super cool with her pale skin and full lips. Yet it made her dainty features look even daintier. But the bold lipstick clashed with my tanned face. Plus, the top of my lip was a tad bigger than my bottom lip, and somehow the lipstick made it look even more lopsided.

Even if the shade didn't look totally weird, I still wouldn't wear it. It was a bit much. Like I was painting a red bull's-eye right on my face. I mean, I did want Ryan to kiss me again, but I didn't need to be that obvious. If he couldn't find my lips without a target, then we had some pretty big problems.

I spotted Ryan's broad back as soon as I walked into the lobby. He was standing halfway across the room at the popcorn topping station. His body was angled away from me and his face was turned downward as he concentrated on drizzling the butter throughout the popcorn tub with the plastic straw, like it was an art piece.

"Hey, there you are." He turned around, and my smile immediately morphed into a scowl. "What are *you* doing here?"

Ian froze for a second or two before glancing around. His hair flopped against his forehead with each movement. "What do you mean?"

"I mean, why are you here? Where's Ryan?"

He gave me a funny look as he picked up the giant tub of popcorn. "What makes you think I'm *not* Ryan?"

I gave him a look and continued scanning the lobby. "Ha!"

"Fine, Ryan's parking the car. But seriously, people usually can't tell us apart. Even friends who've gone to school with us for years." With a slight frown, Ian peered down at me like he'd never seen me before.

He was totally joking, right? He had to be. "I don't know why not. You two are completely different. Like night and day. Soy sauce and water."

Looking surprised, the corner of his mouth quirked into a tiny smile. "You couldn't at first."

My mouth opened for a split second before snapping shut. He was right. Mixing them up was the whole reason I was in this mess to begin with.

At first glance, I *guess* they looked the same. They were twins after all. But there were subtle differences that made it glaringly obvious there were two of them. The dimples on opposite sides of their faces like mirror images. The way Ian's hair was a shade darker and always flopped over his forehead, while Ryan had his hair perfectly styled. Ryan's eyes also had a few more creases around the edges, like he smiled more. And the expressions in their eyes were different. Ian always looked like he knew something, like he was hiding a secret.

Even the way Ian stood was completely different from Ryan. He didn't stand as straight. He didn't slouch or anything, but he was laid back. More relaxed.

Now that I was standing right next to him, I had no idea how I could have confused them. All I could see in front of me was Ian, and he was just . . . Ian.

"It was sunny that day. I couldn't see clearly," I finally said lamely.

Ian shifted his weight from foot to foot like he was lightly bouncing. "Well, most people who *can* see clearly still can't tell the difference between us. I mean, even our girlfriends mixed us up once."

As though to prove his point, Linh came up behind us and waved. "Hi, Ryan!"

"Hi." He turned his head to me with his eyebrow raised as though saying *See?*

I rolled my eyes. "You don't need to be nice to him. This is Ian, not Ryan."

"Oh. *Oh.*" She looked him up and down like she was examining him. The index finger tapped her upper lip. "So this is Ian? *The* Ian? Mr. Unicorn?"

"Mr. Unicorn?"

Resisting the urge to groan out loud, I nudged her side with my elbow instead. Hard. "Don't ask."

"Okay." Ian coughed and tried to keep a straight face. "Judging by the way you said my name, I have a feeling Nina's been talking about me."

Linh giggled. "Oh, you have no idea."

My cheeks flushed. "Well, considering how often I had to borrow Linh's car to run your errands, of course she would know who you are. By the way, you owe her a tank of gas."

"Oh, you don't have to—"

This time he did laugh. "Well, in that case, how about I buy you a slushie? Any flavor you want. My treat."

To my surprise, Linh *blushed* instead of replying with some smart-ass comment. "If you make it a large slushie and toss in a box of Milk Duds, then you can borrow Nina and my car whenever you want."

Unable to help myself, I let out a heavy groan.

Ian glanced over at me with a wide grin. "Well, I can't turn down that deal. Come on, I'll get you the biggest box of Milk Duds that they have." He motioned toward the concession stand on the other side of the room.

With a snicker, Linh leaned over until her lips were right by my ear. "He's so cute. I can see why we spent all that effort tracking him down." She dodged my hand as I reached out to hit her and slid over to Ian's side. "On second thought, I think I might want some Raisinets instead."

"Blah. And here I was just starting to like you."

"That's how most people feel about me. It's okay. The moment will pass."

He laughed and briefly glanced over his shoulder at me with a teasing wink. "Let's see if we can get some pizza, too. Extra olives for Nina. Or maybe we could find some durian and sneak it in for her."

"I dare you to sneak in durian. Everyone will smell you a mile away."

"Great. Then we'll get the whole theater to ourselves."

With a frown, I couldn't help staring at their backs as they walked away. Ian was weird today. Different. Where was the annoyingly sarcastic guy who practically made me his personal butler? I mean, he was still sarcastic, but he was also kind of *nice*? Or at least he was pretty friendly to Linh. Not to mention funny and charming. The way he was with *me*. He was almost like—like the Ian from the hike. The Ian I immediately fell for and had to track down. The one I wanted to—no, *needed*—to get to know.

How many different sides did this guy have? Maybe he was this way with girls he met for the first time. And apparently, I didn't fit into that category anymore.

Maybe it was better this way.

There was no denying the fact that a nice Ian was a dangerous Ian to have around. Especially when I was already dating someone else. Someone sweet and loyal. I don't know what I would do if he turned into the Ian from the hike again, or how I would feel. I could barely handle him now.

Not that I wanted to handle him. I didn't want anything to do with him at all. And I definitely didn't need him to be nice and charming.

One thing's for sure, it was probably safer for everyone if I stayed as far away from Ian as possible from now on.

15

At least that *was* the plan.

Glancing at Ian on my left and Ryan on my right, I struggled to stifle a heavy sigh. Why did these things always happen to me?

The previews had already started when we came in, so the entire theater was pitch-black. It took my eyes a minute or two to adjust as I blindly followed Ryan up the stairs. It wasn't until he moved aside to let me into the aisle first that I saw Ian sitting right there with Linh on his other side.

Judging by the surprised look on his face, Ian wasn't expecting to sit with me either.

I took a step back and stumbled into Ryan. Holding the popcorn bucket to his chest, his other hand landed on my waist to steady me. "Are you okay?" he asked in a low voice.

"Yeah, it's just . . ." My voice trailed off as someone in the row above us grumbled about not being able to see.

Ian glanced at the empty seat beside him before looking back up. Raising an eyebrow, his lips curled up into a tiny half smile, then whispered, "Something wrong?"

With that unspoken challenge, I lifted my chin. "Nope, everything's perfect." As I sat, I made sure to kick his leg, giving him my own half smile when he grunted in pain. Resting my elbow on the armrest between us, I leaned over. "Is there something wrong with you?"

He clenched his chin. "I'm perfect, too. Want some popcorn?"

I had already started reaching toward his bucket when Ryan spoke up. "It's okay. She can share with me."

My hand snapped back like a rubber band.

Damn. That's the second time that Ryan caught me being overly friendly with his brother. If you could call that being friendly. But still, he thought we met just last week. He didn't know that we had been texting and seeing each other nearly every day. And that I've seen Ian more than Ryan himself these days.

It didn't help that Linh chose that exact moment to peer around Ian to smirk at me. She also mouthed something that looked like, *Stop flirting*, but maybe that was just my imagination. Or my guilt.

My face flushed. Thank God for the dark theater.

I wouldn't be surprised if she orchestrated the whole seating arrangement for her own amusement. Especially because she pursed her lips and fully faced us instead of the screen, like we were more interesting. And that's saying a lot, considering her love for Tom Holland.

Definitely suspicious.

Luckily, Ryan didn't seem to notice anything was wrong as he handed me the popcorn. I grabbed a handful and popped a couple of pieces into my mouth. "Yum, perfectly buttered," I murmured.

"Kathy showed us the hack to spread the butter with the straw a few months ago. Works every time," Ryan said with a wink. "Having a sister can be useful sometimes."

Ian coughed on my other side. "Just don't ever admit it to her."

The tension and awkwardness melted away for the moment. Glancing back and forth at them grinning their adorable smiles at me, I couldn't help smiling back. It was impossible not to. Especially when Ian and Ryan were both sitting there looking all handsome, like they were in an Abercrombie ad or stars of some K-drama. Being between them was pretty much like I was in some kind of delicious cute-boy sandwich. Mayo on the side.

Ryan dug something out of his pocket. "Here. For your popcorn."

It was a bag of peanut butter M&M's.

My mind flashed back to our second date at the movies. The concession stand only had regular M&M's, and I had told Ryan how my grandma loved eating peanut butter M&M's with her popcorn. Since we were at the same theater, I didn't check for them this time. "Where did you get this?"

"I picked it up before we got here." With a shrug, he shyly scratched the back of his head. "I remembered how sad you were last time when they didn't have them."

Ian snapped his fingers. "Is that why you made us stop at Walgreens on the way?"

"I can't let Nina be disappointed on two movie dates in a row." Ryan held out his hand, palm side up.

Touched that he remembered something so small, I reached out to take his hand. My fingers curled around his in a tight grasp, and he gave me a bright smile that probably could have melted the M&M's on its own.

Suddenly feeling tingles on the back of my neck that had nothing to do with Ryan's warm hand in mine, I glanced over at Ian.

Something flickered across his face for a split second, and he pulled back. His lips twitched into a mocking smile. "I guess I'll stop butting in on your date. Pretend I'm not even here."

My face flushed for a moment. I had forgotten that this was a date. And I should *not* have been grinning at my date's brother or feeling disappointed that he moved away. Or noticing how the brief flashes of light bouncing off the giant screen only highlighted how handsome he was.

Look away, Nina, look away.

Ryan laughed and reached over to give Ian a fist bump. "Thanks, bro." He tugged me a little closer to him. Even though the armrest was digging into my side, I leaned my head against his firm shoulder and tried to relax.

The theater was dark, but I could feel rather than see Ian's eyes on me again. Not a constant stare. Just a few almost-burning glances here and there that I refused to return, no matter how tempting it was.

16

After we got out of the movie, it started to drizzle. Not enough to get wet, but enough for a light mist to cover the air. It made everything seem kind of foggy and fuzzy, like a dream.

Linh stared at the sky for a full minute or two until her face got all dewy. Finally, she turned to me. "Do you want me to drop you off at home? I assume your date with Ryan is over now, since Ian is here, too. Unless you want to keep flirting with both of them."

"I didn't—I wasn't—" I glanced over at the twins as they stood a few feet away.

Ian twirled the keys around his index finger as he peered out at the parking lot. The wind rustled through his hair, making a couple of dark strands fall on his forehead. On his other side, Ryan was busy typing something on his phone. He bounced back and forth on each foot like he was anxious. His shoulders rolled a bit under his gray polo shirt. It was more fitted than Ian's T-shirt, so I could see the lean muscles on his arms flexing as he typed. He must be typing an essay or something by the way he was going at it. Not that I minded.

"It's okay. I don't blame you." Catching the light blush that crept up my face, Linh winked and called out to the guys, "I'll drop Nina off at home. You guys can go first."

"Are you sure?" Ian asked as he stopped twirling the keys. "I thought you had something to do."

I shook my head as Ryan came up beside me. "It's okay, Linh can drop me off. The house she's babysitting at is in our neighborhood anyway."

"If you're sure . . ." At my nod, he leaned past Ian and kissed me on my cheek. "I'll call you later."

Ian caught my gaze behind Ryan's back, and he looked away. Or maybe I did.

When the guys crossed the street to the parking lot, Linh motioned toward the side of the building where she parked. "Ready? I think the rain's getting lighter."

"Yeah, let's go."

Before we could take a step though, a gray SUV suddenly pulled up and parked right next to us, blocking our way. The driver rolled down the window, and I could hear a Westlife song in the background. Only one person I knew listened to the British boy band religiously.

Dad.

"Hey, girls, I was worried that I would miss you," he called out. His arm hung out of the driver's window as he waved us over. "Come on, I'll drive you home."

I squinted at him like he was a hallucination or something, since he was pretty much the last person I expected to see. Well, him and actual Tom Holland. But at least Tom would have had a better reason to be here, to watch his own movie. Lottery, slim chance, but still better than Dad being here. Something wasn't right. "Why didn't you call me?"

"Oh, I should have, huh? I guess I forgot." Dad glanced away, but not before a flicker of uncertainty crossed his face.

Uh-huh. It was obvious that Dad didn't call because he didn't want me to escape. He was such a horrible liar. I have no idea how he was ever able to have a secret affair with Mom in the first place.

Speaking of Mom, there was no doubt that this was her plan. This had her trademark sneakiness written all over it. Especially because she *knew* that Linh was babysitting tonight. She even asked us before we left for the movies.

Linh's eyebrows rose. "It's okay, Chu. I have my car. I was going to drive Nina home before going over to the Haynes'."

"Oh, don't worry about it. I can take her home," he quickly said. His voice was a little higher than usual as he waved me forward again.

Still holding on to my arm, Linh tugged me aside. "Are you sure you're okay? Maybe you can come babysitting with me instead. Although—"

"Although Mr. Haynes doesn't like it when you bring random people to their house," I finished for her. "I know."

"But you're not a random person. You're my cousin. I'm sure he'll understand. Especially if you don't want to go home right now."

Touched by her loyalty, I forced a reassuring smile on my face. "It's okay. It's just a car ride home. How bad can it be?"

Linh gave me a skeptical look like she knew *exactly* how bad it could be. But she nodded and waved at my dad as she walked away. "I guess I'll see you guys later, then. Text me when you get home."

Letting out a deep breath, I pasted a smile on my face and came around the car to the passenger side. "So why didn't Mom come with you?"

"She was busy. I was hoping that we could get some ice cream or something. Hang out."

My fingers froze on the car door. "Hang out?"

His voice was low and hesitant. "Yeah. I thought it would be nice . . . with just us."

I blinked at him as his words slowly sunk in. The word *us* kept floating around in my head, like it didn't want to be caught or understood.

To be honest, I knew Dad wasn't asking for much. Fifteen or twenty minutes at the ice cream parlor as we got a scoop of strawberry ice cream. And whatever it meant to "hang out." Then home. That's it. Maybe it wouldn't be *totally* unbearable. We could even talk a bit. Have fun. It shouldn't be such a big deal.

But it was. Because I couldn't help thinking about what happens next. What if this became a regular thing next week? And then next month? What if one day, being *us* wasn't that strange anymore, and what if it suddenly stopped? And our outings would become a thing of the past when he moved on without us.

I know these were all what-ifs, but they were what-ifs that I couldn't risk. No matter how much I urged my fingers to open the door to get into the car with him. I just . . . couldn't.

Because one ice cream cone wasn't going to promise anything. It didn't guarantee anything. Nothing could.

"Sorry, Dad, but I forgot I—I have plans," I said quickly, letting go of the handle and backing up. My mind whirled rapidly as I scrambled to find an excuse, any excuse to escape. Ryan's blue car appeared in the distance like a glowing beacon. "I forgot I promised to help Ryan's little sister with a project."

"But—"

"I'll be home by ten-thirty. I promise."

Without a second thought, I dashed across the street toward Ian and Ryan's car. Thank God they hadn't left yet. I didn't know if they were picking music or talking, but it felt like some sort of miracle that they were still here. Ian had started the engine when I banged on the trunk of their car so they wouldn't back up and run me over.

Both of them stared at me as Ryan quickly rolled down the passenger window. "Nina? What's going on?"

Breathing heavily from my sprint, my hand grasped at the open window like it was a lifeline. "So, it turns out that Linh can't drive me home after all."

"Oh, okay. Then do you need us to drive you home—"

I immediately shook my head. "No, I—I can't go home. Not right now. Do you mind if I hang out with you guys a bit longer?"

"We were going back to our house. Dí Mai brought the twins and Ollie over . . ." Ryan trailed off, and for a split second I thought he was going to tell me no.

Anxiously, I glanced over my shoulder at Dad's waiting car. "Please?"

At the look on my face, Ian reached out to lightly touch Ryan's arm. They both stared at each other for a minute or two as though they were having a silent conversation without me. Like some kind of twin superpower. The only thing that moved on their faces was an occasional raised eyebrow and their eyes as they blinked.

I held my breath for what felt like ages—although it was probably barely a minute—and then Ryan broke their eye contact and punched on the unlock button on the car door. "I guess you're coming home with us, then. Come on."

With an inner squeal, I jerked on the car door and dove into the back seat. Ian glanced at me through the rearview mirror. His mouth opened like he wanted to ask me something. Instead, he glanced over in Dad's direction.

Following his gaze, I could see Dad in the other car. He was still parked by the theater. His profile was cast in the shadows, but I could tell by the way his face was turned down, by the way his shoulders were slightly hunched over, that he was disappointed. Sad.

I felt it, too.

For a split second, I almost told Ian to unlock the door. Almost called out to Dad to tell him—everyone—that I changed my mind. And that we could go get ice cream together after all. Maybe we could try to be more than just roommates for Mom's sake. And that I wanted to trust him and be a normal family.

But I didn't. Instead, I buckled my seat belt and looked out the other window until we pulled out of the parking lot and Dad's car was out of sight.

17

In terms of car rides, this one had to be one of the absolute worst. Right up there with the time Linh got carsick on the way home from New Orleans. In the dead of summer with no AC.

It wasn't anything that anyone said or did. It was just so excruciatingly quiet. Painfully silent. Ian even turned the music up louder, but it seemed to just bounce around the empty space and make the awkwardness even more apparent.

Maybe I should have risked the ride home with Dad after all.

I was so relieved when we finally pulled into their driveway that I didn't even notice Ian and Ryan both getting out at the same time. And that they both opened the door for me on their side.

I froze.

Time slowed down as my head whipped back and forth between the two doors. All I could really see were their lean torsos and legs as they waited for me. It was like that iconic wrist-grab scene in all the K-dramas where the heroine was forced to make a decision that would impact everyone and set the course for the rest of the show.

Which was stupid because it was *just* a car door. This wasn't a declaration of love. This was just the guys being polite. I wasn't going to have to marry whoever opened the door for me. And technically, I was a bit closer to Ian's side, so it would be easier for me to get out that way.

Just as I slid toward his door though, Ian suddenly coughed and shut the door. Pretty much in my face.

Okay, now that was just rude.

Glaring at the car door like it was Ian's face, I slid back to the other side. Ryan watched Ian walk away with a slight frown. He shook his head and the frown slid into a smile when I came out. He didn't talk as we walked up the walkway. Nor did he take my hand again.

Once inside, their house was a lot quieter than I expected. I mean, the TV was blaring in the other room, and I could hear voices upstairs. But considering that the last time I was here there were over twenty-five people hanging out in the kitchen, the house was practically empty now.

I was kind of glad that everyone was gone. Okay, really glad. I didn't want an audience to know that I followed Ian and Ryan home like a lost puppy tonight.

Ian tossed the keys on the end table by the door. "Do you want something to eat?"

"I'm not that hungry."

"I guess we could hang out and watch TV or something," Ryan suggested as he ran his hand through his hair. He absentmindedly tugged on the ends a bit, messing up his perfectly styled hair for once. I couldn't help noticing how much he looked like Ian when he did that. "Hopefully Chloe and Ella haven't already camped out in the living room. If they are, then there's no way we can pry the remote from their hands. Do you have anything to do, Ian?"

"Uh, I don't know—"

Kathy came around the corner and let out a squeal when she saw me standing between Ian and Ryan. "I didn't know that you were coming over, Nina," she said, rushing over to our side.

"I didn't plan to . . ."

Ian let out a reluctant snort. "Yeah, it was kind of a spur-of-the-moment thing."

She gave us a curious look, but thankfully didn't ask. "Well, you're just in time, because I was going to start a game of Pictionary."

At her words, they stared at her in horror like she announced she was going to eat a bucket of live frogs. And make a necklace out of their bones.

"You can't—"

"I thought we got rid of that game!"

"I know the uncles did!"

With a wide grin, Kathy moved over to the hall closet. "I bought another set and smuggled it home. I've been waiting ages for a chance to play again."

They both backed away when she pulled the box out and tucked it under her left arm. I half expected Ian to do the sign of the cross or something the closer she came to us. "Cậu Luke is going to kill us if he finds out."

Ryan smacked Ian's arm, making him grunt. "Cậu Luke? What about Bác Julie? She finally stopped glaring at us all the time."

"Wait, I don't get it." My forehead creased in confusion. "What's wrong with Pictionary?"

They all got so quiet that I thought I said something wrong. Which only added even more to my confusion. What the heck was going on?

Finally, Ryan cleared his throat and spoke up. "Pictionary is, uh, kind of banned in our family. Like forever."

"Why?"

"Because it tests marriages, causes betrayal among siblings, and nearly broke our family apart a year ago," Kathy said with a dramatic hand to her forehead as she stared up at the ceiling. "So our family decided to never play it again. It wasn't worth the trouble and heartache."

I laughed because I thought they were joking. It only took me a few seconds to realize that no one was laughing with me. "Wait, you're serious?"

A grim look crossed Ian's face. "It was like any other night. Our whole family came over for Nathan's birthday, and we decided to play Pictionary. After dinner. Boys against girls—"

"Our first mistake," Kathy added.

"And we set up the teams next to each other."

"Our second mistake. A big-ass one."

Ignoring her, Ian continued, "And the guys *may* have bent the rules a bit. There was a lot of finger-pointing and yelling. And both teams ended up getting really pissed at each other."

With a scowl, Kathy tossed the box onto the couch and put both hands on her slim hips. "Cheated. The word is *cheated*."

"Hey, we didn't cheat," Ian said, pointing at her face. "We guessed *secret service* before you guys did. So we won fair and square."

She knocked his hand away. "Uh, you mean you guessed the word when Bác Noah only had two stick figures drawn, while we drew the entire White House and the president with people surrounding him. You copied our guesses!"

"But you still didn't say it first." Ryan shook his head and attempted to look innocent. "I mean, it's not our fault that we *heard* your guesses. There are no rules about eavesdropping on the other team. Besides, if it's anyone's fault, then it's yours for being so loud."

"Oh, now you sound exactly like our uncles!"

"Thank you."

Stepping in between them, Ian held up both hands like he was breaking up a fight. Which made me think that this wasn't the first—or even tenth time—this came up. "Trời ơi, we all know what happened. And we know that this argument will go on forever." He smiled wryly at me. "Now do you believe us?"

My eyes flickered between the three of them. "Yes. And to be honest, I'm a little scared now."

Letting out a deep breath, Kathy shook her head. "We'll be fine. We're more mature now. And I think our uncles are the main troublemakers anyway. Without them, it should be a nice and fun game."

Instead of answering, Ian gave her a skeptical look.

"We don't have enough people to play right now anyway," Ryan pointed out.

"Ollie said he'll play with us. He's not scared of his parents. And Megan—"

At her words, Ian's head whipped up. "Megan's here?"

Before Kathy could answer him, a tall girl came down the stairs with an excited smile. Actually, it was almost like she glided down the stairs. She was so leggy and graceful. Her hair was pulled off her face into a high bun like a ballerina. When she got to the bottom step, she leaped forward and almost tackled Ian.

With a laugh, he easily caught her and wrapped his arms tightly around her waist. The tips of her toes barely brushed the ground as he squeezed her in a giant bear hug.

"I can't believe you didn't tell me you were already in town." Her voice was muffled against his shoulder. "You're such an asshole."

"Sorry, I thought you were still in Florida visiting your aunt. I was going to text you later tonight though."

"Sure, that's what you say now. Kathy said you've already been here for nearly two weeks. Weeks!" The girl—who I assumed was the mysterious Megan—finally noticed me looking at her and pushed Ian away slightly. "Uh, hi."

"Hello."

The first thing I noticed was that Ian's hand was still on Megan's waist. Lightly, like he didn't even realize that it was there. Like he'd done this a thousand times before. And I was annoyed with myself for even noticing that.

The second thing I noticed was that Megan was pretty. Really pretty. Not supermodel gorgeous, but kind of in the normal-girl-next-door-who-everyone-loved way. She had deep chocolate-brown eyes and shiny black hair with a touch of chestnut-brown highlights. Her nose and chin were a bit pointy. She was so tall that the top of her head grazed Ian's ear. I had a feeling that I barely came up to her shoulders.

"Megan, this is Nina. She's Ryan's—" Ian broke off and looked over at his brother like he didn't know how to continue.

"She's my friend," Ryan said smoothly as he leaned against my shoulder. His hand drifted down to play with my fingers. "And Nina, this is Megan Tran, soon to be Nguyen, as she's Ian's best friend and my future sister-in-law."

My jaw dropped, and I stared between Ian and Megan. "What?"

She rolled her eyes. "Don't believe him. He's joking."

"What? It's only a matter of time before you two get together. Everyone knows it. Everyone. Bá already calls you her cháu."

"Sure, if by *everyone* you mean just you. And she calls everyone cháu."

"You wanna bet?" With a mischievous glint, he cupped his hands together. "Ay, Ollie! Come down here for a second!"

A younger boy poked his head out from one of the rooms upstairs. "Yeah?"

Ryan waved the boy forward. "Let me ask you a question. Who's Ian going to marry?"

"Megan," Ollie said without hesitating as he came toward the stairs. He glanced around the entire room like he was searching for someone before shoving his wire-rimmed glasses farther up his nose. "Everyone knows that."

"See?" Ryan smirked in a way I've never seen him smirk before. Now that I thought about it, I've never actually seen Ryan smirk. It was usually Ian smirking at me. "I told you."

"Sorry, but I don't believe that you and Ollie are considered *everyone*."

"I can go around and ask the rest of the family if you want." He nudged Ian's side with a grin. "Hell, I could send a text in the family chat right now, and I bet they'll all say the same thing."

Megan shivered. "Please don't."

To my surprise, Ian didn't say anything through their bickering. Not even when Ryan elbowed him. Curiously, I couldn't help glancing over at him, but his face was blank, almost indifferent, like he wasn't listening or didn't care.

Did that mean that he felt the same way Megan did? Or did he agree with Ryan—and apparently everyone else? I guess it wasn't that hard to believe. Even though we just met, I could already see how close the two of them were. Every interaction, every touch or word they said, reflected how well they knew each other.

I didn't know if I was jealous that I didn't have someone like that in my life, or because of something else. Either way, I didn't like the tight feeling in my chest.

Tearing my eyes away from them, I knelt down beside Kathy as she opened the box and started setting up the game pieces. "Do you need any help?"

"Oh, no, I've got it. You just need to sit on the other side," she said, pointing away from her.

"Why?"

"You're on the other team with Ian."

At that, Ian snapped to attention. "Wait, what? Why?"

"Because you can't be on a team with either Megan or Ryan," she explained patiently, like it should have been common sense. "You and Megan know each other so well that it's almost like you can read each other's minds. And then you and Ryan have that twin thing going on, so you pretty much *can* read each other's minds. Which I consider to be cheating."

Ian spread his arms out wide and smirked. "*Or* I'm awesome at Pictionary no matter who I play with."

"No way. I refuse to believe that. But just in case, that's why you're going to start this game with a disadvantage."

A little offended, my eyes widened. "You mean me?"

"Oh no! Not you!" Kathy patted my arm. "I mean, yeah, you *are* on Ian's team, but I meant Ollie is the disadvantage."

"Gee, I'm glad I stopped playing *Fortnite* for this." Ollie stooped down to sit cross-legged next to me. He was shorter and stockier than the twins, but he had their easy, friendly smiles, minus the dimples. His glasses made his eyes look wide and round, like an owl. "As you can probably tell, I'm the nicer and more polite Nguyen cousin of the family. And apparently also the official Pictionary disadvantage, even though I barely ever play."

Ryan chuckled as he came over. "Yeah, I'm pretty sure that's why Kathy considers you the disadvantage."

"Watch, I'm going to be such a natural at this that you're all going to eat your words."

Laughing, Ian wrapped his arm around his younger cousin's shoulders. "Come on, I'll teach you how to play. You're on the winning team anyway."

After a few minutes of a refresher course for Ollie and me, we all sat down on the floor around the coffee table. Ian sat between Ollie and me so that I could draw first. Not that I *wanted* to go first, but Ian insisted on going second. I have no clue why.

Across from Ian, Kathy sat between Megan and Ryan, taking over the unspoken role as the leader. Her eyes were bright with excitement and her hands kept clenching and unclenching when we started the game.

Earlier, I couldn't really believe that this simple game could cause so much drama in their family, but one look at Kathy changed my mind. She seemed determined enough to ride off to battle. And judging by how the rest of their family was during phở, I can only imagine what it was like to play this with their uncle and aunts.

Only fifteen minutes or so of game time passed before it became painfully obvious to everyone which team was going to win. It wasn't even a close game. And unfortunately for Kathy, the winner wasn't going to be her team. We were already at the end of the game board while Ryan and Kathy's team was only halfway.

Despite the fact that he was so reluctant to play at first, it was obvious that Ian was just as competitive as his sister. He rocked back and forth on his heels throughout the game like he had too much pent-up energy. His right knee rubbed against mine a bunch of times. At first, I moved away, but it kept happening again and again no matter how much I scooted over. After a while—when we continued to steal all the points—I just forgot about it.

At one point, I even accidentally grabbed his leg, but he didn't react, so I figured he didn't even notice.

With a loud whoop, Ian gave both Ollie and me a high five when we scored the next point. "Just two more spaces and we win!"

"Looks like I'm not such a *disadvantage* after all," Ollie boasted with a giant grin. It covered his entire face and all you could see was shiny white teeth.

"Oh please, you aren't even helping," Ryan grumbled. "Ian and Nina are doing all the heavy lifting for your team."

"It's called teamwork. Moral support is important, too."

I patted his arm with a light smile. "You also rolled the dice and got us all those lucky numbers."

With a thoughtful face, Megan tapped on her chin with her index finger as she studied the board. "Seriously, how are you guys so good at this? Are you in a league or something?"

I could tell by her voice that she was only half joking, but I didn't blame her. Surprisingly, Ian and I were actually a pretty good team. It had been a while since I had played, but I know I wasn't *that* great at it. Especially since I could barely draw a straight line. But Ian was a really good artist. Not like a technical artist, but enough to draw exactly what he wanted to in record time.

That, combined with my ability to basically word vomit and blurt out whatever came into my head, made us a formidable team. The other team was barely halfway through drawing when we guessed the answers.

"It's probably just luck," I said with a shrug, trying not to look too happy when they were so miserable.

Ian's face was glowing so brightly. Obviously, *he* had no problem being a sore winner.

"I don't believe it." Kathy narrowed her eyes at both of us as she crossed her arms. "This was definitely a hustle. There's no way that you have never played together before. That's the only explanation."

"Guess some people have automatic chemistry." Ian nudged his shoulder against mine and winked. "Plus, I already told you how awesome I was at this. It's not my fault that you didn't believe me."

"And I still don't believe it."

"You can believe it after we win," he gloated, picking up a card to draw.

Not sure if it was my imagination, but for a split second, he looked surprised at the word on the card. Instead of diving right in like he usually did, Ian leaned back against the arm of the sofa behind us and stared into space.

The only other person who noticed Ian's hesitation was Ryan. Must have been the twin thing. Letting out a low whistle, Ryan flipped the tiny hourglass. "Time's starting, bro."

Chewing on his thumbnail another few seconds or so, Ian finally glanced over at me and Ollie and nodded. "We got this."

Even though he said it to both of us, I had a feeling that he really meant it to me. Which wasn't surprising since I had guessed every picture that Ian had drawn so far. Ollie wasn't kidding when he said he was on the team for moral support.

With a determined look on his face, Ian picked up the pencil and immediately drew a large rectangle on the paper.

"Rectangle. Box. Present. Coffin," I rambled.

A brief smile crossed his face. He shook his head and continued drawing. A couple of lines dissected the box. And tiny boxes in each section like—

"Windows. Building. Office building. Floors. Skyscraper."

"Apartments," Ollie offered.

Ian clapped his hands together and drew a person on top of the building.

"Contractor who fixes roofs," I immediately said. "Daredevil. Bungee jumping."

Letting out a loud snort, he coughed into his fist and shook his head. Then he moved to a different section on the paper and drew a simple airplane. Ian gave me a sharp look and then pointed at the drawing of the plane again.

"Me and a plane. Flights. Flying. Flying over a building." I glanced over at the picture of the person on the roof. "A tall building. Heights."

Ian's eyes widened and he frantically nodded like a bobblehead. He jabbed the pencil at the drawing of the plane again, so hard that the lead point almost pierced the thin paper. He didn't seem to notice though. He continued staring at me, mentally pushing me toward the right answer.

"Heights and planes. Heights and—" Wait, that sounded familiar . . . the list that Ian sent me suddenly popped into my head. "Nightmare. Worst nightmare."

His hand reached out to grasp the top of my arm and motioned for me to continue.

"Biggest fear?"

"Yes!" Ian pulled me in for a tight hug. My face was squished against his neck, but in a nice way. Dang, he smelled good. Like clean soap with a tiny hint of cologne. I didn't know exactly what kind, but it was fresh. I fought the urge to take another long whiff. "That's it!"

Over our head, Ollie jumped up and down in triumph. "We win! We WIN!"

Ryan stared at us in disbelief through Kathy's moaning. "How the hell did you get fear from a building and a plane?"

"I—" I broke off and glanced up at Ian. His arm was still wrapped around my shoulder as he grinned down at me. I couldn't help smiling back at him. "Like I said. Luck. Lots of it."

18

Unlike the uncomfortable car ride from earlier, this ride with Ian was nice. Peaceful and almost friendly in the silence. Thank God, since it was just the two of us in the car now. Ryan ended up having to stay home to help Ollie with *something*. Judging by Ollie's bright red ears and the way he avoided my eyes, I decided not to ask.

At first, I was nervous to be alone with Ian, but the longer we drove, the more my nerves melted away. Maybe it was because of our awesome teamwork during Pictionary, but I felt like there was an unspoken truce between us now.

"Can I ask you something?"

And now the truce was over.

Wryly, I glanced over at him, but Ian was busy checking the rearview mirror as he changed lanes. "Haven't you asked me enough questions already?"

His white teeth flashed in the dark. "One more won't hurt."

I doubted that. "I'll probably regret this, but sure."

"At the theater . . ." Ian trailed off a bit and chewed on his lower lip. "Who was that man you and Linh were talking to afterward?"

Oh.

I turned away to gaze out the passenger window. It was so dark that I could barely see the houses on the street unless their porch light was on. And even then, it was a quick blur.

My thumbnail scratched at the side seam of my jeans. "That was my dad."

Ian was so quiet that I thought he didn't hear me at first. I could see his reflection in the glass though. His head kept turning in my direction as he looked at me. But I couldn't see the expression on his face.

"And are you okay?"

Out of all the questions he *could* have asked, *that* was the one I least expected. And the only one that made me catch my breath. Instead of the whys and hows, he was asking about me and how I felt.

I glanced at him out of the corner of my eyes. "That's another question."

"Consider it a continuation of the first one." He lightly drummed his hands against the steering wheel. "You don't have to answer it if you don't want to."

It was funny, but the fact that he was giving me a choice *made* me want to answer. Was this some kind of twisted reverse psychology? Whatever it was, it was working. I never liked talking about Dad to anyone. Even Linh had to force my feelings out sometimes. But for some reason, I wanted to tell Ian. To talk to him, because I had a feeling that he would understand. Even though a few hours ago, he was literally the last person I wanted to see.

"We don't get along very well," I said carefully. "Not that we fight a lot or anything, but we don't . . . spend time together. At all actually."

"There's nothing wrong with that."

"Oh, really? So you don't spend much time with your dad either?"

"More like the opposite." He fiddled with the volume button on the radio. "I pretty much spend all my time with my dad. I was the only one who decided to live with him after the divorce. Everyone else wanted to stay with Mom."

Surprised, I swung around fully to stare at him. "Your parents are divorced?"

His mouth twisted into a wry grin. "I guess Ryan never mentioned it?"

"No, he didn't." Now that I think about it, we never talked about our families much. Even though Ryan met Mom and Dad, he never asked about us. Or maybe he didn't notice there was anything wrong. And I guess I was so relieved that he never made me talk about them that it never occurred to me to ask about *his* family.

I wanted to know now though. "So you don't live here anymore?" My finger pointed behind me even though his house was long gone by now.

"I'm still in Austin. Sort of. We moved to Marble Falls. Been there for over a year now. Despite what everyone thinks, it's not *that* far from Austin, but sometimes it feels like a world away. Especially with the shitty traffic. This is the first time I've been back for more than a day or two . . ." His voice trailed off a bit. "Even though everything's still the same, it feels . . . different somehow."

There it was again. Without knowing it, he was saying exactly what I was feeling. And from his words, I just *knew* that Ian was the one who wrote the essay. It made me want to lean closer to him, but I forced myself to stay still.

"Why'd you decide to live with your dad? You know, instead of staying here with Ryan and everyone else." I knew I was being super nosy now, but I couldn't make the questions stop. "Seems like things here are pretty great."

Luckily, Ian didn't seem to mind too much. "Because no one else was going to." He let out a short humorless laugh. "Ryan and my other sisters wanted to stay with our mom and the rest of the family. Everyone you met was on my mom's side. My dad was an only child. My Ông and Bá Nội died a few years ago. So he didn't have anybody else. Still doesn't."

"But now he has you."

"Now he has me," he repeated like it was some deep and dark secret. Maybe it was to his family. "At least I get my own room now. That's a plus."

"If you could go back, would you still leave with your dad? Even knowing that it would make things different and you'd feel alone?"

His eyes jerked over to my face. "How did you know I feel alone?"

"I—" Damn, I was mixing up his words and his essay. "I assumed that's what you meant when you said things were different now. Being away from your family."

"Right." Still not looking entirely convinced, Ian nodded. "I think I'd still go with him. My reasons for leaving haven't changed, and there's no point in thinking about what-ifs now."

Everything he said made sense, but I wasn't sure if I was ready to let go of my what-ifs about my family just yet.

"I've only known my dad for two years," I said, offering up my own secret. I tugged on my fingers, cracking my knuckles. A habit that Mom absolutely hated. "My parents weren't married when they had me. Well, he *was* married, but to somebody else. They—he has two other kids."

I wasn't sure why I told him all that. But after everything I knew about him, in the essay and in person, I felt like I wanted him to know me—the real me—too.

Ian flickered a glance over, and I expected him to be shocked. But there was a thoughtful expression on his face. "And that's why you *sort of* have a half brother and half sister."

"Yep. Both of whom I've never met."

"Does he ever talk about them or see them?"

I shook my head. "I don't know if he's not allowed to or if he doesn't want to, but he doesn't. Nor does he talk about them at all. It's almost like they don't exist to him anymore."

"And now he's with your family."

"Now he's with my family."

One side of his mouth quirked up into a half smile. "No wonder you decided to come home with us. I would have done exactly the same thing."

It wasn't *what* he said, but the *way* he said it that made me believe him. I was super grateful that he wasn't pushing for more answers or asking more questions. Or, oh God, giving well-meaning but totally unwanted advice. That was the worst. Instead, he just accepted how I felt.

It was nice.

"If you ever need to escape from your family again, you can call me," he said, holding out his hand. "No judgment. Promise."

And despite the fact that he spent the last few days blackmailing me to keep my secret, my instincts told me that I could trust him.

I reached out and gave his hand a light squeeze. "Thank you."

"You're welcome." His hand squeezed mine back before he let go.

We fell back into the silence again.

"So, any more questions? Do you need to know about my fifth-grade teacher, too? Or maybe when I learned how to ride a bike?" I teased with a grin.

His lips pressed together, and I could see him holding back his grin. "Not right now."

"Okay, so now it's my turn. Why did you ask me all those questions in the first place?"

"To annoy you?"

"Well, if that was the only reason, then it definitely worked."

Grinning, Ian shook his head. "Honestly, I didn't know you. We only met that one time, and suddenly, poof! There you were at my house with Ryan, eating phở with my family. Sitting next to my grandma. And then I realized that you tracked us—me—down, and it was so crazy and weird."

"Oh, sure, but when Prince Charming does it to find Cinderella, nobody called him crazy and weird," I muttered to myself.

"Yeah, well, I'm no Cinderella, and you're no Prince Charming."

I shrugged but didn't say anything, because he was right. I know I would have freaked out if our situation was turned around. Still, the double standards in fairy tales were a bit annoying.

"So, I had to find out more about you. Make sure that you were normal and safe and right for Ryan. I didn't want him to get hurt or anything. He's important to me. Obviously."

"And now? What's your verdict?"

Ian slowly pulled to a stop at a red light and turned to fully look at me. His eyes examined me like he was looking at me for the first time, and I could feel myself turn a little pink under his intense gaze. That didn't stop me from looking straight back at him though. Not sure if I could look away even if I wanted to. Not with him staring at me like that.

He was the first one to break eye contact. And that was only because the light turned green and the car behind us honked.

"I think . . . I'm glad that you found us."

His words made me feel all warm and gooey. And the way he said the word *us* made me wonder if he wasn't referring to Ryan. "I wasn't sure at first, but I'm glad to be here, too."

The grin that he sent me was different from the others. Like he read between the lines and knew that I was glad to be here. With him.

I didn't know whether this secret bubble of ours would pop and tomorrow we'd go back to the way things were before. Maybe the Pictionary game was some kind of team-building activity. Building up friendships as easily as tearing down families. They should really put that on the box.

Probably not the best tagline for the game though.

"Do you ever wonder what would have happened if I didn't have to leave the hike that day?" Ian suddenly asked.

"What?" Surprised, I turned to stare at him, but he was suddenly *super* focused on his driving. His eyes narrowed a bit as he stared at the dark road like our lives depended on it. Which I suppose they did, but it wouldn't hurt for him to glance at me for a second or two. Especially when he asked me *that* question. "I thought you didn't like to think about what-ifs?"

"I don't."

And that's all he said.

Would things be different? To be honest, I wasn't sure. I mean, obviously it *would* be different. I wouldn't have met Ryan or have gone on those dates with him. But would something have happened between Ian and me? Would we still be in the car together like we were now, but *not* like now?

Before I could answer though, Ian massaged the back of his neck with one hand and laughed. "It doesn't matter though. I did leave that day, and you ended up meeting Ryan."

"I did."

"And you're dating him now."

By his flat tone, I wasn't sure if he was reminding himself or me. "Uh, right. I am dating Ryan."

Sort of.

The thing is, I still felt like we were in the beginning stage of getting to know each other. And we've only kissed once or twice since our date in the park. Light kisses and a couple of hugs here and there.

If you took all that away, then I was closer to Ian. And thanks to that dumb list, he knew more about me than Ryan did, too.

That didn't mean I wanted to *stop* getting to know Ryan though. Just because Ian seemed to understand me didn't mean that Ryan wouldn't if I gave him the chance. The more I got to know him, the more he seemed like the perfect guy. Sweet, loyal, and hot. Everything I ever wanted. Who would ever be foolish enough to just throw a guy like that away? And especially for someone who had the perfect girlfriend waiting in the wings?

"What about Megan?" I blurt out. "I mean, how long have you guys known each other?"

Ian looked surprised at the random question, not knowing that I had been wondering about the two of them since she came down the stairs.

He scratched his head. "I guess since we were kids. Maybe six or seven? I don't actually remember her *not* being around."

"Oh. She seems very nice."

"She's awesome."

I glanced over at Ian. After studying each feature of his face, my eyes dropped and lingered on his lips for a few seconds. Three seconds. Five seconds.

Stopping at another red light, Ian leaned back against the seat and rubbed his lower lip with his right index finger like he could feel my gaze on it. Back and forth. I couldn't look away. It was almost like I was hypnotized. Especially when suddenly the image of him leaning over to kiss me popped into my head like a bubble. All shiny and bright and glimmery.

What would it be like to kiss Ian? Would he put a hand on either side of my face and cup my cheeks or would he lift my chin up with one finger until our lips touched? Would he swoop in for the kiss or take it slowly and build up the anticipation?

Catching my breath, I snapped my face forward, and now it was my turn to be super focused on the road. The white lines on the pavement. The speed limit sign that we just passed. Anything but the cute guy next to me. The cute guy who was totally off-limits in more ways than one. And I definitely shouldn't be staring at his mouth like a kid in a candy store. *That* was super embarrassing. Mortifying. Shameful.

Why was it suddenly so hot in the car?

I fumbled with the air-conditioning vents so the ones on my side would blow directly at my face. The cool air hit my flushed cheeks, but it wasn't getting better. I shoved my short sleeves higher on my shoulders. Short of stripping down to my bra, there was nothing else I could do.

Instead, I messed with the neckline of my T-shirt and hoped he didn't notice how uncomfortable I was. "Tell me something."

"About what?"

"Anything about you." I glanced over at him. "You know all my secrets. It's only fair that I know one of yours."

Ian bit on his lower lip as he held in his smile. He reached out to turn the AC a bit higher. "I don't think that's how it works."

Damn, he did notice. I forced myself to stop fidgeting and play it cool. "Come on. You can't tell me one thing about you? You know a whole list of stuff about me."

"So you would feel better if you knew that whole list about me, too?"

"Doesn't have to be that list. Anything about you would be fine."

"Why do you suddenly want to know about me?" he teased.

Yes, Nina, why did you want to know about Ian?

"I just do." My finger traced a couple of circles on the cool glass, around and around his blurry reflection. "We're friends now, and friends should know things about each other."

He raised his eyebrow. "I did tell you one of my secrets. About my sisters dressing me up like their personal doll when we were small. Remember?"

It took a few moments for me to remember what he was talking about. Which was weird, because I used to replay that conversation on the hike in my head, at least a dozen times since we met. "Oh right. Did they dress up Ryan, too?"

"Both of us. I guess technically that's his secret, too." He gave me a small wink that sent my heart beating into overdrive. "Don't tell him that I told you."

I mimicked zipping my lips. "My lips are sealed."

"Thanks."

Ian turned another corner, and I was surprised to see that we were on my street already. Now that our car ride was about to end, a pang of sadness hit—surprising me. I didn't want to go home yet. For more reasons than one.

If only his GPS took him the long way. But I guess that wasn't the point of a GPS. They didn't have an option to take the long route to your destination just so you could continue flirting.

Even though I wasn't flirting.

Ian was pretty quiet, too. Especially when he finally parked. To my surprise, he jumped out of the car before I could say or do anything.

Where was he going?

Turning in my seat, I watched him walk around the car to my side and open the door for me like we were a normal couple coming home from a date or something.

I jumped out and stumbled on the curb like a klutz. Or like the main character would in a movie. Ian reached out to steady me under my elbow. I gave him a small smile that he didn't return. Maybe now that we were out of the car, reality was starting to hit him. Hit both of us.

Ian continued walking with me up the pathway. Not directly next to me, but a step or two behind, so I couldn't see him without turning around. I could still hear each of his footsteps and I could feel that he was there.

I reached the front of the house.

He was still there.

I walked up the steps onto the front porch.

And he was *still* there.

When I reached the front door and had no more steps to take, I turned around to face Ian. He wasn't behind me anymore. Now he was across the porch by the railing. His back pressed against the wooden post with his hands in his pockets. He looked comfortable.

And handsome. Too handsome.

"So, Linh had this crazy idea . . ." I suddenly blurt out.

"What idea?"

My breath got caught in my throat. *Why did I bring this up?* "Never mind. Don't worry about it."

Even though the porch light cast his face partly in the shadows, I could see the glint in his eyes. He leaned against the porch banister and crossed his arms. "Oh, well, now I *have* to know."

"You really don't."

"Come on, how bad can it be?"

Bad. Really bad. Ridiculous. Absurd.

I didn't have to tell him. I could say good night and go inside. I mean, what was he going to do? Follow me into the house and bug me all night until I did? Even Ian wouldn't dare.

But a part of me wanted to see what he would say. How he would react.

So I let out a deep breath for courage and looked away, focusing on the peeling pale blue paint on our doorframe. "She thinks that you like me."

And he didn't say anything.

The quieter it was, the more my courage deserted me.

"Which is crazy because we're friends now, right?" I quickly added with a laugh before daring to look up.

To my surprise, Ian wasn't across the porch leaning on the banister anymore. Now he was in front of me. Barely five feet away. He was too close but also not close enough. If I reached out and stretched, then I could almost touch him. Almost. His eyes pierced me like he was trying to figure something out, figure me out. I felt like he could almost see what I was thinking.

With every ounce of willpower I had, I forced my gaze down to his throat. I had to. After all, I barely understood what I was feeling. I didn't need *him* to figure it out before me.

Suddenly his throat was much closer than before. Did he lean toward me or did I lean toward him? Or maybe we both did. Either way, we went from being five feet apart to being two feet. Then one foot. Then . . . then . . .

"Right."

My head jerked up. "Right what?"

He swallowed before answering again. "Right. We *are* friends."

Pop!

And just like that, his words woke me up. They popped our little bubble and unraveled our cozy cocoon and brought both of us right back down to reality.

Of course we were friends. I don't know what I was thinking. For a second there, I was being stupid. There was no way that I had feelings—could ever *like* Ian. And he definitely didn't like me. After all, he had Megan, and she was *awesome*. Plus, I had Ryan and he was awesome, too. In more ways than I could ever count.

Maybe it was the adrenaline of winning the Pictionary game. That had to be the only reason why my emotions were going crazy.

"Did you forget your key or something? The camera in the driveway said you've been home for—oh!" Mom poked her head out the front door and clapped a hand to her mouth when she saw us standing there. Still too close together. "Sorry, I didn't know that you were out here with somebody."

My feet shuffled backward. "It's okay. Ian was just leaving."

Immediately taking the hint, he stumbled backward. "Uh, right. Bye, Nina. Chao Co."

Mom nodded and waved at him until he was across the lawn. The smile on her face didn't even budge when she asked, "Ian? So now there's an Ian again?"

"Don't ask."

"It's still early. There's a carton of brown sugar boba ice cream in the freezer if you want to talk."

Unlike Dad's invitation to get ice cream and hang out earlier, Mom's invitation was much more appealing. But I *didn't* want to talk about Ian or Ryan. "Maybe tomorrow. I'm kind of tired."

"Okay." Taking my left hand between hers, Mom played with the tip of my ring finger, massaging the soft skin like she's done thousands of times before to comfort me. Except I didn't need comfort this time because there was nothing going on. "Nina, what's wrong?"

"It's funny," I said, watching as Ian got back into the car and drove off without a second look or a wave in my direction. "But I just realized that Ryan's uncles were right."

"Right about what?"

Pushing down my disappointment, I pasted a bright smile on my face. "A game of Pictionary really isn't worth the trouble and heartache."

19

Just as I promised Mom, we had our talk with ice cream the next day. It wasn't a long deep talk or any secrets spilling. I explained to her that Ian and Ryan were twins and I had mixed them up in the beginning. Pretty much the short non-stalkerish version without any of the complicated feelings.

Nice and simple.

To be honest, things did seem better once I was finally able to get some sleep. It took me a while. I stared at the shadows on my ceiling for hours as I listened to Linh snore. She swore that she didn't, but she totally did. Not a loud and obnoxious snore, just really heavy breathing. It was kind of soothing actually. My room at home was too quiet.

But seriously, now that it was a new day, I could see everything so much better. Clearer. And it was obvious that I was swept up in the moment last night. Ian was being nice and sweet, and I got carried away. Plus, let's face it: He's pretty easy on the eyes, so it's not hard to get fluttery around him. But there was nothing going on between us except the fact that we were friends now. Something that he made *very* clear before he left.

But I wasn't mad about that. I was happy. *Content. Delighted. Jovial.*

In fact, I was happy enough to help Mom polish off the carton of boba ice cream and a couple of Girl Scout cookies that Linh had stashed away in the back of the pantry. Along with the shrimp chips that Aunt Sarah loved. It sounds gross, but the salty and sweet snack was pretty delicious, and it hit the spot.

Mom licked the back of her spoon before tossing it in the sink. "So, I was hoping to talk to you about your dad."

"What about him?"

"It's . . . you know that we're engaged. And while we're not in a rush to get married or anything, we *were* hoping—well, planning—to move in together. Maybe even get a house instead of renting another condo. Those are getting too small for us anyway."

"Move in together," I repeated with a blank look on her face. My half-eaten cookie was forgotten in my hand. I could feel the chocolate melting on my warm fingers. "All of us?"

"Well, yeah, unless you were planning to move out next month," she joked half-heartedly. "And then maybe, when we're living together, things can change."

Her voice may have been casual, but she had that determined look in her eye. The look that indicated that she wanted to have the TALK. Last time she had the TALK about our future, she convinced me to start calling him Dad. The time before that, we moved to Houston to be closer to him.

I didn't want to know what she had up her sleeve now.

"I don't know. Maybe I should get my own place. The real estate market is really hot right now. And the interest rates are low, so that's always good," I said, changing the subject to distract her.

It worked like a charm. She loved to talk about houses. Sometimes it helped to know her so well.

Mom laughed. "And what do you know about the real estate market and interest rates?"

"Only what they say on HGTV. I only understand half of it, but I figure that people on those shows are always buying new places, so it can't be that bad, right?"

"You can barely afford a car, and now you want your own place?"

"It's an investment, Mom. All the cool kids are doing it."

She patted the top of my head and swept my bangs off my face like I was ten again. "Please stick to high school for now and leave the real estate stuff to the actual Realtor in the family."

Letting out a heavy sigh, I propped my chin on my palm. "And I thought you would be happy if I joined in on the family business."

"Right now, I would be thrilled if we could be one big happy family."

I knew that she meant with her and Dad. But when she said happy family, I only pictured our life here before Dad. Linh and I would hang out in the kitchen all day while Bá cooked. Mom and Aunt Sarah would stay up on the weekends to binge-watch their shows. Sometimes Linh and I stayed up with them as we did our nails, or we read in the living room. The Lifetime movies weren't my thing, but I didn't mind the cop shows. It was better than the nights when they caught up on *The Bachelor*.

Bá would always pop in midway, and they'd have to explain the entire plot to her. And then she would get bored and leave before it ended.

The times when we were *actually* a big happy family.

Mom and I tried to keep up with the movie night tradition when we moved, but it wasn't the same. And Dad always ended up watching his sports or game shows instead.

Although we've been here for nearly two weeks now, Mom and Aunt Sarah hadn't watched anything together. Maybe because everyone knew that things were different now.

But that didn't mean we couldn't try.

"Do you think there are any Lifetime movies on this weekend?"

She chewed on her lower lip. "I don't know." My face must have dropped, because Mom grabbed her phone. "But I could always look. Or we could stream it on the TV. Maybe there's a special Christmas-in-July thing. Although I know you don't like the Christmas ones—"

"I don't mind," I quickly said. "I miss it. How there's always that one person who adores Christmas and has to show the other person the spirit of Christmas through shiny tinsel and fudgy hot chocolate."

She laughed. "Don't forget the gingerbread contests and light festivals."

"And ice sculptures. Those are the best."

Looking almost excited now, she got up and started packing away the snacks. "We'll need to restock the snacks if we're going to have a movie night. If your aunt finds out we ate all her stuff, she's going to freak out."

"I can pick some up tomorrow." My phone buzzed and I dug into my pocket.

"Linh needs more chicken to marinate for the lunch boxes next week, so we were going to go to the store anyway."

To my surprise, I got a text from Ian. Just two short sentences.

My favorite meal would have to be bun bo hue. With lots of sate and pig's feet, the way my mom makes it.

Okay, that was super random. Why would he—

Buzz. Another text.

I have two older sisters, Anh and Grace. One younger twin brother, Ryan, who is exactly seven minutes younger than me. We were born around midnight, so we actually have different birthdays. And I have one younger sister, who you already know too well.

And I agree with you. This question is a bit of a waste, but you answered it so I have to, too. 😌

That's all you get for today.

I had to reread his texts over a few times to be sure. But once I realized what he was doing, a reluctant smile crossed my face. I picked up my phone to text him back, but I couldn't figure out what to say.

Seeing my smile, Mom peered over my shoulder. "Who's that?"

My hand shifted a bit to cover the screen. "Oh, Ian. He was texting me about something we talked about yesterday."

Her right eyebrow lifted into a perfect arch. "Uh-huh. So let me get this straight again. He's the one you met on the hike and liked at first."

"I didn't *like* him. I thought he was nice. And funny. And kind of cute."

"But you're dating his brother, Ryan, now. After you saved his life."

Not liking where this conversation was going, I gathered up the bowls and moved toward the sink. "Sort of . . ."

"Yet *Ian* was the one who drove you home yesterday and walked you to the porch. And he's texting you now." She cleared her throat a few times. "And none of this is weird to you?"

"No, because he's my *friend*." At least he was as of yesterday, but she didn't need to know that.

Mom didn't say anything else. Not until I turned around to face her. Her arms were crossed against her chest and she smirked at me. "Friend, huh?"

My eyes narrowed. "What?"

One of her shoulders rose innocently. "I think it's interesting, that's all. Can't I take an interest in my favorite daughter's life?"

"I'm your *only* daughter. And no, not with that look on your face."

"What look? This is my face!"

Before I could explain to her exactly what the *look* was, Linh poked her head into the kitchen. Her hair was swept up into a messy bun that flopped back and forth behind her head. "Hey, Nina, someone's here to see you."

"Who?"

"Ryan."

Beside me, Mom snorted loudly. Twice. "Of course. That sounds right."

Deliberately NOT looking at her, I pulled my hair out of the ponytail and combed my fingers through my hair. "I'll go talk to him. You two stay here."

"But—"

I whipped around and pointed my finger at Mom. "And don't watch us on the doorbell camera. Yesterday was bad enough."

Linh's eyes widened, and she slid in the kitchen closer to Mom. "Wait, what happened yesterday?"

Shooting a quick glance at me, Mom shook her head. "Nothing happened. What should we eat for dinner? Do you think we should call your mom? Or maybe order some pizza?"

"Oh, I don't know if she'll—"

She didn't fool me one bit. I knew that as soon as I left the kitchen, Mom would tell Linh everything. But at least the gossiping would distract them enough so they wouldn't spy on me. It was the lesser of two evils.

Ironically, Ryan was leaning on the porch banister in the exact position that Ian was in last night. Even though I knew they looked different—that they *were* different—there was no denying that there were times when they looked the same. The way they lifted their head to look at me. The little smile on their faces that were mirror images of each other. Even the way they shoved their hands in their pockets was the same.

Okay, Mom was right. This was a little weird.

I carefully shut the door behind me and stood right in front of the doorbell, blocking the camera with my back. Just in case. "Hey, what's going on? Was everything all right with Ollie?"

A confused look crossed his handsome face. "Why would anything be wrong with Ollie?"

I shrugged. "I don't know, you guys seemed so secretive after I left."

"Oh, *that.*" Amused, he leaned to the side and peered behind me. Worried that Mom and Linh were lurking again, I almost turned around to check. "Apparently, he saw the picture that Linh posted of us at the movies yesterday and had an instant crush."

"Not on me, right? I mean, he's a sweet kid, but I don't—"

"On Linh."

"Oh." Well, that made more sense. Thank God. I had enough problems with Ryan and Ian on my plate. I couldn't handle another family member. "Again, he's a sweet kid, but I don't know if Linh is right for him."

With a chuckle, Ryan pushed himself off the banister. "You know the sweet *kid* is only a year younger than us."

"That's it?" I blinked at him in surprise. Maybe it was because of the way everyone affectionately pushed him around, but he seemed so much younger. That meant that he was the same age as Linh. But I knew Linh's usual type, and Ollie wasn't it. "Still—"

"She'd walk all over him," Ryan finished with a huge grin. "I didn't have the heart to tell him though. This is the first time he's come to me for advice. So I promised to invite him along the next time we hang out with Linh, and he can figure it out for himself."

"Good idea. A couple hours with my cousin should make that crush disappear," I joked with raised crossed fingers. "If you're not here to be a wingman for Ollie, what are you doing here?"

"I wanted to drop something off for you." Ryan twisted around a bit and grabbed a brown paper bag that was balancing on top of the rails. He came over to stand in front of me and gently placed it in my hands like it was something delicate.

"What is this?" I reached in and pulled out . . . allergy medicine. Specifically the nondrowsy kind. "How did you—"

He grinned. "Kathy is allergic to practically everything. From pollen to eggs to certain soaps. So I know what being passed out on allergy medicine looks like."

My cheeks grew warm, and I dropped my gaze to his feet. His sneakers were super shiny, like he recently cleaned them. "You knew this whole time?"

"It was kind of obvious." His feet tapped on the ground a couple of times. "I mean, Austin's pollen count has been crazy lately. Kathy's been popping the medicine like candy. I figured you were too nice to cancel on our first date." He reached out and tapped the box in my hand. "This is a good brand though. I did my research. You won't need to worry the next time you walk Chrissy."

And just like that, last night and Ian melted from my mind. All I could think was how sweet Ryan was and how lucky I was to have him in my life. And how I could probably tell him everything now and he would totally understand. I know he would, and it probably wouldn't even matter to him. Even though Ian had already promised not to say anything.

But that was another reason I wanted to tell Ryan the truth. I didn't want another secret, another connection to Ian.

Darn it, now I was thinking about Ian again.

Swallowing at the lump in my throat, I glanced up at him. "I have a confession to make."

"You do?"

Here goes nothing. I let out a deep breath . . . and chickened out. "I probably won't ever walk Chrissy again. I don't even like dogs." Oh God, that sounded horrible. I shook my head and tried to backtrack. "I mean, I *like* them. Who doesn't like dogs? I'm not a horrible person like Cruella de Vil or something. But I like them at a distance. Preferably a long distance and away from me."

Ryan froze when I started talking. In fact, he barely even blinked when I was done. It was like he blanked out as soon as I started talking.

Tempted to snap my fingers in front of his face, I almost reached out to poke him when he let out a booming laugh. The kind that goes deep from the pit of your stomach and makes you cry. And you feel like you're almost choking because air isn't coming in fast enough.

Now it was my turn to stare. Damn, I broke him somehow.

There wasn't anything to do but wait for him to finish laughing. Which took a few minutes. Every time I thought he was almost done, he would look up at me and start laughing again.

Finally, he wiped his eyes with the back of his hand. "Sorry, but if you hate dogs—I mean, only like them from a far distance—why did you bring Chrissy to the park for our date?"

“Because you li—” I stopped myself before I blurted out that I had seen his dog key chain, which would open the whole Pandora’s box of secrets. “Because everyone loves dogs, and I wanted you to like me.”

His face softened, and Ryan took a step forward. Slowly he reached out and tipped my chin up with one finger until I was looking straight up at his face. “I *do* like you, Nina. Dog or no dog.”

That was pretty much the perfect thing to say. And Ryan was the perfect guy to say it. Who else would think to bring me allergy medicine? Plus, it was so easy to be around him. Easy to *like* him. Sure, I wasn’t overwhelmed with emotions, but I wasn’t confused, and I didn’t doubt myself either. And I liked who I was with him.

The tip of his finger slid down my neck and made a trail to curl around my shoulder as I took a step closer to him. Our faces were barely a foot apart now. It wouldn’t have been difficult at all for him to lean down or for me to tiptoe up. I could reach out to hold on to his arms to balance myself. Our lips would have been touching within seconds.

But neither of us moved to take the first step. We stayed in that position for ages. Seconds. Minutes. It all felt the same at this point. Slowly, Ryan let go of my shoulder and stepped back. My skin instantly felt a shock of cool air instead of his warm fingers.

With a shy grin, he held out his hand in my direction like a peace offering. “Well, now that we don’t have to worry about the medicine anymore, do you mind if I take you to my favorite place in Austin?”

Ian’s face flashed in my head, and I mentally pushed him away as I reached for Ryan’s hand. “Sure.”

20

Wrinkling my nose, I stepped out of the car and let out a low whistle at the packed parking lot full of tourists. "This is your favorite place in Austin? No offense, Ryan, but I'm kind of judging you a bit right now."

Laughing as he shook his head, Ryan reached out to lace his fingers through mine, instantly warming them with his touch. "I know this place is a tourist trap and the food sucks, but it does have some good points."

"Like what?"

Instead of answering, his grin just widened as he tugged me along. Past the front entrance of the Oasis, with the vivid blooming flowers and little statues, up the stairs, and along the corridors. I barely had a chance to glance in the colorful store windows before we zoomed by.

Finally, we stopped at a long stretch of balcony with a glass railing that showed off the shimmery blue lake in front of us. The sun danced off the water, making it look deep indigo in some areas and pastel blue in others. And all the different blues made the greens and browns of the shore even brighter in contrast. It was like a perfect postcard of Lake Travis at its finest.

I stepped forward and leaned against the top of the rail. "Okay, this *is* pretty nice." My voice was low, as though the noise might startle the serenity of the lake.

"So, I didn't lose any points?" Ryan asked as he stepped up next to me. It was so crowded on the balcony that his elbow rubbed against my arm. Not that I minded.

"Nope. In fact, I think you might have gained some." A gust of wind blew a couple of strands of my hair into my face. "Although if I knew we were coming up here, I would have brought a jacket."

"I can help you with that." In one smooth move, he lifted his arm and slid behind me until both of his arms were around me, partially shielding me from the wind.

Twisting my head around, my cheeks grew warm when I saw just how close his face was to mine, barely an inch away. If I tilted my head slightly to the left, his lips would be touching my forehead. And if I raised up on my tiptoes . . .

A burst of laughter behind us made my gaze snap back to the lake. "Something tells me that I'm not the first girl you've brought here."

"No, you're not."

Surprised at his honesty, I giggled. "Wow. You know, it's okay to lie sometimes."

His chest rumbled against my shoulders as he laughed. "No, I would never lie to you."

Even though that could have just been a total line, I had a feeling that Ryan was telling the truth. Just like I instinctively knew that he meant what he said and would be there when I needed him. He just had that comforting, dependable quality. Plus, I never had to second-guess how he felt, since he just *told* me, which was super nice. He didn't do one thing and say something else, like other people who shouldn't be on my mind.

Nope, not on my mind at all.

Without a warning, Ryan stumbled to the right, causing me to trip over my own feet at the sudden movement. The older couple beside us didn't even apologize as they jostled us out of the way as though their lives depended on getting the perfect shot for their Instagram or whatever.

"Are you okay?"

"Yeah, I'm fine." I stepped back, and our prime view was immediately swallowed up by the crowd.

His handsome face twisted, and for a second I thought he was going to say something. But Ryan just let out a deep breath and turned back to me. "You know, that's one of the reasons I don't come here as much as I would like to."

That was one of the reasons I never came here at all. "Do you come here a lot?"

"Maybe once or twice a month." He dropped onto one of the nearby benches. "In case you haven't noticed, it's kind of hard to get time to yourself at my house."

"No kidding." Instead of just sitting down beside him, I turned to curl my legs beneath my butt and faced him. My elbow rested on the back of the bench. "At least you have your own room now. Ian told me he moved in with your dad," I added at the surprised look on his face.

"I didn't think he—well, yeah, I do have my own room, but just because my door is closed doesn't mean I get left alone," he said with a short laugh. "I love them. I really do, but they can be a bit smothering sometimes."

There was something different about his laugh. It was a bit off, almost like he was annoyed, but Ryan never got annoyed with anything. I studied him more closely. He was watching the crowd with a slight absent smile like he didn't have a care in the world. I almost thought I was wrong until I saw his finger scratching into the bench like there was an itch he couldn't scratch.

Reaching out, I lightly touched his finger with my own, and he immediately stopped. "Why didn't you move with Ian and your dad? I'm sure their place probably has more than two bedrooms, right?"

"It has four. My dad has an office, and the last one is Ian's game room. The lucky bas—duck."

"Oh, I know Ian. The other word is definitely more fitting, but I get it. We're in a family place, after all."

Ryan laughed and twisted his body so he could fully face me. Now he watched me as I watched him. The wind lightly ruffled through his hair, making it a little less perfect. I was tempted to brush it back.

Who cared about the picturesque view behind us? Mine was way better.

His finger still didn't move beneath mine, but it did stop scratching at the bench. "I guess I just knew that I was needed at home. To be there for my mom and my sisters."

"For support?"

"Yeah, but also *physically* be there. You know, my mom didn't even know how to mow the lawn? She didn't know that our lawn mower needed gas and actually broke it when she tried. My uncles would help with stuff around the house now and then, but she hated asking them for help."

"And you stayed to help her," I said when he didn't continue. "Without her asking."

Instead of answering, he just shrugged, but the silence said so much. For once, his face was closed off, and I wanted to wrap my arms around him to hug him. Instead, I hooked my finger around his for a small embrace.

It's funny how Ian left so his dad wouldn't be alone, but Ryan stayed because his family depended on him. They both sacrificed for their families, and yet somehow they were both still unhappy. Did they ever talk to each other about it?

I had a feeling the answer was no.

They both made different choices, and I respected both of their decisions. But I definitely preferred one more than the other. Someone who stayed and was dependable. That was what I craved in my life. Who else did I have to depend on? Probably Linh. I knew she had my back, but I was also starting to learn the hard way that she couldn't always be there for me. And who else was there? Mom? Definitely not Dad.

"What do you want to do?" I suddenly asked.

Ryan blinked. "You mean right now?"

"No, I mean next summer. After high school. What are your plans?" With a dramatic sigh, I held up a finger. "And I know you probably hate that question. I know I do."

Pursing his lips like he was trying not to laugh, Ryan finally took my hand in his. His thumb stroked back and forth across my inner wrist. "If you hate the question, then why are you asking?"

My mind drifted back to the night before with Ian, and for the first time that day, I felt guilty. "I don't know. We've been on a couple of dates, but I don't think we've actually talked that much."

Ryan studied me for another minute or two before leaning back against the bench, like he was getting comfortable. "Okay, so let's talk. I'll go first. Next year I'll probably go to UT just because it's in town. I'm not sure what I'll be majoring in though. Definitely not premed like Bá wants. Or biology like Ian."

"Ian wants to do pre-med?"

"Yeah, is that surprising?"

It was. I didn't think of Ian as the studious type, but I guess it made sense that he would be interested in that field. He was so attentive with caring for me the first time we met. I couldn't tell Ryan that. "So, you're not sure what you want to do?"

"No." He grimaced. "Is that bad?"

With a wide grin, I threw my arms around his shoulders. "No, that's awesome. Finally, someone else who's just as lost as I am!" I pulled back from my hug. "No offense."

This time Ryan did laugh as he pulled me back against his side. His arm draped around my shoulders, fitting together like two pieces of a puzzle. "Thank God. I thought you'd be one of those people who had a plan for every month of the year."

"That's definitely Linh."

"People like her suck." I could almost feel his smile against the top of my head. "No offense."

"I don't mind. She's not here. So, no plans at all?"

His body tensed up beneath me. "Well, I do want to travel. Maybe blog about the things I see. Maybe write a book. Not a mystery. I'm not that creative, but just something. Anything. I probably wouldn't be able to."

I tilted my head up to look at him. "Why not? I think that sounds awesome."

"Because I'm needed at home. Remember?"

Despite the fact that I had just decided that I liked Ryan more because he was dependable and stayed, I couldn't help leaning up to give him a kiss on the cheek. His cheek was smooth and cool against my lips. "I think you should travel if you want to. Maybe you could just teach Kathy how to mow the lawn."

He bit his lower lip. "You really think so?"

"Yeah, she's a smart girl. She could handle it. Just make it a competition, and she'll learn in five minutes."

His lips curled into a half smile. "I meant, do you really think I should try to travel? A friend of mine has been bugging me to go on a trip with him before school starts. Pretty much texting me about it all the time."

My mind drifted back to our movie date. "Is that who you were texting with during the movie?"

"Yeah, and every day since. Super annoying." He tried to laugh it off, but I could catch a slight wistful tone in his voice.

"Where is he planning to go?"

"He doesn't really have a plan. He just kind of roams. Makes stops when he wants to, or continues driving until he sees something cool."

That sounded completely awful to me. Then again, I was also the type of person who hated making pit stops, especially for no reason. I would rather not drink water during a long car ride than take a pee break. My only exception was Buc-ee's, and that was because of my obsession with their mini cookies. Crispy bits of butter in a tub.

My hand patted his shoulder. "I think it's okay to think about yourself sometimes and do what you want to do. As long as you always come back."

Grasping my hand, he kissed my fingers. "Thanks. I'm still debating, but it's nice to know I have someone in my corner."

"Anytime."

We sat there quietly for a few minutes, lost in our own thoughts. But it was a comfortable sort of silence. Not nervous and tension filled like in the car with Ian. There were definitely more layers to Ryan than I expected. He wasn't just a nice guy. I mean, he still was, but he was also *more*.

And the more I found out about him, the more I wanted to know.

He reached out and brushed my bangs out of my eyes and smiled. "What else should we talk about?"

"Everything."

21

Even though I swore to myself that I would focus on Ryan from now on, that he was the right—the better—choice for me, I didn't expect Ian's text the next day. Nor could I stop myself from responding.

IAN: You know, I thought that the favorite hobbies question would be an easy one, but it's pretty hard.

NINA: See? I told you. It's super difficult to find an answer that isn't totally boring or lame.

IAN: Like your answers?

NINA: ☹

IAN: I'm just kidding. Your answers were fine. A tiny bit boring, but perfectly acceptable.

NINA: Oh yeah? And what would your intriguing and insightful answer be? Obviously not playing the piano.

IAN: That's a low blow.

NINA: . . .

NINA: I'm waiting for your answer.

IAN: Give me a second . . .

NINA: Time's up. You're as boring as me.

IAN: Okay, so I like to hike. Nothing crazy. But it's nice to be alone outside. Especially since our family is so huge. I love them, but sometimes it's too much.

IAN: Although now that I don't live with them anymore, I kind of miss it. And I like to cook. I'm no Top Chef, but I think I'm okay at it. My dad hasn't died from my cooking so far.

IAN: I also like to watch anime. Not just the stories, but the technical side of things. The voice acting. How they perfectly sync the voices to sound and look like they belong. I've watched a couple of the voice acting panels online and the process is pretty cool. Did you know that they have to go frame by frame to make the mouth flaps fit? And they started with Dragon Ball Z with the VCRs and wires and stuff.

IAN: Sorry, you probably don't even know what I'm talking about.

NINA: Not about the VCRs, but the other stuff sounds cool. Everyone loves Vegeta, but I'm more of a Trunks girl.

IAN: 😮

IAN: I have never liked you more than I do now.

NINA: I'm surprised you like me at all.

IAN: . . .

IAN: . . .

NINA: So anyway, I didn't even know they had panels online. The only things I watch online are K-dramas and food-eating videos.

IAN: Lol

NINA: Fine, I'll admit that was a pretty good answer. Long, but still pretty good. You win.

IAN: I usually do.

NINA: 🖕

IAN: Next question. My worst nightmare would be if the zombie apocalypse actually happened.

NINA: Seriously?

IAN: Yes, seriously. Can you imagine what life would even be like? Constantly on the run. Wearing the same dirty clothes every single day. Not being able to buy stuff whenever you need it? My emergency pack would be emptied in days.

NINA: So you're MORE concerned with the everyday things rather than the FLESH-EATING MONSTERS who are constantly after you?

IAN: Well, yeah, that part sucks, too. But that's only if they catch you. I'm talking about the days when they're not around and you STILL have to suffer through life.

NINA: I thought you like to hike and be outside.

IAN: I do, but even I have limits.

NINA: Omg, it's an apocalypse. You can't be that picky.

IAN: So you're telling me that you would be fine with being outside 24/7 in Austin? No AC. No shower. No toilet. Just you and the bugs in nearly 100-degree heat.

IAN: Forever.

NINA: . . . Okay, I get your point.

IAN: Thank you. And I'm not even going to get into the politics of everything.

NINA: Please don't.

IAN: Let's see . . . if I won the lottery. To be honest, I think I would buy myself a car, too. My car is pretty old and shitty. That's why I have to borrow Ryan's car all the time.

NINA: Ha! So at least one of my answers is right.

IAN: There are no right or wrong answers.

NINA: You made me redo the questions the first time because they were wrong.

IAN: Not because they were wrong. Because you were being a smartass. Honestly, I liked your first answers.

NINA: If you liked them, then why did you make me redo them?!

IAN: Because I wanted to see what the real you was like.

IAN: And because I'm an ass. 😌

22

"So how should we divide up the teams?" Ian suggested as we stood outside the laser tag entrance. His hand fidgeted with the strap of his vest to tighten it.

Before anyone said anything, I immediately scooted over to Ryan's side. "I'll be on Ryan's team."

Ian looked surprised and a tad disappointed, but he didn't say anything. This was the first time we'd seen each other since he drove me home last Saturday night, but we've been texting every day this week. Pretty much all day, actually.

It was a mistake to respond to Ian's text that day. And the day after that. Even though our texts were perfectly innocent (Linh read them and agreed that they were innocent and kind of boring), they were like a drug. And I couldn't make myself stop replying. Every message, every joke, made me want another one.

Each time I would tell myself that *this* was the last one. And then the *next* one would be the last one. It was like the never-ending text message.

I was determined to set boundaries in person though, and it was imperative to stay away from him. Thankfully laser tag was the perfect way to do that.

Running and hiding from each other was pretty much a requirement if you wanted to survive.

The rest of us separated into different teams—Linh was on my team with Ryan, while Ollie and Megan were with Ian. After Linh won rock, paper, scissors against Ollie (Go, rock!), we got to go in first. Our team had a minute to go inside before Ian's team came in. Once everyone was inside, the lights would dim and our guns and vests would glow in our team colors.

Ryan took my hand and pulled me into the room. He let go when we were halfway through the first room. It was a giant maze with walls of varying heights. Lights glinted off the wall in the corner like it was a reflective mirror.

"Do you want to separate or find somewhere to ambush them?" he asked with his arms crossed like he was ready to do battle.

Linh immediately shook her head and backed away from us. "You guys can go ambush them if you want. I'm a loner. I'm going to go find myself a good hiding place as high as I can go. You know, the Katniss Everdeen strategy."

My left eyebrow rose. "So, we're going all Hunger Games now?"

"Minus the squirrel steak." She turned her face slightly and flashed me a quick wink that I hoped Ryan didn't notice. Obviously, her strategy had more to do with leaving us alone rather than actual laser tag tactics.

Before she could race away, I reached out to grab her sleeve. "Don't forget, we are the shadows."

Her loud sigh practically knocked me over. "And the smoke, we rise."

With a grin, we turned to Ryan. His eyebrows scrunched together as he stared at both of us. "I feel like I'm missing something."

"You didn't give him the Sylvester memo?" Linh shook her head. "What do you guys even talk about on your dates? Or do you just make out the whole time?"

My cheeks burst with the heat and I waved her away. "Just get out of here before I shoot you myself."

Laughing, Ryan kissed his three middle fingers and waved them in her direction as she backed away. "May the odds be ever in your favor. At least I know that movie reference."

I patted his arm. "Don't worry, you'll learn."

"As long as you'll be the one to teach me."

Before I could respond, the overhead lights flashed twice, signaling that the other team was about to enter in another minute or so. The game was about to start.

With a deep breath, Ryan took my hand. "Let's get a bit farther in so they don't run right into us."

"Good idea." I followed closely on his heels as we zoomed through the maze and found ourselves in a room full of barrels and random doors. Symbols and pictures were drawn all over the place in bright neon colors.

We barely crossed half the room when suddenly the lights went out and came back very dim. I could barely see Ryan's face if it weren't for the purple lights glowing on the lining of our vests and arm pads. The neon paint on the walls and barrels gleamed.

Everyone was inside the arena now. My stomach immediately dropped.

Catching my breath, I immediately ducked down to crouch behind two large barrels. Ryan followed me as we heard someone rush through the doorway. Maybe two people. They were kind of loud.

My heart pounded frantically. I wanted to cover it with my hand in case I needed to muffle the sound, but I didn't dare move.

We stayed frozen as the footsteps grew closer to us. Step by step. Finally, they stopped a few feet away. I waited for them to pass us up or leave, but they stood there like they could sense us. We were all frozen for so long that I swear my foot started to fall asleep.

Unable to stay still any longer, I leaned forward to the left toward Ryan and peeked through the little seam between the two barrels covering us. There were two shadowy figures in front of us, looking around the room, but my eyes immediately zoomed in on the person on the left.

Ian.

Of course, it would be him. Maybe his twin sense knew that Ryan was nearby.

Sucking in a deep breath, I slunk back so he wouldn't see me. I poked Ryan and pointed past the barrel and at his face. I think he understood because his eyes widened and he glanced around the room again.

As I crouched there, I couldn't help leaning back to peek at Ian again. Ironically, I thought it would be safer to be on Ryan's team so I wouldn't have to be close to Ian. But somehow my plan backfired. Just because I wasn't physically *near* him didn't mean I would stop thinking about him. Especially now that he was on the opposite team, and I was actively *looking* for him.

Finally, Ryan pointed at me and motioned toward the other side of the room. I thought he meant for us to go over there together, but he suddenly stood up. Before I could even yank him back down, he bolted in the opposite direction toward the stairs heading upstairs. Ian and the other person quickly ran after him.

"Hey, Ryan, wait up! I have something to tell you!"

His laughter seemed to bounce off the walls. "Like hell you have something to tell me! You'll have to try to catch me first!"

Red lasers bounced all over the place, and even though I knew they were harmless, I plastered myself against the metal barrel as they passed me.

Now that I was alone, I jumped to my feet. My right foot was still asleep, and I gritted my teeth together and forced myself to move toward the other side of the room. Painful tingles ran up and down my foot and leg with each step.

My fingers clenched the laser gun tightly in my hands, and I peered around a tall door. There was a ramp that went straight up. I didn't know what was up there, but it was either this or the stairway the guys went down.

There was no choice but to go up. Especially after Ryan used himself as bait so I could escape.

I edged along the wall and tried to blend in, despite my glowing vest. Shifting the laser gun to my right hand, my left hand covered my chest to hide as much of the light as I could with my fingers.

When I reached the top of the ramp, I realized this was one of the main floors. And this room was *huge* compared to the one I was just in.

The arena had three floors, but the first floor was mainly the waiting area and equipment room. The second and third floors were where the real game started. The smaller rooms had themes whereas this room was a mixture of everything. Mini mazes with ramps that went up and down, barrels that ranged from huge to tiny ones, doors, and half walls to hide behind. There were even mini turrets with towers and windows overlooking everything.

Deciding to get to one of the turrets so I could keep a lookout, I headed for the ramp on my left. It took less than a minute for me to reach the top. Before I could duck into the turret though, I heard a small thump beneath me.

My heart pounded in my ears, and I held my breath as I crept around the giant boulder to hide. I didn't see or hear anyone else around me, but I knew that there was still *someone* out there.

The hairs on my arms were sticking up by now. My nerves were tingling in overdrive as I dropped down to my stomach and army-crawled over to the balcony. Inch by inch, I peered over the balcony and spotted someone standing near the ramp. A guy. He glanced around the room with his laser gun held loosely at his side. His face was in the shadows though.

Recognizing the dark hair, I almost called out to him when I realized his gun and vest were glowing red. Wait, that wasn't Ryan. It was Ian.

With a soft gasp, I ducked down again before he could catch sight of me. My body was plastered to the floor as the handle of the laser gun dug into my side.

There were two choices. I could either attempt to sneak away before he noticed me, or I could stay and get revenge for being his butler last week. And for all the times he annoyed me. Which were a lot.

It was a pretty easy choice. I didn't even have to think twice about it.

Leaning forward with the laser gun gripped in both hands, I positioned myself against the floor like a sniper. When Ian turned slightly away from me, I took aim and fired.

I missed the first time. The red beam hit the wall behind Ian. He swung around to stare at it. Before he could react, I pressed the trigger of my laser gun a couple more times. Finally, one of them hit Ian's chest plate.

He glanced down at his flashing blue vest in dismay. The lights on his equipment and gun shut off. Pretty much putting himself in time-out for thirty seconds. "Shit!"

Ducking inside the turret, I collapsed against the wall and shoved a fist against my mouth as I struggled not to laugh out loud. Tears gathered in my eyes instead as his frustrated face flashed in my head.

Linh and Katniss were right. It was way better to be up here looking down at everyone.

Still crouched on the floor, I crept over to peek out of the bottom of the window. He was half-standing behind a short wall now. His head whipped back and forth as he searched the room for his enemy. He didn't think to look up though.

When his vest glowed again to let him back into the game, I knelt by the window and took aim before he could go anywhere. This time it only took one shot. His chest plate flashed three times and shut off again.

"God, seriously?!"

This time I did laugh. I couldn't help it. Only for a second or two, but I saw Ian's head snap up at the sound. With a sharp gasp, I ducked beneath the window before he could catch sight of me. There was a minute or two of silence.

Not sure if I was tempting luck, I debated between shooting him one more time as I peeked out the window again. He wasn't in the same spot though. In fact, I didn't see him anywhere at all.

Where did he go?

Grasping the ledge with both hands, I leaned farther out the window and looked around, but I didn't see Ian anymore. Maybe he left in case he got shot again. I'm sure he didn't hear me though or he would have run up the ramp.

I checked my watch. Five minutes left. Jeez, fifteen minutes sure went by quickly in this game. Maybe I should keep moving.

I had reached the bottom of the ramp when my foot got caught on a low barrel. With a squeal, I pitched straight toward the floor as someone grabbed my arm and pulled me to the left. My weight must have knocked them off-balance, too, because I ended up sprawled on top of them. The top of my head knocked against something hard and immediately started throbbing.

"Damn it!" A voice muttered over my head.

Lifting myself slightly upright, I peered up into Ian's grimacing face. He kept one arm around my shoulders and rubbed the bottom of his chin with his other hand. Surprised at how close our faces were, I froze. I could see the faint dark stubble under his chin. It would have been barely noticeable if I weren't so close.

"I think your hard head gave me a bruise," Ian complained. "I guess I should be lucky that you didn't give me a concussion."

And just like that, I unfroze. "Well, it's not my fault that your pointy chin broke my fall."

"That's not exactly a thank-you."

"That's because it wasn't supposed to be one."

He tried to look annoyed, but his dimple flashed, betraying him. "You know, we're breaking the rules of the game."

"What rules?"

"No physical contact. They said it at the beginning of the game. Weren't you listening?"

His arm was around me and his hand was stroking my back. So gently that I almost wouldn't have noticed it if it weren't for the heat from his fingers. I could feel it through the thin fabric of my shirt. How did he manage to find the *one* spot on my back that wasn't covered by the giant vest?

"You're the one still holding me." I poked at his arm around my shoulder.

His grin was wide now. "Because you're still laying on top of me."

Realizing that not only was he right, but my hands were tightly clenching his shoulders, with a deep flush I scrambled to get off him. I might have accidentally kicked him, too, because he groaned out loud. Since I wasn't sure, I didn't apologize. I had just rolled to my side when Ian towered over me. How the heck did he get up so quickly? Was he a cat in his last life?

Reaching down, he brushed my bangs out of my eyes. It was so quick that if I blinked, I would have missed it. He held out his hand to help me up. I hesitated for a few seconds before I took it. His tight grasp pulled me upright until I was back on my feet. But he still didn't let go. And he didn't stop smiling at me either. It momentarily distracted me, and I almost forgot what we were doing.

"Sorry."

"What for—"

Then he shot me on my left arm plate with his other hand. My vest glowed blue a few times and my laser gun shut off.

I immediately dropped his hand and shoved him. "What the hell?!"

"That's payback for following me around and shooting me this entire time."

"How did you know it was me?"

"I didn't." He wiggled his dark eyebrows. "But you just admitted to me that it was."

My mouth snapped closed. Damn, he caught me.

"So now that I know it was *you*, I think I'm allowed to get another free shot." He dramatically cocked the laser gun upward.

"Excuse me, the first one was not *free*." I grabbed his arm so he couldn't aim at me again.

"Again with the physical contact." Ian let out a low whistle and shook his head disappointedly. "You have to learn how to play by the rules if you want this to be fair."

"I don't play fair."

"I've noticed." His eyes sparkled happily. Suddenly he leaned down until his lips were right by my ear. My breath got caught in my throat as I could feel rather than hear his words now. I tried to ignore the shivers that were dancing up and down my spine. "Well, now that I know that . . . neither will I."

Pulling back a tiny bit, he stared straight into my eyes and gave me a slow wink . . . before he shot me again—on the chest plate this time—just as the lights came back on to signal the end of the game.

I let out a loud gasp and he bumped his forehead against mine with a snort of amusement. "There. We're even now."

Closing my eyes, I counted to ten in my head to calm myself down so I wouldn't give him a kick where it would really hurt. Luckily for him, I glared at him instead. "You could try to be less of an ass."

"I could try, but it probably won't work."

God, it wasn't even possible to insult him.

I tried to sweep past him to leave, deliberately digging my elbow into his side. "By the way, you're supposed to wait a minute or two after my stuff turns on again before shooting at me. That's very unsportsmanlike of you." I knew I was being a hypocrite, since I had done the same thing to him a few minutes ago, but I was too annoyed to think clearly.

He stepped to the right to block my way. "Ah, so you DO know the rules. Or at least how to break them. This should make the next game a lot more interesting now. Are you ready?" Ian asked innocently, already walking away before I could answer.

Not wanting to give him the satisfaction of following him, I stayed right where I was. My jaw was clenched so tight that the sides of my neck were sore. I wanted to stomp up and down in frustration, like a little kid. He was so arrogant and irritating and . . . and . . .

I was so mad that I couldn't even think of the words, and that never happened to me. And I had thought Ian was getting a tiny bit nicer. I should have known that it was just a fluke.

There was no time to throw a tantrum though. Not when I had a game to win.

Now that the lights were on again, my eyes scanned the room and tried to memorize all the hiding places and paths between the boulders like my life depended on it. Which it did if I let Ian beat me again.

Okay, if he wants to play again, then we'll play again.

Game on.

23

"So not only are you two amazing at Pictionary, but you're also a pro at laser tag." Megan shook her head as she popped a french fry into her mouth. Her lips pursed into a round circle as she breathed in and out to cool the hot fry. "Is there seriously anything that you and Ian *can't* do together?"

I searched her face for any sign of jealousy or annoyance, but there was nothing. Either she didn't feel *that* way about Ian, or she was *so* confident about their relationship that no amount of laser tag or Pictionary could ever shake it.

Probably the second one.

She was right though. I hated to admit it, but today turned out to be pretty fun. The most fun I had in a while—and it was mainly because of Ian. He was a worthy opponent.

Even though our entire group was playing, the game became a challenge between us to see who could find the other person first. Who would have the most points in the end. Honestly, Ian and I would have kept playing after everyone called it quits, but we couldn't just play with the two of us. We'd already asked.

"Technically, we weren't *playing* together," I said, glancing at Ryan and Ian at the snack stand out of the corner of my eye.

"Thank God, or you two would have squished the rest of us like bugs," Linh complained as she swept her hair off her forehead.

Ollie nodded but didn't say much. His eyes kept sliding over in Linh's direction, like they'd been doing all afternoon. And he only spoke to her. "Do you want to check out some of the other games, Linh? Maybe shoot a couple of zombies?"

"Sure."

They were already strolling off when I called out, "We'll stay here. Thanks for asking."

Without looking up, Linh waved over her shoulder as Megan snickered. "Guess Ollie's little crush isn't fading anytime soon."

Not surprised that she noticed, since he *was* being pretty obvious, I shook my head. "I hope she lets him down gently. I'd hate for Ollie to have his heart broken."

"A little heartbreak won't kill anyone."

I didn't totally agree, but it'd be rude to start a debate so I just nodded.

And then . . . silence. Now it was just us left at the table. Megan and me. Me and Megan. She seemed content with munching on the french fries, but I *felt* like I should say something. Anything. The silence enveloped me, bugging me like an itch that I couldn't scratch. It was all I could think about.

"Do you think you and Ian will ever start dating?"

Choking a bit on a fry, she gave me a surprised look. "What are you talking about?"

I flushed. That was probably the wrong thing to ask. Maybe I should have left the freaking itch alone. "Oh, I was just wondering. Everyone keeps talking about how you two will get together someday, so, you know . . ."

"Right, that. If you ask me, they're rooting for the wrong ship. To me, he's *Ian*. We've been friends for so long that it's hard to imagine being anything else, you know what I mean?"

"Uh, not really."

She studied my face for a few seconds before smiling. "I mean, don't get me wrong. Ian is awesome. He's smart and funny and the sweetest guy ever. Any girl would be lucky to have him. Any girl. Don't you think?"

Why was she gushing about Ian to me?

"Uh, yeah, I guess." I shook my head. "I mean, I don't know about the 'sweetest guy' part, but everything else seems pretty much right. Not that I see all those qualities much."

Megan leaned on the palm of her hand. Her index finger tapped against her pale cheek. "That's because you bring out another side in Ian. I've never seen him act that way with anyone else."

"You mean he's only rude to me? Gee, thanks."

She laughed. "It means that you're different to him. In fact, if you ask me, I think—"

Just then, Ian and Ryan came back with an armful of drinks in each hand. Megan stopped talking so I didn't get to finish hearing what she thought. Although she was probably planning to list more of Ian's invisible qualities again. Sorry, not invisible, just none of the good qualities that he never bothered to show me.

"Thank God, I'm dying of thirst over here," Megan complained as Ian handed her a plastic cup. She immediately poked a straw through the lid and slurped it down.

"That took so long, I swear they were waiting for the ice to freeze or something. Iced tea, half and half. Extra ice." Ryan handed me a cup and glanced around. "Where's Ollie and Linh?"

My hand waved over my shoulder. "They said they wanted to go shoot zombies or something."

"Ah, probably *House of the Dead IV.* He's determined to finish that game, even if he has to spend his entire college fund on it."

"Not sure his dad will be very happy about it." Ian dipped a fry in the ketchup and popped it into his mouth. "Not to mention, Cậu Luke will probably kill us, too."

Ryan shrugged like death threats didn't bother him. Although I'm pretty sure death threats were very common in their family, so maybe he was used to them.

"Maybe Ollie will become some sort of rich professional gamer on YouTube," Megan suggested as she set her drink aside. "Although I doubt his dad will like that either."

"He'd probably kill Ollie after he kills us," Ian announced with a grimace.

"Oh, well, let me know when to send flowers." She leaned her arm against his shoulder and grabbed his drink straight out of his hand. "Sorry, I already finished mine."

A brief smile crossed Ian's face. "It's fine. You always steal my drink anyway. Why do you think I get an extra-large all the time?"

Her eyebrow rose. "If you were smart, then you would save both of us the trouble and get *me* the extra-large."

He laughed. "You're right. I never thought of that before. What would I do without you?"

Megan patted his head like a puppy. "It's okay. That's what I'm here for, buddy." I couldn't help noticing that even after she gave him back his drink, her arm stayed on Ian's shoulder.

And as I watched them talk, I could totally see why Ian's family expected them to start dating any day now. The way they sat next to each other—her elbow on his shoulder and his body angled toward hers—it was like they gravitated toward each other without thinking. Their bodies knew that they should be together, even though they denied it.

And it wasn't just physical. It was like they knew exactly what the other was thinking before they even finished talking. They danced from subject to subject as easily as flowing water. There was no awkwardness or confused feelings.

And I felt like the other person looking in.

Yeah, she definitely didn't see me as a threat. Not that I was one. After all, I was dating Ryan. I shouldn't care what Ian and Megan did. At all.

But why did my stomach feel so heavy all of a sudden?

Unable to watch them flirt anymore, I swung around in the stool to face the other direction. Ryan came over to sit with me. The slightly annoyed expression on his face probably reflected my own. But what did he have to be pissed about?

Following his gaze, I thought he was looking at Megan and Ian, too, but he wasn't. He was looking past them at another group at the next table. There were four girls sitting with three other guys. They looked like they were around our age, although one of the guys looked a bit older. Maybe nineteen or so.

When one of the girls laughed, Ryan frowned darkly and turned toward me. "How are you with basketball?"

"Not great." I snuck a curious glance over at the other table.

"It's okay. I can teach you. Come on."

He was already on his feet and walking away, so I had no choice but to follow him. With a frown, Ian watched me hop to my feet. His gaze moved to his brother's back, like he was trying to figure something out, when suddenly he glanced over at the group. His face froze.

My curiosity doubled. Tripled. Who were they and why did they bother Ryan so much? Even Ian seemed uncomfortable to see them.

By now I was bursting to ask, but I waited until Ryan started the game and shot a basketball through the hoop first. "So, who are those people at the other table?"

He paused mid-throw and grimaced. "You noticed that?"

Uh, I'm pretty sure everyone did. "A little bit."

His eyes were glued on the basketball as he bounced it against the side of the machine a few times. "My ex-girlfriend, Liv, is over there with some friends."

My eyebrows rose and it took every bit of willpower I had not to whirl around to stare at the group again. Instead, I picked up a basketball and handed it to Ryan. "Which one is she?"

"The blond in the center," he said without looking up.

"How do you know she's in the center?"

"She's always in the center."

Trying to look casual, I swept my hair over my shoulder and looked behind me. My eyes immediately zoomed in on the pretty blond girl. Ryan was right. Liv was right in the middle of the group. Her head swung back and forth as though she was trying to be in two conversations at once. Or maybe everyone was just trying to talk to her.

Man, she was pretty. She looked petite, even shorter than me, but she stood out in her group. Maybe it was the way her hair was so blond that it almost looked platinum. Or her wide eyes that were a bright glittery blue. Even from this distance, I could see that her skin was clear and perfect. Something that I could never achieve—not even with daily face masks and Linh's fanciest makeup.

"Eh." I turned back to Ryan and shrugged like I wasn't impressed.

The corner of his mouth curved into a smile and he tossed the ball. It swished neatly through the hoop without touching the net. "We broke up nearly a year ago. Well, she dumped me. She said I was too nice for her, and she wasn't ready for a relationship. After we were already together for six months."

Ouch. "How could anyone ever be *too* nice?"

"I know, right?" With a slight laugh, he shook his head. He looked a little happier, more like himself for a second. "You'd be surprised how often I'm called the nice twin. That was the first time it's ever come back to bite me in the ass though."

It wasn't *that* surprising. I had met them only two weeks ago, and I always referred to Ryan as the "nice twin" out loud and in my head. But it also didn't help that his brother was *Ian*. It wasn't too hard to be considered the nicer one. I didn't know until now that Ryan considered it a bad thing though.

"It's not your fault. That's a sucky excuse to break up with someone."

"I know. She ended up going out with someone else barely a month later, so obviously not being ready was a lie, too." He shrugged like he didn't care, when he obviously did.

Not knowing what to say to comfort him, I leaned on his shoulder instead. The side of my head pressed against his arm. He straightened his back and turned his head to press his chin against the top of my head. We stayed that way for a few seconds before the buzzer rang loudly as the time on our game ran out.

Ryan laughed and pulled away. He dug into his pocket for the little plastic card. "Sorry, but I need to get a better score. My ego can't leave the score like that,"

"No problem."

As he shot basket after basket, I glanced over at Liv and bit my lip. It was obvious from his intense reaction that he wasn't completely over her. But if that was the case, then what did that make me? Did he like me, or was I some kind of rebound?

He was almost done playing when I couldn't help asking, "Ryan, do you still have feelings for her?"

"What? Oh, no. I'm completely over Liv. Now I'm *glad* that we broke up. But sometimes . . ." He broke off and glanced over at her with a downcast look. The basketball was pressed between the palms of his hands. "It just sucks to be the one who got their heart broken, you know? And without knowing why."

I did know. I had been dumped before. Sort of. My first boyfriend, Alex, moved away with his family, and he didn't want to do the long-distance thing. Didn't even want to bother trying. Even though we were pretty much kids, it still hurt. No one wants to be abandoned.

Just then, Liv let out a laugh that echoed across the room. Ryan picked up a ball and tossed it toward the hoop. And missed again. He cursed under his breath as the timer ran out.

Her laughter seemed to swirl around us as it taunted Ryan. It almost didn't seem fair how Liv appeared perfectly fine while he was obviously still hurt. He didn't deserve any of this. He was a ni—he was a *good* guy. And good guys like him should be treated better.

I fought the urge to defend Ryan. To march across the room, snatch the drink out of her pretty hands, and order Liv to leave so he wouldn't have to see her anymore. And tell her what a big mistake she made by letting Ryan go. But I couldn't do that, not without getting kicked out myself. Besides, he wouldn't want Liv to know that she still bothered him.

Yeah, there was nothing I could do to her. There was one thing I could do for *him*.

Placing a hand on either side of his cheeks, I leaned up and kissed him. It wasn't a long kiss, but I kept my hands on his face as I beamed up at him.

He jumped at my sudden kiss but didn't pull away. "What are you doing?"

"Showing Liv that just because she doesn't want you anymore doesn't mean that someone else wouldn't grab on to you." Finally, I let go of him and dramatically fluttered my lashes. "You deserve the best."

"And you're the best?"

"Maybe not the *best*, but pretty darn close to it."

His grin was so wide that his dimple was practically a crater in his cheek. "Pretty darn close is good enough for me."

When I glanced over to see if Liv noticed us, my gaze collided with Ian. He gave me a small smile that didn't reach his eyes. Suddenly feeling uncomfortable that he was watching, I looked away. I smiled at Ryan for another few seconds before taking a step back, naturally letting go of his arm. He didn't even notice anything was wrong as he moved on to another game.

Following him, I couldn't help glancing back over at Ian.

He wasn't looking at us anymore. He was watching Megan as she told him a story with lots of hand movements and gestures. Even though he wasn't looking at me, I had a feeling that he was still aware of my every movement.

Like I was aware of each of his. Though I wished in my heart that I wasn't.

24

"Thanks again for driving us home," Ryan said as he leaned against the back seat. His hand was so close to mine that we were practically holding hands. Although our pinkies and ring fingers were touching, so maybe that counts. I wasn't exactly an expert at hand-holding etiquette.

Linh wiggled her fingers in the air over her shoulder. "It's no problem. We couldn't let you guys waste your money on an Uber when you're treating us to dinner next week."

"We're going out to dinner?"

Instead of answering me, she just shot us a big grin in the rearview mirror as Ian snorted loudly from the front seat. "I guess we have to now. And let me guess, we're going somewhere fancy?"

"Well, I haven't had steak in a while, but I'm partial to lobster, too."

"Stop teasing them." I leaned forward and patted Ian's shoulder with my other hand. "You can take us out for Korean BBQ instead. Maybe the karaoke one on Lemon Street? I've been dying to try that place."

Turning his head to glance back, he smirked at me. "Oh, we *can* take you out? That's sweet of you." I hope you won't let us pay, too, 'cause then that would be way too generous.

Ian started to reach up like he was going to touch me, but his eyes drifted down to Ryan's hand and mine. It felt like time in the car froze as the laughter faded from his face for a split second.

And then it was suddenly gone like it was a trick of the sunlight in his face. Ian gave me a quick grin and jerked forward to fiddle with the radio buttons. My hand fell away from his shoulder like a heavy weight.

Ryan laughed. "So you girls get to hang out and sing while we do all the grilling? I don't know if this ride is worth all *that*."

Linh turned her head and winked. "Hey, you can get out here if you don't like the deal. We're pretty close to your house anyway."

"Nah, I'm already looking forward to showing off my cooking skills. Gotta get some more points in." Ryan glanced over at me like he expected me to say something, but my mind was suddenly blank, wiped clean like the blackboard on the last day of school.

Instead, I gave him a half smile that felt entirely too forced and not at all convincing. His brow wrinkled in confusion. "Are you okay?"

"Yeah, just a little tired," I lied.

He leaned closer and patted his shoulder. "This pillow is available whenever you need it."

Normally I would take up his offer, but it just didn't feel right. Blinking rapidly, I glanced again in Ian's direction, but he was busy talking to Linh. "I'm good, thanks."

Still looking uncertain, he nodded and sat back in his seat. His finger tapped a steady beat on the car door. "By the way, did I tell you that I talked to my mom about taking a year off to travel before starting college?"

"You did? What did she say?"

"Oh, she almost fainted," he said with a chuckle. "You know how moms are. Plus, no one ever just delays college in my family. Or anyone we know actually. To be honest, she kind of freaked out. I almost backed down, but then I remembered what you said about doing what I want, and I just went for it."

Both of my hands gripped his arm when he didn't continue. "And . . . ?"

"And we're going to keep talking about it." His lips flashed into a quick grin. "I don't know if I *will* take a year off, but at least the idea's out there. It's actually just really nice to have my voice heard for once."

Unable to help myself, I gave him a tight hug. "I'm so happy for you. And whatever you decide to do, just remember that I'm always on your side."

His breath rustled the hair by my ear as he laughed and hugged me back. "So does that mean that you'll help me teach Kathy how to mow the lawn?"

I grimaced. "Uh . . ."

Just then Ian got everyone's attention. "Hey, what is Bá doing?"

We all turned to look out the window as Linh pulled up to their house. Their grandma was standing by one of the cars—only two were in the driveway today—with nearly a dozen grocery bags at her feet. She bent over and looped several of them over her arms and straightened up. Or at least she tried to.

Without waiting for Linh to put the car into park, Ian and Ryan leaped out and were at her side within seconds. They each held on to her arms and pulled her upright before taking the bags away. With a stern look on his face, Ian looked like he was giving her a lecture while Ryan nodded every few seconds. Rolling her eyes, Bá smacked their arms and tried to take the bags back, but the brothers just brushed her away.

The concerned looks on their faces actually made my heart swell a bit. It was so cute to watch. Forget about the grilling skills, grandma love was getting both of the guys a ton of points.

Linh gave me a knowing smile like she knew what I was thinking. "Come on, let's go help them."

"Okay."

Between the four of us, we were able to get all the bags inside in one trip. I didn't know what their Bá had bought, but some of the bags were actually pretty heavy. Even Ryan struggled with them. I had no idea how she expected to bring all this inside herself.

"This is a lot of ground pork," Linh commented as she dropped the bags on the kitchen table with a loud thud. She stretched her arms up over her head, and they made a popping noise.

"Thank you. I'm making giò for the family this afternoon."

At her words, Ryan and Ian froze with horror etched across their handsome faces. They shot each other worried looks and practically stumbled over themselves to escape the kitchen. Or at least they tried to. Their grandma was already blocking the doorway with her arm as she smiled expectantly. "If you're not doing anything today, then you can all help me."

"Oh, we would love to, but we—"

"—there was this place we needed to go—"

"—to pick up before it closes—"

Unable to help myself, I leaned against the counter and crossed my arms. "That's funny. You both told us earlier that you didn't have anything to do."

Linh was right there alongside me with an identical grin. "Isn't that why you lent Ollie your car?"

"That's . . . right. I forgot. Thanks for reminding us," Ian said dryly with an annoyed look on his face.

"You're welcome." I had to swallow my laughter as Ryan just looked resigned and started to unpack the bags on the table. The more stuff he took out though, the more I was starting to understand why they were trying to escape. There were at least thirty pounds of ground pork on the table with bottles of fish sauce, bags of sugar, and a bunch of small pink bags that I couldn't read. "How many pounds is this?"

Bá pulled out several different spoons from the drawer by the stove. "About thirty-five pounds."

Ah, my guess was pretty close.

Across the table, Ryan groaned under his breath while Ian groaned out loud and flopped onto the chair next to his brother. "This is going to take hours. Why do we have to do this again?"

"Bác Noah's parents are visiting this weekend, and I can't let them leave empty-handed." Bá shook her head and pulled out a gigantic tub from the pantry in the corner like a magician. "Plus, we need some more giò for banh mì this weekend anyway. Unless you don't want any."

"I do want some banh mì," Ryan admitted. Ian shot him a look of betrayal, and he held both hands up in surrender. "What? You know you want some, too. It's one of your favorites."

"Yeah, but it doesn't mean we have to admit it."

To be honest, I was starting to feel overwhelmed, too, as Bá piled the meat into the tub. It was like a never-ending pink gooey glob.

Linh, on the other hand, was so excited that she started rocking back and forth on her heels. Her fingers wiggled like she was itching to get started. "How many giò would this make?"

"About twenty-five large ones. And then a few smaller ones. Oh, and we have to save some uncooked aside to make bún mọc."

"Oh, that's it?" I couldn't keep the thread of sarcasm out of my voice.

Luckily, Bá just laughed. "It takes a lot of work to feed this family, but I love them. Ian, why won't you set up the two food processors with your girlfriend?" She gestured toward the other table with a wave of her hand.

At first, I thought she meant Linh, but she was looking right at me.

Ian started coughing like he was choking on something. "Bá, Nina's not—she's not my girlfriend."

Her startled glance bounced between the both of us. "Oh, sorry, I thought she was your girlfriend because I saw her name pop up on your phone a few times last week."

Now it was my turn to choke. I don't even know what I was choking on. Air, spit, embarrassment. Either way, my cheeks burst with heat as everyone turned to stare at both of us. Me in particular, since I sounded like I was almost dying.

Ryan looked confused as he got up. "Do you need some water?"

"No, I'm—actually, yes. Water would be nice." At least drinking water would give me something to do.

Chewing on her lower lip, Linh studied the three of us with a suspicious glint in her eyes. I could practically imagine all the thought bubbles around her head like in an anime. And none of them were good.

Avoiding her gaze, I gave Ryan a grateful smile when he handed me a glass of water. Thank God, he didn't seem too bothered by Bá's comment. Ian, on the other hand, was studying the wall next to his elbow like the tiny cracks had the answer to all life's questions. The tips of his ears were pink though, so I know he was paying attention to us.

I had just taken a big gulp when Bá spoke up again.

"If you're not Ian's girlfriend, are you Ryan's girlfriend?"

Jeez, she was really on a roll today.

I spat the water out on the table, and both Ian and Ryan had to jump out of the way to avoid getting splattered. Horrified, I wanted to apologize, but this time I was actually dying for real as water went down the wrong pipe. My throat and cheeks were all on fire as I gasped for air. Both Ian and Ryan moved over to my side. Ian lightly patted my back, while Ryan grasped my shoulder. "Are you okay?"

"Yeah, I'm fine. Dying of embarrassment, but fine."

Not deterred by my near-death experience, Bá still wasn't going to let her question go. "So, whose girlfriend, are you?"

"I'm not—" I glanced back and forth between the two brothers. Both were standing so close to me that I could feel their heat from either side. Ryan's hand was still grasping my shoulder, while Ian's hand was just rubbing my upper back now. It was still hard to catch my breath, but now it was for an entirely different reason.

Being in this cute-boy sandwich wasn't turning out to be as much fun as I imagined.

From across the room, Linh's eyes met mine and she smirked at me.

So annoying.

Finally, Ryan seemed to notice something was wrong as he glanced back and forth between his brother and me. Or maybe the tension in the room was suffocating him like it was doing to me. I doubt that he could even imagine that there was actually something going on between Ian and me though. That there was so much more to the story then anyone could ever know.

And Ian . . .

Still silent, he practically jumped across the table to get away from us. His cheeks were burning red now as he turned back to the wall. His Adam's apple bounced up and down. I had a feeling that he was struggling to not look at me. Or maybe I just wished that he would. Even a tiny glance. Everyone else in the room was looking at me except him.

I answered Bá the only way I could honestly. "We're just all . . . we're all friends, Ba. Ian, Ryan, and me."

With her brows furrowed together like Ryan, Bá opened her mouth again, and I braced myself for the interrogation just as Linh jumped in. "And me! I know I'm your cousin, but I'm everyone's friend, too. Most of the time, as long as you don't bother me before breakfast."

Bá finally turned to Linh. "What's your name, con?"

"Linh." She looped her arm through Bá's like they were the best of friends and picked up a spoon. "So how much fish sauce do you need for all this? And where do you even buy a bucket of fish sauce that big?"

Once she steered their grandma out of the way, I concentrated on wiping down and scrubbing all the water I had spat out on the table until it was sparkling clean.

With a tight smile, Ryan waved me away. "This part is pretty nasty. Ian and I can handle the food processors since we already know how. Why don't you go help Bá and Linh with the measuring and mixing?"

"Oh. Okay."

As much as I liked their grandma, I was reluctant to help her after she kept putting me in the spotlight. Thankfully, once everything was prepped and ready, the food processors were so loud that Bá couldn't ask me any more questions even if she wanted to. None of us could talk at all. Although that didn't stop the twins from giving each other looks like they were having their own silent conversation.

Wishing I could know what they were saying, I turned to Linh and leaned in close. "Took you long enough to save me, but thanks."

"Yeah, just wait until we get home." She gave me a slow smile that made goose bumps tingle up and down my arms. Especially when she squeezed my hand. "You won't be thanking me then."

Oh no. I was in trouble now.

25

Two unread texts. One from Ryan and the other from Ian.

I glanced over at my phone for what felt like the hundredth time, but I couldn't bring myself to read the messages. Or even open them. Not because of what they would say, but because I didn't know whose text I should read first. Who I would answer first.

It seemed like such a simple thing, but right now it felt like the hardest thing in the world to decide. I don't know why it was so important, but it was.

"I don't think I'll ever eat pork again." Linh sniffed her fingers and grimaced.

"Seriously, same here."

"Okay, tell me the truth. Between Ryan and Ian, who is the better kisser?" she asked as she pulled a giant T-shirt over her head. Her fingers yanked the hem down until it fell around her knees. The shirt had a giant smiley face on the front that was identical to the one on her face.

Startled, I almost spat out the toothpaste all over the bathroom counter. "What are you talking about? I haven't kissed Ian yet!"

Hearing the word *yet*, she pounced on it like a lion spotting its prey. "But you want to, don't you? I can tell that you like both of them."

"I don't." But even I could hear that the words sounded unconvincing. Like something was caught in my throat. I waved my foamy toothbrush at her like a sword. "Seriously, I don't! That's just crazy."

"Okay, fine." She shrugged delicately as she pulled the towel off her head. Her damp hair fell over her shoulders in a tangled mess. "I was going to suggest making a list to help figure out who's better for you. But if you're not interested . . ."

"I'm not."

Staying silent, Linh gave me a tiny smile as she brushed her hair. Slowly and meticulously, as though getting every little tangle and bump out was the most important thing in the world to her right now.

Finally, after I finished brushing and rinsed out my mouth, I turned toward her. "But if I *did* make a list, I wonder who would be in the lead?"

That was all the encouragement she needed. Tossing aside the hairbrush with such force that it should have left a dent in the wall, Linh rummaged through one of the drawers. She pulled out a box of cotton swabs. "There's no use in wondering. Let's find out!"

"What are those for?"

"We have to keep points somehow." She laid them out on the counter in front of us and patted on either side of the sink. "Ryan's side will be in front of you, and Ian's side will be in front of me."

"Okay." I picked up a cotton swab and placed it in front of me. "Ryan is super sweet. And I guess they both get a point for being handsome. Can't say one is cuter than the other since they're twins."

Linh nodded and put a cotton swab on each side. A mischievous grin crossed her face. "Although, if we're going to be technical, I think Ryan should get an extra point for all his swoony muscles."

"Linh!"

"Are you going to pretend like you *haven't* noticed them? I've seen you hold on to his arms more than once."

My mouth opened and closed, but since she was right, I gave Ryan an extra point.

"Who has a better personality?"

"Ryan." She started to put one down on his side, when I held up a hand to stop her. "But I do like to talk to Ian. When we're not fighting, we actually get along really well . . ."

"Then Ryan gets one for being nicer, but Ian has more of a connection." She dropped one on each side and tapped on her chin. "What else? Ryan can cook."

"So can Ian. I mean, that's what he told me. And he's referenced *Top Chef* at least twice, so he probably watches that show."

"Oh, he obviously has good taste then. Okay, then that one should go to Ian."

"Ryan should get an extra one because he likes me, while Ian . . ." I broke off and shook my head. "I don't know how he feels about me."

Linh nodded and slid a swab onto Ryan's pile. "Then Ryan should get one for being honest about his feelings. He's straightforward. It sure makes things easier."

"Definitely."

"We don't even need to count up the points. It's obvious that Ryan wins." She glanced over at me. "Are you okay with that?"

I glanced back and forth at the two piles. She was right. It was clear who the winner was. "That's pretty much what I expected anyway. Ryan is an awesome guy."

But then so was Ian. It was hard to compare the two. On paper, Ryan was so much better. But sometimes things weren't as clear-cut, and it couldn't be sorted out on a list. Did Ian get an extra point because he seemed to know me better? But I'd only started to open up to Ryan, and he was just as easy to talk to. And Ian was super sarcastic, but sometimes that wasn't such a bad thing.

The more I stared at the cotton swabs, the more confused I became. It was like two parts of me wanted different things, different people.

"I don't know. I just . . . don't."

Linh gave me a sympatric smile and patted my shoulder. "If you don't know, then I think *that* might be your answer. It doesn't matter who has the most swabs if you don't even care."

It made sense, but that wasn't the answer I wanted.

"You forgot about Megan," I said with a sigh.

"Uh, is she a point for or against Ian?" She picked up another swab.

"She's someone who could wipe out all his points." At the blank look on her face, I took the cotton swab out of her hand. "Hypothetically, what if what I want is already taken by someone else?" I reached out and moved Ian's pile out of the way. Almost out of my reach. "Or worse, it's waiting for that someone else, and I'd be a mistake along the way. And then I'm left behind in the end."

"Okay, first of all, you think way too much. And second, instead of thinking of all these hypotheticals and what-ifs, why don't you just go ahead and ask him?" Linh crossed her arms and leaned against the back of the door so I couldn't escape.

With a sigh, I gathered up all the cotton swabs and shoved them back into the box. "Do you ever wonder if our parents' failed relationships screwed up our own love lives?"

"You mean, if I'm traumatized by my dad ditching us?"

"Kind of."

"Nope, not at all, because I would never fall in love with someone like my dad." She shrugged. "I love my mom, but he sucked. No, sucks, present tense, because I know he's still a bad person somewhere in the world. And technically, your parents didn't have a failed marriage. They're trying to make it work now."

"Considering everything that happened, I don't know if we could count it as a successful one. Love shouldn't be that hard," I said with a frown.

"There's no rule on how love should be." Linh tilted her head to left and pursed her lips together. "But you would prefer the easier route."

"What do you mean?"

"Just that you've always been that way with relationships. When there are problems or a chance of you getting hurt, you back out. You're not a risk-taker. Then again, I don't know if you've ever actually been in love."

"That's not true—"

Her eyebrows rose. "Oh, really? Think of your exes. Did you love any of them? Been truly heartbroken when it didn't work out?"

There was her blunt honesty again.

Maybe it was true that I'd never actually been in love. I was sad whenever I broke up with someone—especially that one time I was dumped. But I always got over it. And honestly, after a few weeks, I never really thought about them again.

"You've never been heartbroken either," I pointed out lamely.

"That's because I've never been in love. Believe me, when I do, I'm going all in. Risks and heartbreak and all. Nothing is going to stop me." She shrugged like it was no big deal. "But everyone is different. There's nothing wrong with the easy route. If it makes you happy, then do it. Just don't settle for something just because you don't want to get hurt. That's not fair for anyone. Remember, live for nothing or die for something."

I know she was expecting me to agree with her, but I couldn't.

There's no denying that my parents were very happy and in love *now*. Anyone could see that. Even though Aunt Sarah hated Dad, she knew how much Mom loved him. But I also saw everything that she went through, and I wasn't sure if it was worth it. Especially when it could all disappear again.

Yet now I couldn't help wondering if maybe it was. Maybe it just depended on who it was all for. Live for nothing or die for something.

I wished there was a third option.

26

Linh hopped onto the center of the couch with the bowl of popcorn and a giant bag of peanut butter M&M's. A couple of kernels fell onto her lap, and she swept them into her mouth. "I call dibs on the couch."

"You can't call dibs *after* you jumped on. You're supposed to call it *before*," I complained, sitting on the love seat across from her. I snuggled into the thick comforter on my lap.

"Before or after. Either way, it's mine." She grinned and popped another handful of popcorn in her mouth.

I rolled my eyes, but I didn't really put up a fight. Honestly, I didn't really care where I sat. I was just glad that we were finally having our movie night again. Plus, the love seat fit me fine since I was shorter than everyone else. All I had to do was curl my legs up a bit, and it was perfectly comfortable and cozy.

Mom and Aunt Sarah came into the living room. Their arms were full of snacks and drinks that they piled onto the ottoman.

"I found two movies. Do you want to watch *The Christmas Mix-Up* or *The Mistaken Bride*?" Mom asked as she pulled out her phone to stream on the TV.

"The Christmas Mix-Up," Aunt Sarah and I both said at the same time. She gave me a surprised look since everyone knew I hated the holiday movies like black olives—something I was *very* vocal about growing up.

I shrugged lightly. "For some reason, I'm in the Christmas spirit tonight."

"Yeah, despite the fact that it's 92 degrees outside right now," Linh said with a grin. "And the sun's already been down for twenty minutes."

"That's why we're inside and not outside."

"It is nice for us to finally be together. Just us for once." Aunt Sarah looked around the room. "I can finally relax again."

I glanced at Mom, but she didn't say anything or even look up at the subtle snub at Dad. In fact, I wasn't even sure that she heard her.

A lack of response didn't stop Aunt Sarah though. It never did. And it didn't matter to her that nobody was listening or that Dad wasn't even here to defend himself. After all, she's done this a ton of times before. With or without him.

Like Mom, I usually ignored her until she ran out of steam. Sometimes it only took a few minutes. Other times it took much longer.

"Mom would have been so mad if she knew I let him stay here with us this summer." Aunt Sarah perched on the arm of the couch and sighed. Linh scooted over to get out of her way. "If you didn't beg me, Beth, I wouldn't have agreed."

This time I knew Mom heard her. Her mouth tightened a bit, but she didn't say anything.

"Is the movie ready, Mom?" I asked loudly, hoping to change the subject.

"It's taking a little while to load."

With a sympathetic glance in my direction, Linh grabbed a can of soy milk and pressed it into her mom's hands. "You look thirsty."

"Thank you, con."

But Aunt Sarah didn't take a drink. Not when she wasn't done. If anything, she was only just beginning. "I don't know why you bother with him though. Once a cheater, always a cheater. Even if the person he was cheating with was *you*. Lord knows why you got together with him in the first place. But you should be even more worried since you know what he's *really* like. Only a foolish person lets themselves get abandoned again."

Even though she wasn't saying anything that I hadn't secretly thought about Dad before, I hated the fact that she used him to make backhand insults at Mom. Although it wasn't even backhanded tonight, that was a full-frontal insult to the face.

Thank God, the movie was finally starting.

"In fact, if it were me, I would have—"

"God, shut up," I muttered under my breath.

Or at least I thought it was under my breath.

Even though the first scene of the movie was a loud Christmas party, everyone in the room turned to look at me. Linh's mouth dropped in shock as Aunt Sarah's eyes narrowed into fierce slits.

"What did you say?"

Crap, I guess I wasn't quiet enough.

I could have backed down. Just shook my head and apologize. But I was so tired of overthinking everything and having all my emotions bottled up in a jumbled mess that I just exploded. "It's just . . . could we watch the movie instead of talking about my dad? Everyone knows you hate him, so you don't need to say it again."

I didn't think it was possible, but Linh's jaw dropped so low that it looked painful for her face to stretch that much. I couldn't blame her though. I could barely believe the words that were coming out of my mouth. No one *ever* talked back to Aunt Sarah. Occasionally Dad would fight with her, but even then, he always backed down. The only person who could make Aunt Sarah speechless was Bá.

And now me. Someone should give me an award or something.

That didn't mean I wasn't scared to death though. My palms were clammy and tingling. Especially when Aunt Sarah started tapping her foot against the sofa. She usually did that right before she was about to start shouting.

"I'm sorry. I didn't mean to—" I quickly stood up and moved across the room. "I have to go to the bathroom."

Hopefully I could hide in there until the movie distracted her enough. Or maybe I'd camp out in there all night. That felt like the better option. The tub could be cozy.

When I passed Mom, her hand swept out to grab my arm, stopping me from my escape. Surprised, I looked up at her. She gave me a hard stare for a minute or so, like she was seeing me for the first time. Or maybe she was seeing something *in* me for the first time.

"You don't have to apologize." Finally, Mom looked over at Aunt Sarah and scowled. "Your aunt should be apologizing to you. To both of us."

Holy. Crap.

I don't know who was more shocked at her outburst—Aunt Sarah or me. Although Linh would have been a close second, too. With Mom and Aunt Sarah on either side of her, she looked like she wanted to melt into the cushions and disappear.

I bet she was really regretting calling dibs on the couch right now.

Straightening her shoulders, Mom marched right over to her sister and stared down at her. I hadn't noticed until now that she was taller than Aunt Sarah. A lot taller. At least three inches. I always thought that Aunt Sarah was the taller one, but maybe it was because Mom's never stood up straight around her before.

Now her back was straighter than a ruler.

"And I would appreciate it if you would stop insulting David—Nina's dad and my future husband—in front of us. In fact, stop talking about him. Period."

Aunt Sarah blinked at her with wide eyes. "But after what he did to you . . . what he did to us . . ."

"He didn't do anything to me. I did it to him. And he still came back to us. If we can accept him—" Mom stopped and gave me a quick glance. Her voice wavered a bit. "If *I* can accept him, then you have no choice but to accept him, too. At least if you want us to be a family again."

Even though she was talking to Aunt Sarah, I felt her words hit me, too. Like an arrow right at the target.

"But *we're* your family," Aunt Sarah cut in just as Mom held up a hand.

"If you were really my family, then you would want us to be happy. And trust that I know what I'm doing. That I'm making the right decision."

"But what if you're wrong?" Aunt Sarah scowled. "And it's the wrong decision? What happens if he leaves you again?"

Mom lifted her chin. "Then I'll deal with it. It's not like you're the queen of perfect marriages either. At least my David's here with us now."

Ouch. Even I knew that was a low blow. Mom's eyes blinked rapidly like even she couldn't believe what she had said. Her hand halfway reached up toward Aunt Sarah before dropping again.

For the second time that night, Aunt Sarah was speechless as she stared at Mom.

As much as I loved my aunt—she was basically like another mom to me—everyone knew that she was a bit of a bully. But kind of in that aggravating way that you knew she still meant well and had good intentions, so you couldn't get *too* mad at her. It felt good to finally see someone stand up to her. And for that someone to be Mom, well, that was icing on the cake.

While a bunch of emotions crossed my mom's face—guilt, doubt, and nervousness—Aunt Sarah's face was strangely blank. "Then don't expect me to wait around and pick up the pieces for you again," she said in a low voice.

Mom immediately looked away, and I thought she was going to back down like I did. Instead, she squared her shoulders and nodded. "That's fine. I don't need you to help me, because it's my decision. And if you can't deal with it—without your snarky comments—then I don't think we should stay here anymore."

With that said, she turned and glided out of the room like she was a queen dismissing her servants.

Despite the fact that a giant feeling of dread settled in the pit of my stomach like a heavy weight, I knew I had never been more proud of her.

After we packed our clothes, I expected Mom to go to the nearest hotel. Instead, she drove straight downtown toward the Waldorf Luxury Hotel. It was super fancy, but that was expected, since the word *luxury* was right there in the name.

The lobby itself was as huge as my school's cafeteria. And there were fancy water bottles lined up on the counter. Not the cheap ones that you got at the corner stores, but the expensive kind that came in mini glass bottles. Probably flown in from a secret magical spring halfway around the world. And they were set up on a shiny gold tray next to a plate of freshly baked cookies the size of my hand.

This hotel was the kind of place that housed celebrities on vacation and rich heirs who were in town for multimillion-dollar business deals. Not for a semi-successful Realtor and her teenage daughter to escape to after a family fight.

But Mom strolled in as though she owned the place and booked a room like she did this every day. All I could do was wordlessly follow her. But not before I grabbed a couple of bottles of water and the whole plate of cookies to shove in my purse. And a few mints from the jar on the side.

The receptionist glanced over at me but didn't bat an eye. The celebrities who came in here were probably on diets anyway. They didn't need warm, heavenly smelling cookies in their lives. My mouth watered at the sweet and luscious scent.

After a couple of wrong turns—one that took us to the pet spa (yes, a pet spa)—we finally got to our room. When the door closed, Mom collapsed on the bed with a loud groan. Her face was fully pressed against the fluffy white pillow.

"Oh my God. I can't believe I did that."

Or at least that's what I assumed she said. It was sort of hard to tell with her voice all muffled.

Finally looking a lot more like the mom I knew, I handed over one of the still-warm chocolate chip cookies. She shoved nearly half of it into her mouth and let out a heavy sigh.

Kicking off my shoes, I climbed into bed next to her. I propped up a couple of pillows behind my back and popped a mint in my mouth. It instantly melted into liquid spice on my tongue. "I think you were great. Aunt Sarah's probably still sitting in the living room in shock. Actually, I know she is. Linh texted me."

For a brief second, Mom stopped chewing and smiled. "I know I should feel guilty for making her so mad, but man, that kind of felt good. Really good. And it was so long overdue. But I know I'll regret it tomorrow. Like eating that last piece of double fudge cake last night."

For once, I felt like the parent as I patted Mom's arm. "It's okay. We'll deal with it later. Let her be pissed for the night, and we'll go back home to grovel tomorrow."

"But I don't want to grovel." The leftover cookie crumbled in Mom's clenched hand. "She's the one who was wrong. Sarah shouldn't have talked about your dad that way. And especially in front of us. I *had* to say something."

"Why?" I couldn't help asking. "I mean, why now? Aunt Sarah's been crapping on Dad for years. It's her thing. But it never seemed to bother you before."

Instead of answering me, she set the broken cookie pieces on the nightstand and brushed off her hands. "And you? Why did you say something first?"

I didn't have an answer to that, so I shrugged like it was no big deal. "I just didn't feel like hearing all that tonight."

"Me neither. It bothered me. Always has. But I figured it was easier to stay quiet than start a fight." Mom leaned back against the headboard beside me. "But when you stood up to your aunt today . . . I don't know. It made me feel like I *had* to say something, too. Like I owed it to you, to myself, and to your dad *not* to stay quiet anymore. Especially when everyone's been so wrong about him."

"What do you mean?" I turned to my side so that I would be facing her. The bed sunk with each of my movements like we were on a fluffy cloud. "And what did you mean earlier when you said that he didn't do anything to you? That you did something to him?"

With a heavy sigh like all the air was collapsing out of her, Mom turned her head away. Her cheeks were stained pink. "You know how your dad and I were . . . together, even though he was married. It just happened. I'm not proud of it, but I didn't end it either. And when I got pregnant, I was scared and . . ."

She didn't seem like she could continue, so I finished her sentence for her. "And you moved back to Austin with Bá and Aunt Sarah, because Dad couldn't leave his other family. I know." We all knew this story. I didn't know why she was telling me this again though.

Her voice was so low that I almost didn't hear her at first. "He didn't know."

"What?"

"He didn't know that I was pregnant. I never told him. As soon as I found out that I was, I ran away. I changed my phone number and shut down all my social media."

Shoving myself upright, I stared at Mom in shock. "You ran away . . . and ghosted him?"

Her lips curved into a brief smile. "Pretty much."

"But why?"

She tilted her head back and stared at the ceiling as if the answers were written up there. "Because I was ashamed. Not of you. I would never be ashamed of you. But the whole time, I knew that I shouldn't have been with your dad. That we shouldn't have had the affair. That we shouldn't have let it go so far. And once I realized I was pregnant, I couldn't face him anymore. I could barely face myself by that point. The level of guilt multiplied by a hundred. A thousand."

I still didn't understand. "Because you were scared that he would leave you?"

"Because I was afraid that if he knew, he would leave his family for *me*." Mom shook her head. "I know it sounds stupid, but I couldn't let him do that. I already hated being the other woman, but I would despise myself if I was the cause of his broken family. We didn't even reconnect again until over a year after he got divorced. And that was purely by accident."

There were so many thoughts whirling through my brain that it hurt to think. It felt like my brain was about to explode, and all I could do was focus on my breath and breathing at this point.

Everything that Mom said, everything I thought about Dad—felt about him—was a total lie.

Like Aunt Sarah, I blamed Dad for leaving Mom. For abandoning *us*. And in reality, he didn't. He didn't even know I existed. He wasn't even given the chance to know. And once he did know, he came right back into our lives. On his own free will, *after* he left his other family. He didn't family hop. He didn't change his mind on a *whim*. And he never told me *any* of this.

But then, it never occurred to me to ask him either. Most of the time I didn't even try to talk to him. Not in the two years that he's been in my life, because I assumed I knew everything.

I swallowed the lump in my throat. "But why? Why did you lie to everyone? Why did you lie to me?"

Her fingers played with the edge of the white comforter between us. "I was scared, and I didn't want your Bá to blame me for running away. It was easier to just say that your dad left us. To make him the villain. She was still mad, but she also felt sorry for me. And then you came along, and everything was okay for a while. Perfect. But when you got older, I didn't want you to get mad at me either, so I ended up keeping the truth to myself. I didn't think it would hurt anyone. Until I met your dad again."

"How did he find us?"

"We have a mutual friend who gave him my new number. And when he found out about you—" She broke off and sucked in her breath as her flush slid down her neck. I didn't think she could look any guiltier, but somehow, she did. "He wasn't happy. Especially when I told him that everyone thought he abandoned us. But eventually he agreed to play along because I asked him to. I think he was worried that I would take you and run away again."

Frustrated, I ran my fingers through my hair, both massaging and tugging it at the same time. "Okay, and why tell me now? What's the point of telling me this when you hid it from me all this time?"

"Because it's not fair to your dad. He's not—he's not the villain. And I'm tired of seeing him treated this way. Especially by you." Her fingers were gripping the covers now. "I thought things would get better once we moved to Houston with him. Once we were away from your Bá and your aunt Sarah and started our own family. Then we could start over. But it hasn't gotten better. You still haven't accepted him."

"Of course I haven't." My hand dropped to my side. And the words poured out of me. Faster than I could even say them. "And do you know why? Because I couldn't let myself believe *even* for a second that I *had* an actual dad. I've been so freaking afraid that if we let him into our lives he'll disappear again. Because what if he suddenly decided that he didn't want to be in our family after all and ran off with another family. Because he'd done it before. But no, wait, he didn't. He didn't leave his other family to join ours. He didn't abandon us in the first place, because he didn't even know about *me*. Because you never told him!"

I was practically yelling by the time I was finished. Something that I've never done to Mom before—to any adult. Bá would have kicked my ass for being so disrespectful. Rude. Insolent.

But I think even she would give me a free pass if she were in my shoes right now.

I could feel Mom's eyes staring at me, but I couldn't look at her right now. I didn't want to see her big sad eyes watching me. I didn't want to forgive her. Not yet. Not when I felt this overwhelming guilt at how I'd been treating Dad all this time. How he must have felt.

Oh God, I should have gotten ice cream with him that day.

"I know it's not fair—"

"None of this is fair." Rolling onto my side, away from Mom, I tucked myself into a little ball and squeezed my eyes shut. "Just . . . leave me alone."

Mom stayed in the same position for a long time before she got up. She came around the bed and paused by my side for a few seconds before going into the bathroom. I heard the water running for a few minutes, but I still didn't open my eyes. Not even to take out my contacts, even though I knew I would regret it tomorrow when they burned and were stuck to my eyeballs.

After what felt like forever, the door opened and Mom shut off the lights. This time she didn't try to come over to me. She went straight to her side of the bed and lay down.

After a minute or two, she lightly touched my arm. Her voice was soft. Sad as it drifted over to me. "I am sorry. For everything."

I didn't trust myself to answer her. Not yet. But I didn't move away either.

Hours later, I knew that neither of us were asleep. Our breathing was too even, too controlled, like we were trying too hard to pretend to be asleep. It was better than admitting that we were awake.

"So, were you telling the truth when you threatened not to see Aunt Sarah anymore?" I finally asked out loud. Careful to stay away from dangerous topics like lying moms and misunderstood dads.

She let out a sigh. "It was just an empty threat. We'll have to see her sooner or later if we move back."

Her words hung in the air between us for a few seconds. "What do you mean if we move back?"

"Uh . . ." Mom hesitated like she was afraid to tell me. Like she hadn't already dropped enough bombshells on me tonight. What could possibly be worse than lying to me my entire life?

"Your dad and I have been talking, and we've been thinking about moving back to Austin permanently. So we could be close to family. Although at this moment, I doubt Aunt Sarah will be very happy with us right now." Now it was her turn to word vomit. It was easy to see where I got that particular trait. "Your dad interviewed for a position at the University of Texas a few days ago, and I've been house hunting in the meantime. There's a nice one about fifteen minutes from your aunt's house that's within our budget. It's a one-and-a-half-story with the primary bedroom downstairs, so you can have the entire upstairs to yourself. Your room has a cute little dormer window for you to set up your desk or bookshelf. A few rooms need to be repainted, but that's an easy fix. You could even paint your own room. You don't have to if you don't want to though. It's just an idea."

Turns out that Mom had one last bombshell up her sleeve.

But compared to the other secrets, this one wasn't so bad. In fact, it was actually nice. I mean, I could have—should have—been mad that she was uprooting me *again*. That we would have to move. That I would have to change schools. Start my senior year at a new place.

But the idea of moving back to Austin, of being back home, overshadowed all that. Despite living in Houston for a year, I never considered it to be my home. I never bothered to get to know anyone or make any friends. I never even got a toll tag in Houston because I never needed one in Austin. Instead, I took the longer routes and inside roads because getting an *actual* Houston toll tag made things seem too permanent. Too real.

"So what do you think?"

"I think . . . I think that sounds nice."

The mattress creaked as she rolled over to look at me. The room was still too dark to see her face. There was only a faint bit of light coming from the night-light in the bathroom. "Really? 'Cause we could even make one of the other bedrooms a guest room for when Linh stays over."

"She would probably like that." Actually, she'd probably love it. "But what about Dad? Would he be okay with being so close to Aunt Sarah?"

"He's not looking forward to it. But since it's important to us, he understands." Mom laughed out loud. "And it definitely helps that he'll have his own house to escape to instead of a tiny room."

I nodded, even though I knew that she couldn't see me. "As long as he's okay with it. He's done . . . enough for us already."

"He has," she said softly. I could hear the emotion and affection in her voice. And I knew no matter what she did or said, I couldn't stay mad at her for too long. "By the way, if we move back, then you can see Ryan a lot more. Or is it Ian this week?"

I snorted at her innocent tone. "Yeah, I'm not going to talk about that. You don't deserve any gossip about my life tonight."

"Fine. When do you want to go back to your aunt's house?"

"Whenever she's not pissed anymore."

"So never?"

"Yep."

"Sounds good to me. Your dad will probably enjoy staying at the hotel for a few days. Finally have some peace and quiet. Maybe visit the pet spa."

We both laughed this time. Not so much at the weak joke, but more at the relief that both of us felt. It was like a weight was lifted off our chests, as corny as that sounds.

"Nina?" Her voice was cautious in the darkness. Like it was testing the waters between us. "Do you want to go see the house with us when your dad gets back?"

Such a simple request, but I knew it wasn't that easy. If we got a house here, we would be closer to Aunt Sarah and Linh. We wouldn't be able to keep our families separate anymore. Our two families, the two *separate* families, would have to combine to be one. We'd be living in the same house and putting down roots. We'd be taking that step forward. Together.

And as scared as I still was, I owed it to Dad to try now. No matter how much the thought terrified me. "Yeah, I do."

27

IAN: So I've been thinking about my superpowers. And I'm torn between shape-shifting, time travel, or telepathy.

IAN: With shape-shifting, I could pretend to be anyone I want. That's super cool. Think of all the secrets I could find out. All the things I could do. Or I could time-travel and change the world. Or try that mochi donut place before it got so popular and crowded. Hell, I could even invent mochi donuts before it became a thing and be rich!

NINA: Do you even know how to bake?

IAN: That's not the point. You know what? Scratch shape-shifting. I already know what it feels like to look like someone else. So now that leaves time travel and telepathy. With telepathy, I could read people's minds and manipulate them. Professor X makes it look super cool.

NINA: You could even skip everyone in the mochi donut line. And they wouldn't even get mad at you.

IAN: Now you're thinking. Okay, I pick telepathy as my superpower.

NINA: And the world rejoices.

NINA: You do know that you don't actually GET the superpower, right? It's what you WANT to have.

IAN: Just let me dream this one time.

IAN: Now, if I killed someone, I would definitely need Ryan to help me hide the body. And he'd bring the shovels without asking any questions. Plus, if anything ever got linked back to us, then our DNA are identical, so they wouldn't be able to prove which one of us actually did it.

NINA: It's a little disturbing how well thought out this is. I feel like this isn't the first time you've considered this question.

IAN: Hey, I never do anything halfway. Kathy would definitely have to help find the best spots to bury the body though. Neither Ryan nor I are very good with directions. Unless you want to help us?

NINA: Nah, I'm good. I have my own skeletons to bury.

IAN: Great, we could do it together. Teamwork makes the dream work.

NINA: What makes you think I wouldn't lead the police to the bodies and pin everything on you?

IAN: That's just wrong.

NINA: Why not? I feel like it would be the perfect crime. After all, you said that with your identical DNA, you wouldn't be convicted anyway. This way we could test out your little theory to see if it would work.

IAN: And if it doesn't?

NINA: I'll make sure to drop off some bun bo hue at the jail for you at least once a week. With the mochi donuts.

IAN: At least you're not totally heartless.

28

"Guess you couldn't help getting back into your stalker habits, huh?" Ian asked with a grin as he scooped some corn onto a plate and held it out to me. "Although you're doing a pretty bad job today. You're supposed to *pretend* that you didn't know I was here."

Taking it from him, I poked his chest and shoved him backward. "Don't flatter yourself. I'm just here for the steak."

"That's better." He laughed and swept his hair off his face. "Admit it. I'm too irresistible for you to send to jail. You'd miss me too much."

I resisted the urge to stick my tongue out at his smug face like I was ten years old again. "Never."

Turning away to sit at the small table by the piano, I couldn't stop the smile from drifting across my face. But I made sure it was gone by the time I turned around to face Ian again. That didn't stop my beaming from the inside, though.

This morning, the sun was barely up when Mom bolted out of the room. She claimed that she had to run to the store for some important stuff like pads and tampons. Or at least I think that's what she said over her shoulder as she left.

I spent all day at the hotel on my own, but Mom never came back. I knew she was fine, since every time I texted her, she answered with a different emoji. A thumbs-up. A jogging woman. She even texted a picture of a turtle and some vegetables. Either she was planning on getting a pet turtle or eating one for dinner. I was afraid to ask.

By midafternoon, I decided to leave the room so that Mom could finally stop avoiding me. It didn't take *that* long to buy pads and tampons. Then again, maybe she forgot how to, since she's never had to buy them before.

Ironically, we never had to worry about buying those things when we were at Aunt Sarah's house. With her couponing skills and hoarding tendencies, we were always stocked up in that department. And with lotion. Even though she was a bit of a bossy bully, Aunt Sarah always took care of us.

Thinking of the tampons made me think of Ian (which was something I never thought I would ever say about a guy), and I decided to visit him at the Shamrock Patio. He did promise to be a distraction from my family. Without any judgments.

Besides, there was nowhere else to go, since Linh was still with her mom. She promised to text me when Aunt Sarah wasn't mad anymore. So far, nothing yet. And Ryan was finally taking my advice and teaching Kathy how to mow the lawn. I hoped that meant he was planning to go on the trip with his friend, too.

I was almost done with my steak when Ian came strolling over. Leaning one hand against my table, he stole one of the pieces I had cut and stuck it in his mouth. "So, what have you been doing today besides stalking me?"

I rolled my eyes. "You're really making me wish I stayed at the hotel."

Dropping his teasing act, Ian gave me a concerned look. "Hotel? Why were you at a hotel? What happened?"

"My mom and aunt got into an argument, so we're staying at the Waldorf Luxury now."

Again, I expected him to ask about the argument, but he glanced over his shoulder to make sure he wasn't needed before sitting down in the chair in front of me. His arms crossed on the table as he leaned forward. "Are you okay?"

"Yeah, it wasn't my argument." I stopped and frowned a bit. "Well, I *did* start it, but it was mainly between them. It's . . . a long story."

He flashed me a brief smile. "You always say that about your family."

"Because nothing's ever simple with them."

"Nothing is ever simple with anyone," Ian pointed out with a raised brow. "Come on, how bad can it be?"

"You'd be surprised." Not sure if I wanted to prove him wrong, or if I was just dying to talk someone—anyone—about what happened, but I ended up blurting out everything. Including the conversation with Mom and how she lied to everyone. I gave him an expectant look when I was done. "Well?"

He scrunched up his face and finally nodded. "Okay, that's pretty bad. Like almost K-drama type of bad. At least there's no shocking birth secret. What are you going to do?"

I poked at the pile of potatoes left on my plate. "What do you mean? I'm just here to eat my free steak."

"First, your other steak was free. This one isn't. We're not running a charity here. And second, there's tons of stuff you can do. First, you can forgive your mom, but that's a given."

"Why?"

"Because you're you," he said like that was enough of an explanation. He took the fork from me so I would stop stabbing the potato lumps. "And there's tons you can do about your dad. *With* your dad, now that you know the truth."

"Well, technically he still left his other family—"

"But you don't know why. Maybe there's an explanation for that, too. You won't know until you ask him. And that means that you need to talk to him first."

I grimaced. Ian was right, but hearing the words out loud didn't make it easier. Sure, all the reasons for avoiding Dad were gone now. And I didn't know why he got divorced. Just like I was in the dark about how he didn't abandon *us*. And I knew that after the way everyone in our family treated him all these years, how I treated him, I was obligated to try to make it up to him now.

If only it were so simple. I've avoided him for so long, I didn't even know what to say or what to do anymore. And after being angry for two years, I couldn't switch my feelings that easily.

"I've kept him at a distance for so long that I don't even know how to start. It's weird."

Ian gave me a smile so gentle that I almost forgot what we were talking about. "You can start with some ice cream."

"Ice cream?"

"Yeah. Get a scoop of ice cream with him and see where it goes."

Sigh. "Fine, I'll try," I finally said. "Now you have to tell me a family secret."

"Why?"

"Because that's how we do things. I tell you something, and then you tell me something. It has to be good though."

He looked amused and leaned back in his chair. "I don't remember ever making this deal."

I poked his arm repeatedly. "Come on. Come onnn . . ."

Swatting my hand away, Ian rubbed his forearm. "Fine. Let me think of something."

A couple of minutes went by and he still didn't say anything. Since I wasn't wearing a watch, I pointed at my bare wrist, and Ian sighed loudly. When about five minutes had passed, I leaned forward to poke him again, but he grabbed my finger with his hand so I couldn't move.

"Fine, this is kind of stupid, but has Ryan ever told you about his ex-girlfriend?"

"Liv? Sort of."

Ian chewed on his lower lip. "Well, she broke up with him because of me."

I jerked backward so suddenly that my chair almost knocked over. I barely noticed though. All I could do was blink at him. "What?!"

His hands rose like he was defending himself. "Shit, nothing like *that.* I would never do anything like that to Ryan." He raked his hand through his hair. "One day she found me at his locker before lunch. I was borrowing his history book because I left mine at home. She must have thought I was Ryan, because she grabbed my arm and kissed me."

"And then what?"

"And then nothing! When I jerked back, she realized that I wasn't Ryan and was super embarrassed. We both were. And we promised never to tell him what had happened. But then they broke up a week or two after that."

I shook my head. "But that doesn't mean it's your fault. Maybe—"

Now it was his turn to fiddle with the potatoes with my fork. "Later she told me that kissing me made her realize that she wasn't that into Ryan. Not that she liked me or anything, but just that if she was *really* in love with him, then she should have been able to tell us apart."

"Oh." It was kind of hard to argue with that logic. "She was probably ashamed that she couldn't tell you guys apart. I know I would be."

He glanced up at me. "But *you* could tell us apart."

"Not in the beginning. And after I found out there were two of you . . ." I shook my head and laughed. "If Liv even felt a tiny bit the way I did, then she must have been mortified."

"Oh, she definitely was."

"And you never told Ryan?"

Ian shook his head.

Crossing my arms, I leaned back in my seat and chewed on my thumbnail. "Maybe you *should* tell him. He thinks that she broke up with him because he's too nice."

"He told you that?"

"That's what she told him, but he knows it's a lie." For a moment, I wondered if it was right for me to tell Ryan's secret like this. Especially one that he didn't even tell his own brother, but I felt like this was something Ian needed to know. "He said he doesn't care, but I know that he does. I think it would really help him to know the truth."

Ian didn't say anything for a long time. All he did was rub his lower lip like he did so often when he was thinking of something. "I guess sometimes wondering can be worse than actually knowing."

"That sounded almost philosophical," I teased, glad that it seemed like he was going to take my advice.

He grinned. "Thanks, but don't expect it to happen very often."

"That's not true. You're really good at expressing yourself. Like in your essay."

"What are you talking about?"

Oh crap. I didn't mean to say that.

I lowered my eyes to the tabletop and scratched at the peeling paint in one corner. "Well, when I was looking for you to return your stuff, I looked through the flash drive on your key chain and saw the comic and . . ."

It took him a few seconds to realize where I was going. Peeking up, I could tell when it hit him as his fingers tightened on the fork. "*That* essay."

"Yes."

"And you read it."

Was he asking me or telling me? Either way, I gave him a weak nod.

His jaw clenched and his lips pursed together into a straight line. It was so tight that I saw his right dimple pop out. I didn't even know that it was possible to show off a dimple without smiling.

And then silence.

For ages.

"How do you know it's mine and not Ryan's?"

His question made me pause. How did I know? There wasn't a name on the essay. And the *Spider-Man* comic was Ryan's. But somehow, I *knew* that those were Ian's words. That he was the one whose words touched me.

"I just do, and I'm sorry that I read it, but I'm also not sorry." I shook my head because I knew that I wasn't making sense. "Because when I read your essay, I thought it was amazing."

He raised an eyebrow and scoffed. "Amazing? It was barely a rough draft. Half of it was me rambling to myself. That's why I didn't finish it. I didn't really know where I was going with it."

Even though he was brushing it off, I knew the essay was important. To both of us and he needed to know it.

I reached out to touch his arm. "But what you *did* write was amazing. Even though it wasn't much, it was enough." I let out a short laugh. "It's the main reason why I decided to track you down and accidentally found Ryan instead. Because—because I didn't understand how you could feel the same way that I did. It was almost like I was writing the words down myself. Except you expressed it way better than I ever could. And I had to find out if you had figured things out yet."

Looking much nicer now, Ian shook his head. "I haven't. I'm still trying to find out who I am without my family around. But the more I do that, the more I feel like I'm almost betraying them. Like wanting to distance myself makes me *not* a part of the family anymore."

"That's not true. You can be your own person and still be a part of your family. It's not one or the other." I grinned. "Whether you're here 24/7 or visiting once or twice a month, you still have Bá's phở broth running through your veins."

"I know, but . . . it's still a work in progress."

"Will you let me know when you figure it out? I could use some life-changing revelations with my family, too."

Finally, the corners of his mouth quirked up a tiny bit. "So basically, I do all the work, and then you swoop in and reap the benefits."

"I'll give you credit for it," I joked with a wink.

He laughed, and I brightened at the fact that I was able to cheer him up. "I'm surprised you cared about that stupid essay enough to track me down."

"Because I care about—" I broke off and shook my head. "Because your essay made me get invested. Like a good book. You should definitely add that to your list of hobbies."

Ian started to say something else, but Mr. Alan came over and clapped a hand on his shoulder. His other hand tossed a dirty towel over his shoulder. "Did Ian tell you about that new song he's been practicing for you?"

"New song?" I glanced over at Ian as his face flushed. Seriously, it went from gorgeously tanned to tomato red within seconds. "No, he didn't."

"I didn't practice it for her," he muttered as he looked away. His head ducked down a bit as though he didn't want to look me in the eyes.

This was surprising. I thought I knew all of Ian's different sides, but I've never seen the shy side of him before. It was sweet and kind of endearing.

Mr. Alan laughed. "Sure, you didn't. Why don't you show her anyway?"

Ian looked like the *last* thing he wanted to do was play the piano for me. So obviously, I did the *first* thing that came to my mind. I dragged my chair over to the piano and patted the seat next to me. "Well, come on. I want to hear it."

Tossing his piano teacher an annoyed look, Ian dragged himself over to sit next to me like he was going to his own execution.

"Come on, it can't be as bad as the last time you played for me. Nothing could *ever* be that bad."

I expected him to give me a cocky or sarcastic retort, but all he did was roll his eyes. It wasn't until he fiddled with the volume and keyboard settings for a few minutes before I realized that he was nervous. Super nervous, like he was performing at a recital or something. His leg bounced beneath the table, kind of distracting me. I was tempted to touch him to calm him down, except I still didn't know why he was so anxious in the first place. It was just Mr. Alan and me. And obviously Mr. Alan had heard him play tons of times.

His fingers curved over the keyboard lightly. Ian let out a low deep breath and started to play. The first few keys were shaky and slow. It took a little while for me to catch the actual melody.

Ian's forehead creased as he concentrated on the right notes, and I was tempted to smooth it out with my finger. I didn't though, in case it would mess him up. At least his leg stopped shaking for the moment.

It was a slow and sweet song. There were a bunch of off keys here and there as Ian pressed the wrong ones, but I could tell that it was a love song. Even without any words. The melody was smooth and warm, like being caressed or enveloped in a big hug.

When he was done, I clapped my hands together in a light applause. "Well, that wasn't half bad."

The leg tapping came back. "Gee, thanks."

Trying to look sincere, I gently poked his leg until he stopped. "Hey, I'm serious. That was pretty good. What song is it? I've never heard it before."

Ian suddenly looked shy again. "It's called '27. May' by Yiruma. He wrote it for his wife, because that's their wedding day."

"I could tell it was a love song. You could almost feel the heart and emotions in the notes. It reminded me of being in love." I glanced over at him. "Have you ever been in love?"

He shrugged. "To be honest, I don't know, but I guess if I don't know, then that would be my answer, right?"

"I guess." Not knowing why his answer bothered me, since I've never been in love either, I scooted my chair closer so I could reach the keyboard, too. My right arm rubbed against his as I laid my fingers on the keyboard. "Teach me how to play that song. What's the first note?"

Moving my hands around, Ian repositioned them until my fingers hovered over the right keys. "And press down on these fingers first and then this." He tried to move my hands again, but almost jabbed me in my face with his elbow. "Hold on."

To my surprise, Ian got up and stood behind me. With his arms around me, he laid both of his hands on top of mine. They were so big that they dwarfed my hands, but amazingly gentle and light as he helped me press down on the piano with each finger.

My breath got caught in my throat at the sudden feel of his warm hands on top of mine. That combined with the cool keys beneath my fingertips. Surely that was the reason goose bumps trailed up and down my arms. Not because his chest was pressed against my back, almost like he was cradling me. Or that I could feel his face hovering over my head.

Not over my head.

My shoulder.

Ian was barely inches away from my face. Especially when I turned my head to peek over at him. Our eyes locked as our fingers froze in place. His breath was on my lips like a light warm breeze, and it caused me to melt back against him a little bit, bringing us even closer. Something I thought wasn't even possible.

The expression on his face changed as he glanced down at my lips for a split second. But a split second was enough to make the tingling rush up to my neck. Especially when his face got closer. His breath smelled like peppermint.

I closed my eyes and then . . . and then . . .

"Hey, are you all done with the steaks tonight?!"

The shout hit me like a bucket of water. Hit both of us as we jerked our heads back and stared at each other. For a few seconds, we didn't move.

I knew that the moment was gone, but I was reluctant to move. Maybe Ian felt the same because he stayed hovered over me for the longest time. Half holding me in the position, like he was hiding me. Protecting me. My heart was still beating in overdrive at our almost kiss, even as my stomach sunk in disappointment.

Damn. I wanted to kick the person who interrupted us. Or at least give him an evil glare once I was able to pry my eyes away from Ian's face. His lips were tightened into that annoying line again. Just a minute ago, they looked so soft and inviting.

Ian let out a low shaking breath. "I think that maybe you should learn on YouTube instead. I can barely teach you when I don't know how to play myself."

"That's probably a good idea."

Finally, we both pulled away at the same time.

"That was . . . Nina . . ." His voice was even softer than a whisper. I wouldn't have even heard him if I hadn't been watching his mouth so closely. He slowly swallowed, and my eyes flickered down the line of his throat before going back up to his face.

"Yes?"

Ian stared at me for a long minute. His eyes were barely blinking, but I could see a rush of emotions flood his face before he turned away from me. "I think I should go home."

And he did.

And for the first time that week, Ian didn't text me that night.

29

The next morning, I was in the lobby trying to read, instead of obsessing over Ian and our almost kiss, when Dad found me. Not sure how, since I was pretty much tucked away in the corner armchair behind a giant plant.

Not that I was trying to hide from him or anything. At least not intentionally this time. I wanted to give my parents some privacy until the hotel moved us to two rooms with a connecting door. Mom was fine with me having my own room, but only if she was next door. She was worried that I would sneak in a boy or throw a raving party. This coming from the woman who kept an earth-shattering secret from her family—her own daughter—her entire life.

But I was over *that* now.

Mostly.

The first place I went to go be alone was the pool. The hotel boasted seven different pools in their facilities. All ranging from inside, outside, and kiddy to wave. One pool even ran from the inside *to* the outside. Plus, they had these lounge chairs that swallowed you up like you were laying on a fluffy cloud.

I would have stayed out there, but the tanning butler kept coming over to offer me sunscreen every five minutes. He couldn't seem to understand that I didn't need his services.

At first, I thought he was flirting with me or something, but he was in his forties. And then I saw him kiss the lifeguard on the other side of the pool. A really hot lifeguard, too, who could put the Hemsworth brothers to shame.

So *obviously* I wasn't his type, but way to go, Mr. Tanning Butler.

Not to mention, he seemed very sweet and was genuinely worried that I would burn. Or maybe that the hotel would get a bad review if I did. Either way, once he chased me inside, the only other place I knew in the hotel was the lobby. Or the pet spa. And I couldn't stay there with my allergies. Plus, it would be super weird if I did, considering I didn't have a pet with me.

A shadow loomed over my shoulder. "Do you mind if I sit down?" Dad asked.

"Sure."

I assumed that he was going to sit in the seat next to me—I already scooted over a foot—but Dad decided to sit in the seat across from me instead. He clasped his hands together and leaned on his knees with his forearms. His mouth opened and closed slightly like he was trying to figure out exactly how to start.

Deciding to help him out, I switched off my Kindle and placed it beside me. "What's Mom doing?"

"Oh, she's at the spa. Normal one, not pet," he quickly added. "Since we're still not sure how long we'll be staying here, she thought she would make the most of it in the meantime."

I grinned. "Considering she also went to the spa yesterday, I think she's definitely making the most of this."

Dad made an exaggerated grimace. "Yeah, we need to get out of this hotel soon or we'll end up spending your college fund."

"Or your retirement fund."

"Oh, no. We're not touching that," he joked with a laugh. It slowly died as he cleared his throat. "Your mom told me that she confessed to you about . . . everything."

"She did."

His hands were clasped together so tightly that his knuckles were turning white. "I don't want you to blame your mom. She did what she thought was best at the time."

I was almost surprised that the first thing he did was defend her, but I shouldn't have been. I mean, he basically let himself be the villain in our family for years and probably wasn't ever planning to tell me the truth. So of course the first serious talk we'd ever had would be about forgiving Mom.

But in my heart, I knew that Ian was right. I couldn't stay mad at her. In a way, I didn't even think I was anymore. Not that much anyway. But that didn't mean that I could totally forgive her. It's not like I could snap my fingers and *poof!* everything would go back to the way it was before.

"I don't blame her, but it's going to take a while for me to . . . accept everything," I said slowly. "It's a lot right now."

"I know. You've always been her rock. And she's been yours. And it's going to stay that way no matter what happens." One of his hands lifted and I thought he was going to reach out to me, but it hovered in the air for a few seconds before falling back onto his lap again. "But now that you know the truth, I want you to know that I'm here, too. I may not be able to be your rock, but I would like to be here for you. Just a tiny pebble, if that's what you want."

"Thanks."

"And I do want us to talk." Dad looked a little hesitant, like he knew this would be a bad idea, but he took the plunge anyway. "About anything you want."

There were so many questions, so many things I wanted to know about everything. It was like I was starving and someone plopped me down in front of the biggest buffet in the world. With a homemade pasta station made from scratch and a chocolate bar with hundreds of different varieties and flavors. And sushi.

So much sushi.

Maybe I was hungry. Skipping breakfast probably wasn't the best idea.

I let out a deep breath. Better to take it one thing at a time. "I want to know about your other kids. I want to know about Lucy and Adam."

He instantly nodded like he knew exactly what I was going to ask before I even did. "They're great. You would like them. Adam is loud. Outgoing. He's everyone's best friend. And he loves to build things. Model planes. Random stuff around the house. He would nail and glue everything together. There used to be Legos all over the place when he was small. I stepped on so many of them that the bottoms of my feet don't even feel pain anymore. And Lucy . . ."

His voice got a bit softer when the subject turned to Lucy. I was almost fascinated by the change in his voice, his facial expression. I'd never seen him like this before. Then again, I normally went out of my way to avoid him. "She's like you, actually. She's smart. Almost too smart for her own good. But she's not a nerd. And she loves to pick fights with her brother. They can spend all day fighting about who's more annoying. But you can tell that they love each other.

"And now . . . now they're even better. Lucy is going to a dental internship in New Orleans next month, and Adam has a new girlfriend. I think she's the second one this year," he said with a laugh. "Or maybe third. I couldn't really tell."

"I thought . . ." Leaning forward, I stared at him. "I thought you don't keep in touch anymore. How do you know all that?"

"You're not the only one who's good at stalking."

For a split second, I thought he was talking about Ryan and Ian, and all I could do was blink wordlessly at him. "I don't—what are you—"

"Mom told me that you check on Lucy and Adam's Instagram accounts all the time. In secret. I do, too." He shook his head. "I really should tell their mom that they post way too much stuff on their social media, but if they didn't, then I wouldn't be able to still be a part of their lives. Even if it's just a tiny invisible part."

Not even realizing what I was doing, I mirrored his position. Hands clasped together and arms pressing against my knees. "Do you miss them?"

Instead of answering me, Dad stared into space. Or at least I thought he was until I followed his gaze. He was watching a little two-year-old girl and her dad across the lobby. The little girl seemed determined to climb up her dad's leg like a monkey. At first glance, he looked like he was ignoring her, but the corners of his mouth kept twitching until finally he grabbed her under her arms and swung her around. Her sweet laughter echoed through the entire lobby, making everyone smile along with her.

So did Dad. "Did you know that Lucy's team won the regional Science Bowl a few months ago?"

I did. She posted about it for weeks both before and after their win. There was even a post about her family and how she—

"She thanked her dad. Her *other* dad," Dad softly said without looking over at me. "Her mom remarried pretty soon after we got divorced. To a friend of mine. A good friend, so it wasn't like she married a complete stranger. And I'm happy for them. I really am. But . . . I do miss them. A lot."

"Then why don't you call them? Or see them?"

"'Cause I think they're probably mad at me." He let out a soft laugh. "No, I *know* they are. Even when we were still a family, we didn't—I wasn't a good dad. We weren't happy. In fact, I wouldn't be surprised if they were happy when we split up. That's partially why I'm determined to make it work with your mom. And with you. To make sure I don't mess up my family like I did before."

I swallowed at the lump in my throat. Now that I could see how vulnerable he was, guilt burned away at me at all the times I avoided him. Blamed him for no reason. "Lucy seems very cool. I wish I was as motivated as her. I still don't know what I want to do with my life."

"You'll get there someday. It's not a requirement to have things figured out right now." He shook his head. "In fact, I think it's better that you don't know what to do yet. This way, you can grow a bit first and live life. It's better than rushing into a decision and regretting it later on."

"You mean it's okay if I just drive along aimlessly and waste gas?"

"It's not wasting gas if you're moving. Sometimes just the drive alone can be good enough."

Besides Ryan, this was the first time that someone ever told me that what I was doing was okay. That I didn't have to have everything figured out and it was fine to not have a goal in life right now. And the fact that *Dad* was the only person who actually understood and accepted me made my chest tighten almost painfully for a second or two before all the air and stress flowed out of me. *Whoosh!*

For the first time in over a year, my shoulders felt light. "Thanks."

"No problem." He grinned at me. "Besides even if you have a plan, it doesn't mean that it's always the right one. Believe me. Things have a way of surprising you."

"You mean like suddenly finding out you have two teenage daughters instead of one?" I was proud of the fact that we were able to joke about this now.

Dad let out a bark of laughter. "Yeah, pretty much."

With a deep breath, I took the plunge and reached out to take his hand. This was the first time we had touched each other, aside from the occasional bump in the halls or passing the remote or ketchup bottle. "I'm sorry I was being such an ass—sorry, a brat—before. I was scared that you would abandon us like your other family. And in a way, I think I was mad at you for choosing them over Mom."

"I didn't."

"I know."

He let out a sigh. "But I did abandon them. Even if it was for their own good."

I shook my head. "Still, it wasn't fair of me to be that way. Especially since I didn't know the whole story. And maybe they don't know the whole story either. Instead of wondering if they're still mad at you, why don't you ask? The worst thing that could happen is that you're right. If you ask me, wondering is worse than actually knowing." For some reason, Ian's words rolled off my tongue as naturally as though they were my own.

"Maybe you're right. Not today, though. I think reconnecting with one daughter is enough for one day." He squeezed my hand when I opened my mouth. "But soon. I promise I'll call them and I'll tell you all about it afterward. Deal?"

"Deal."

Letting out a deep sigh of relief, Dad let go of my hand and stood up. He lifted his arms over his head and stretched from side to side. "Now I have to go and attempt to pry your mom away from that massage table. Are you going to stay here?"

Nodding, I saluted him. "Good luck with that. Maybe we could get some ice cream later?"

"I'd really like that." Dad started to walk away when he stopped and turned his head back to smile at me. "You know, I think you and Lucy would get along pretty well. Maybe someday you can meet her. And Adam. Although I think we should keep him away from Linh. Just in case."

Even though I knew he was joking, I snorted with laughter at how accurate he was. Dad didn't know, but I had shown Linh a picture of Lucy and Adam before, and she swooned onto the bed before calling dibs on Adam. It didn't matter to her that he was over a year younger than her and sort of my brother.

After Dad left, I pulled out my phone to text Ian to tell him about what happened. I had to tell him about the tiny step that Dad and I took together. It wasn't much, but it felt like the start of something. I knew Ian would be proud of me, and most importantly, I *wanted* him to be proud of me.

It wasn't until I pulled up his number that I realized with a pang that we weren't talking anymore. Or rather, *he* wasn't talking to *me*.

But overshadowing my disappointment was the sudden realization that I had automatically turned to Ian first. Why was my first instinct to talk to him and not Linh or even Ryan? When had Ian become so important in my life that he was the first person I turned to? When did I start depending on him so much?

Almost in shock, I slumped back against the cushions. The edge of my Kindle dug into my side, but I didn't move, because the answer to my own question was staring me smack in the face.

I didn't just like Ian, I was in love with him. He became my person.

I've liked people before, but it wasn't the same with Ian. My previous boyfriends didn't make my heart swell three times its size just thinking about them, like I was the freaking Grinch on Christmas Day.

Despite the fact that Ian was so frustratingly annoying, stubborn, and . . .

wonderful, I still loved him. Even when I didn't want to, which was pretty much most of the time. Despite all the problems it caused and all the people we would hurt.

Oh my God. Especially Ryan. How was I going to tell him—tell anyone—that I fell in love with his brother? *Twin* brother? Which was on its own different level of weirdness. I still liked Ryan. Like really liked him, and I thought it was enough. It should have been enough. But the way I felt about Ryan was different from my feelings for Ian. Less intense and consuming. With Ian, everything was just . . . more. And I couldn't deny it anymore.

But I still didn't know how Ian felt about me.

I mean, I *think* he liked me, too. He definitely wanted to kiss me yesterday and would have if we weren't interrupted. But it wasn't just that. It was the way he looked at me sometimes. How his face brightened when we talked, like I made his day better by being there. Or the way he touched me . . . he had to feel *something*, at least. As cheesy as it sounded, Ian and I had a connection. Chemistry.

Although the fact that he was ghosting me now wasn't exactly very encouraging, but the fact that he *did* want to kiss me was. Oh God, it was all so confusing.

It was ironic how different the two of them were about their feelings. Ryan had always been pretty upfront with me about everything. While Ian was not.

Why couldn't I have been in love with Ryan instead? It would have been a thousand times easier. But no, my stupid heart had to fall in love with stupid Ian. Who wasn't even talking to me anymore.

But I needed to know. Needed to find out once and for all how he felt. If maybe he felt the same way I did.

After all, wondering was worse than knowing.

Maybe it was time I took my own advice.

30

"Are you sure she's not going to kick my ass as soon as she sees me?" I asked Linh for the tenth time as we lingered outside Aunt Sarah's office.

She hitched the giant box in her arms a bit higher. "Yes, I told you already. The safest place is at work so she can't make a scene. Every time I need to confess something, I come to her office. It gives her time alone to simmer, but she's too busy to obsess over it. And by the time she comes home, she's usually okay. Even her coworkers know to distract Mom for me after I leave."

Despite my fear, I smirked a bit. "You do this pretty often?"

"Often enough." Linh grinned for a moment before nodding toward the glass door in front of us. "Now, can you open the door before my arms fall off?"

Shifting the two bags of lunch boxes to my left hand, I grabbed the door and yanked it open. The heel of my foot held it open as we ducked inside. "How do you manage this each week?"

"This is the biggest order I've ever had. Must be the truffle flatbread I messaged everyone about. I hope they're not disappointed because I'm not providing any refunds. I already ordered a new knife set for myself."

She marched into the giant office and plopped the box onto the receptionist's desk. "Hi, Ms. Susan. I'm here with the lunch boxes."

A curly-haired woman popped up from her seat and let out a heavy sigh. "Thank goodness! I was late this morning so I skipped my breakfast, and that smells so heavenly. I'm probably going to inhale it all right now."

With a wink, Linh reached into the box for a lunch box marked with a smiley face. "I know. I made your flatbread extra doughy and cheesy. And I included some strawberry shortcake that I made the other day."

Ms. Susan looked like she was about to cry as she snatched the box from Linh's hands. "Bless you, sweetie."

Linh continued to unpack the boxes and waved a hand toward an office on the right. "Mom's in there. Harper might be in there with her. She temps during the summer. Just say that Ms. Susan needs her to fax the case file. That's code for her to give you some privacy."

"Are you sure you don't need help? I could pass out forks or even—"

"Will you go? You're wasting this opportunity." Linh shoved me forward when I continued to stand there.

Letting out a couple of deep breaths, I tiptoed toward Aunt Sarah's door.

This was pretty much the last place I wanted to be. But like I knew I had to forgive Mom—and how I had to give Dad a chance—I knew I also had to fix our relationship with Aunt Sarah, no matter how much I wanted to run away. I was trying this new thing where I actually talked to people instead of assuming things.

Knowing all this didn't make it any less terrifying.

Aunt Sarah hung up the phone when I knocked on her office door. "Hey, Aunt Sarah, are you busy?"

With a shocked expression, she twisted in her seat to look out the door behind me. "What are you doing here?"

My legs were shaking like Jell-O. I gently placed the lunch box on her desk and slid it forward like a peace offering. "I'm helping Linh with her delivery today."

Her eyes narrowed a bit as though she saw right through the ploy, but she accepted the box. She didn't open it right away, though. She moved a couple of folders and paperwork around on her desk before turning to stare at me, waiting for me to continue.

Wondering if I should sit in the seat across from her, I shifted from one foot to the next. "I also wanted to say that I'm sorry. For . . . the other night. I didn't mean for it to get out of hand. I shouldn't have said anything."

"You already apologized that night. The rest is between your mom and me."

Jeez, she wasn't making this easy at all. "I know, but I still wanted to say again that I *am* sorry."

"Okay."

And that was it. Okay. Nothing else to continue the conversation. And definitely no apology on her behalf—although I wasn't really expecting one.

While I searched my brain for a subtle way to bring up Mom again, Aunt Sarah was the one who spoke up first. Her eyes studied the polish on her nails. "Where are you both staying?"

"Waldorf Luxury."

To my surprise, she snickered. "Your mom's been dying to stay there for ages. I should have guessed that she would use this fight to go there. Even when she runs away, she runs away in style."

"Mom didn't run away." I cleared my throat. "I mean, we left, but we didn't run away."

Her brow rose, but she didn't argue with me. Instead, she clasped her hands on the desk in front of her. "I didn't mean to say all those things, you know," Aunt Sarah said before shaking her head, "Well, I did, but that's not how I meant it to come across. How I wanted to end things."

Taking that as a sign of encouragement, I sat down on the chair in front of her and she didn't stop me. She continued studying her nails like the polish color was fascinating to her.

"Your mom was always the risk-taker between the two of us," she suddenly said. "When we were small, she would ride all the roller coasters and run off to her new classes even though she didn't know anyone. She even got her license before me and ended up chauffeuring me around for two years before I got mine. And she went to college out of state while I stayed at home with your Bá."

Not sure what brought this up, but I nodded as she continued.

"You don't know what it was like when your mom suddenly came back home. Pregnant. Scared. She didn't know what to do or how to handle things. I've never seen her that way before. She was totally different. And I had to be there for her. For once, I was the big sister who took care of things. Who took care of *her*. Both of you."

I scooted forward until my butt was on the edge of my seat so I could touch the surface of the desk. Even though our hands were two feet apart, I felt like I could reach out and touch her. "And you did. You're more than an aunt to me. Half the time, you're like another mom to me."

The edge of her mouth twitched. "Well, someone had to discipline you. Your mom and Bá spoiled you too much. Both you and Linh. They always made me the bad guy."

I shrugged but couldn't deny it. When I was a kid, whenever Mom gave me candy or permission to watch TV, I always looked at Aunt Sarah first to make sure it was okay. It was instilled in my brain to have her approval. There was a reason she still terrified me even now.

"When your dad came back, I was scared of your mom was going to get hurt again. Of her making another mistake. Especially now that we had you, too. There was too much to care about. So, I pushed him away until he left. But this time your mom went with him." Aunt Sarah rubbed at her eyes like she was fixing her contacts, but I could see that her fingertips were damp with tears. "And I was angry at him, but mostly at *her* for abandoning us. For leaving our family and everything we did for a man who had already left her before. It's like we didn't matter to her anymore."

I longed to tell her that he wouldn't. That he never left us in the first place, but I couldn't. That wasn't my secret to tell.

Seriously, I was pissed at Mom for not telling Aunt Sarah the truth from the beginning. This wasn't Aunt Sarah's fault. Sure, she complained about Dad and was super rude to him, but she had plenty of reasons to be. But maybe if she knew, then things would be different for them. For us.

I never realized how alike we both were. What Aunt Sarah said out loud, I held on to in my heart. And we both were scared of accepting that our lives were different and refused to let Dad in. It was easier to stand aside than to have that faith like Mom that everything would be fine.

Unable to help myself, this time I leaned forward and grabbed her hand. Her fingers were slightly moist, but I held on until she looked up at me. "I know what you mean. I've been mad at my parents all year for making us move and for leaving our little family. And I missed you every day. You. Linh. Bá. You were my family. You guys were everything I had, and I didn't want to go."

Aunt Sarah finally smiled. "It's been hard for everyone. I know your mom is happy now, but sometimes I wish that your dad had never come back."

"Me too. But no matter how mad I get—or how alone I feel sometimes—Dad makes Mom really happy. And I'm grateful for that."

"I suppose I should be, too," she admitted with a grumble. "And he isn't as bad as I imagined. But he still has a long way to go to prove that he's good enough for our family."

"I'm pretty sure he's up to the challenge."

"We'll see." Aunt Sarah made a face and turned her chair away. "I have to go back to working now."

She started shuffling through stacks of papers like she had already forgotten I was there. I waited for another minute or two before getting to my feet. Guess we were done.

Before I could leave though, she spoke again without even looking up. "Tell your mom to come home. There's no use wasting all that money on a hotel when I have a perfectly good house for her."

My fingers curled on the back of the chair I had been sitting in. "And my dad?"

Her breath was uneven, but she nodded her head. "I can't let my family stay in a hotel. Your Bá would haunt me forever."

Knowing how much effort it took for her to call Dad family, I wanted to give her a hug, but knew I shouldn't since she was at work. Instead, I settled for two thumbs-up as I grinned like an idiot. "I'll go back to the hotel and pack for Mom myself if I have to. We'll even pick up some dinner tonight."

As I got to the door, Aunt Sarah glanced up at me. "Oh, by the way, tell Linh that we'll be getting a new intern next week and she won't be faxing any case files for Ms. Susan anymore. In fact, I'm going to start locking my office door when your cousin comes." A brief smile crossed her face. "She'll have to find another way to confess crimes to me from now on."

31

Wondering was worse than knowing.

Time to finally test out that theory.

Once I was able to check Dad and Aunt Sarah off the list of people to talk to, the next person was Ian. He wasn't as easy to track down though. When my texts and calls to Ian went unanswered, I had to resort to stalking him again. Like Linh said, full-on stalker mode this time, with some vital help from Kathy.

Unable to stand still, I paced back and forth outside the supermarket as I waited for Ian to come out. I still wasn't exactly sure what I was going to say. I mean, it wasn't like I could just blurt out that I was in love with him. That may work in the movies, but real life was totally different.

Finally spotting him coming out of the entrance with a plastic bag, I popped out at him from behind the carts like a jack-in-the-box. "Finally! You took forever in there."

Ian jumped back a foot and let out a heavy deep breath. "What are you doing here?"

"Waiting for you. We need to talk." There was no use pretending. Ian usually saw right through my lies anyway.

His eyes narrowed. "But how did you—did Kathy tell you that I was here?"

"Maybe."

"Seriously? Did she even need zucchini and alfredo sauce for tonight's dinner or was it a trick to get me here?" he asked suspiciously, holding up the bag like it was a bomb.

"I have no clue."

I hoped that once I saw him face-to-face, then we would be able to have an honest talk. That our conversation would flow like it always did. But now that he was right in front of me—all handsome and a little annoyed—I was so overwhelmed with my feelings that I didn't even know how to start. All the words that I wanted to say were jumbled up like there was a traffic jam in my throat.

It was an extremely frustrating feeling.

His eyes softened a bit like he could tell. "What do you need, Nina?"

"You never finished answering all the questions from the list," I finally blurt out.

"I didn't know there was a deadline for it."

Why did I bring up the list? Shaking my head, I took a step toward him and he immediately backed up so the distance between us didn't change. "Why have you been avoiding me?"

He edged toward the parking lot. "I'm not. I've just been busy."

"Too busy to call? Or text? Definitely not too busy to get zucchini."

Ian's face scrunched up like he was in pain, and he turned away. His stride was so large and fast that I was practically running to keep up with him across the parking lot. "I don't know what you're talking about. But I really have to get home. I bought some ice cream and it's going to melt."

That was the lamest excuse I'd ever heard.

The urge to roll my eyes was overwhelming. Why was he the one who was mad? We both leaned in and almost kissed that day. Yet somehow he was acting like the victim. I was tempted to give him the silent treatment, too.

Instead, I reached out to open the passenger door. "Great, then you can drive me home, too."

His hand came down and blocked the door from opening. "I can't take you home."

"Fine." Glowering at him, I crossed my arms and didn't budge. "Then I'll take an Uber to meet you at your house instead. Sooner or later, you will have to talk to me."

We had a stare down for another minute or two before Ian eventually let out a sigh hard enough to blow me over. He went to the other side of the car and tossed the groceries in the back seat—not seeming to care where the precious ice cream landed now.

Step 1: Get Ian alone. Done. I was back in the car with him.

Again.

The tension in the car was so thick that it was almost hard to breathe. Honestly, I was starting to hate this car. Each time I was in here, things got worse and worse. Maybe it *would* have been better to Uber to Ian's house.

As I looked over at Ian's profile for the hundredth time that night, I couldn't help feeling like this might be the last time we'd be in the car together. Judging by the way he was gripping the steering wheel and how far he leaned away from me—another inch and he'd go flying out the car door if it weren't closed—I wouldn't be surprised if I never heard from him again. With or without Kathy's help.

And if that was going to happen, then I had only one chance to make the most of it. Especially because Ian seemed to be speeding through the streets to get me home as soon as possible. Already we were barely five minutes from my house. "Can I ask you a question?"

"No."

My hands gripped together on my lap and I dove ahead anyway. "So, we almost kissed the other day."

"That's more of a statement than a question."

"And you're mad that we almost kissed."

"More statements." He let out a deep breath, too. "And no, I'm not mad."

"You are."

"No, I'm—"

Rolling my eyes, I jabbed my thumb back to point behind us. "You just ran that stop sign back there."

His head whipped back to look as he slammed his palm against the steering wheel. "Oh, shit."

"It's okay. There weren't any cars."

"It would have been nice if you warned me *before* I ran the damn sign," he grumbled.

Annoyed that he acted like even *this* was my fault, too, I slumped back against my seat and glared at him. "Or maybe next time you shouldn't run the damn sign."

"Sorry, I was . . . distracted."

"Because of my question?"

"You haven't asked any." Ian cleared his throat. "But you were going to ask why we almost kissed, right? It was a mistake. Maybe it was the damn piano song. We got caught up in the moment. It happens. We should forget all about it."

"That wasn't my question." I glanced at him out of the corner of my eyes. "By the way, even if *you're* not mad, now I am. Very mad."

He looked started. "About the kiss? I'm sorry—"

"Not about the fact that we almost kissed. I'm mad that we *didn't* kiss and you're already acting like everything was a huge mistake."

That immediately shut him up. But now that it was out there, there was no backing down. Not that I wanted to.

"Well?"

"I'm sorry."

Scoffing, I resisted the urge to hit him. "Will you please stop apologizing? There's nothing to apologize for. Like you said, we didn't even kiss."

Ian rubbed the back of his neck with one hand until his skin turned red. "I know, but I'm sorry. That's all I can say right now."

I don't know what was more frustrating, the fact that he was avoiding me or the fact that he wouldn't say anything else except "I'm sorry."

Before I knew it, we were parked in front of my house. Knowing that I missed my chance, my fingers played with the door handle since I couldn't bring myself to look at him. "Fine, answer one question now. You said you've never been in love *before*. What about now?"

I could hear his breath catch in his throat. "Why are you asking me that?"

"Why do you think?"

Instead of answering, Ian stared at me with a hard expression on his face. Unreadable. And I thought he was going to turn away from me again. But suddenly he reached out and pulled me to face him. His hands wrapped around the top of my arms, digging into my shoulders. But it didn't hurt. If anything, his touch made me feel a little lightheaded, like I ate too much sugar.

He let out a deep shaky breath as he said my name. "Nina."

So softly that it was barely a whisper.

And I felt it all the way down my spine. Tugging me closer and closer, his face hovered inches over mine for a split second, and he stared at me so hard and for so long that I thought he was going to reject me again.

Not wanting to give him that chance, my hands came up behind his neck and I pulled him in for a kiss. That long-awaited kiss.

It was explosive.

And definitely worth it.

As soon as our lips touched, everything happened at once. Ian's hands slid up to my face, holding me, angling my face a tiny bit to the left so we could fit perfectly together. So he could kiss me even deeper. Harder. His tongue traced my mouth until my lips parted and I couldn't help letting out a soft sigh against his lips. Pulling back, Ian briefly smiled against my cheek before swooping in for another tingling kiss.

I could barely concentrate on anything but him. My hands ran down his shoulders and his lean muscles tensed beneath my fingertips. And now it was his turn to let out a heavy breath as he pulled me even closer. I'm not sure how it was even possible since we were pretty much plastered together by now. Nothing could get between us.

And he didn't seem to mind. His lips slid over mine. Over and over. It was both hard and soft. Gentle and firm. And everything in between. It made my head spin even as I was rooted to him. And I didn't care that we were just fighting. I didn't care that we were parked in front of my house and my entire family could be watching. I didn't care about anything as long as Ian was here with me. In this moment.

While my hands moved from his shoulders, to his neck, around his waist, Ian's hands stayed on my face as he cupped my cheeks. Gently holding me together as though he were afraid that I would fall apart, which I probably would have.

After what felt like ages, when I thought he was going to end the kiss, Ian murmured my name against my lips. Feather soft in that way that made me want to swoon in his arms. Which I did. And the kiss went on. And on. And on.

Until finally, he pulled back.

I knew before I opened my eyes that Ian was already regretting our kiss. All of them. And it hurt that something so beautiful, so wonderful, would make him feel so bad. I already knew that I would be dreaming about these kisses for a while.

"Don't you dare say you're sorry again or I'm going to have to kick your ass,"

I announced before he was even able to pull completely away. "You can't say that was a mistake."

Ian let out a reluctant chuckle and for a second, I thought he was going to pull me back into his arms. But no such luck. "Of course I want to kiss you; I want to kiss you more this very moment. I would be crazy *not* to want to kiss you. But we can't."

I swallowed at the lump in my throat. "Because of Ryan?"

"Yes. I told you before that I would never hurt him. I can't. He's my brother." Ian rubbed his forehead between his fingertips. "And you're dating him. But even if you weren't—if there's only a 0.1% chance that he likes you—then we can't be together. I can't take that risk of him being hurt. I can't betray him like that."

I should have seen it coming. In my heart, I knew that he was being a good big brother. Protective as he's always been. And in a way, that made me love him even more. So much more.

And in a way, he was right. It wasn't right to betray Ryan like this. He didn't deserve any of this. As amazing as this kiss was, it was a mistake, and it probably pushed Ian away even more.

But I couldn't help how I felt. And although I had a thousand things to apologize for, I wasn't going to apologize for following my heart.

"The last thing I'd want to do is hurt Ryan, but I'm not his girlfriend. We've only gone on a handful of dates." Frustrated with Ian and myself, I shook my head. "I'm not saying that it's right, and I *will* talk to him, but how I feel about him and you are two entirely separate things."

"But you were with Ryan first."

"And I met you first. But none of that matters." My eyes narrowed. "It's not like you guys can call dibs on me. I have a right to my feelings, too."

"I know, but—" Ian ran a shaky hand through his hair and tugged on the top strands. "We just can't, okay? I think we should—"

"Forget this happened?" I let out an empty laugh. "Yeah, I've heard that before."

Turning his head to face the window, he leaned his forehead against the glass. I could see the reflection of his narrow chin. His lips were pursed together so tightly that no words could come out. Our time together was up.

Even so, knowing now that all the problems in my family, between my parents and Aunt Sarah, were all because they kept secrets from each other, I knew that I couldn't leave without telling Ian how I felt. At least one last time.

Letting out a deep breath for courage, I looked straight at him, almost memorizing his face. "You know, I thought I had been in love before, but it turns out that I never was. Because it's nothing compared to how I feel about you now. Even though I know you're the one walking away from me. From *this*."

He glanced up at me. His eyes were rimmed with sadness, but I could tell that he wasn't going to change his mind. "Nina . . ."

Before he could reject me again, I flung the car door open and jumped out. Without a backward glance, I rushed up the walkway, almost tripping over my own feet. But I kept moving forward. Each step was faster than the last.

Because with each second that passed—each step that I took—Ian didn't follow me. He didn't call me back. He didn't do anything. He sat in the car until I was safely inside the house and then drove off.

32

"Guys suck," I announced, flopping onto the bed so hard that Linh bounced twice.

"Yep, they sure do." Without looking up from her phone, she held out her hand and I automatically gave her a high five.

Despite how depressed and annoyed I was, I was so glad to be home. And double glad that no one but Linh was here to witness my embarrassment.

After I talked to Aunt Sarah at the office, I rushed to pack my things to move back. Mom and Dad opted to stay in the hotel for another day or two. They said they wanted some alone time—eww—but I honestly think that they wanted to give Aunt Sarah a little more space.

Or maybe Mom and Dad really *did* want some alone time.

Again, *eww.*

Then again, it must be nice to have the person you love *want* to be with you and love you back. Not kiss you senseless and leave you. Not like—

Linh leaned forward and pointed at me until the tip of her nail touched my nose. "You're NOT allowed to cry over him."

"I'm not."

"Seriously."

"I'm serious."

"Then why are your eyes leaking?"

My hands flew up to my face and I wiped away two tiny tears at the corner of my eyes that I didn't even notice were there. As soon as they were gone though, two more appeared against my will.

"I don't understand why you're sitting here crying." With a scowl, she crossed her arms and glared at me. "You're not a crying-over-some-guy-and-staring-into-space type of girl. You hardly ever cry. Remember Nancy, that girl in elementary school who bullied you into giving her your lunch money? When she tried to make you cry, you kicked her so that she would cry first."

I sniffed. "Are you suggesting that I kick Ian's ass until he cries, too?"

"If you don't, then I will."

As the image of Linh attacking Ian popped into my head, I couldn't help giggling a little through my tears. "Well, I'm allowed to be a little sad. The first guy I've ever been in love with rejected me. Who I'm *still* in love with, even now, when I'm heartbroken." Just saying the words out loud made my eyes well up with more tears. Seriously, I was like a faucet with a broken handle. "Damn it!"

With her eyes widening, since she's never seen me like this before, Linh shoved a couple of tissues into my hands. "Okay, okay, let's talk about something else for a minute. Did I tell you that I'm going to the mall with Ollie tomorrow?"

That instantly got my attention. "As a date?"

"What? No, as friends."

I played with the soft fringe of her blanket. "I don't know if that's a good idea. I don't know if you noticed, but Ollie sort of . . ."

"Has a crush on me? Yeah, we talked about that." She pursed her lips together and tapped her index finger against the bottom one. "Although, I guess it's *had* a crush, since it's all in the past now."

"Are you sure?"

"Yep. That's why we're going to the mall," Linh said with a smirk. "I'm going to give him tips on how to get a girlfriend, and he's going to help me carry the new cast-iron pots from Williams-Sonoma to the car. The truffle flatbread was such a hit that Ms. Susan ordered a tray for her sister's baby shower. And she paid ahead of time."

Sitting up, I wrapped an arm around her for a half hug. "Nice! So, you're going to start catering on the side now? Along with everything else you're doing?"

She shrugged. "Probably. It'll look good on my internship application. I'll just have to make it work."

It's funny, but I expected to feel the usual twinge of jealousy whenever Linh talked about cooking, yet after the talk with Dad, now all I felt was pride. My cousin was kicking butt as she chased her dream. And now she had a new friend to cheer her on along with me.

Speaking of Ollie, it must be nice to be able to erase your feelings so easily. No matter what I did or who I was with, the last conversation with Ian danced in the back of my mind. I finally understood what Linh meant when she said that I had never been in love before.

But whoever said that it's better to have loved and lost than never loved at all was a freaking idiot.

Seeing the tears in my eyes again, Linh quickly changed the subject again. "Are you excited about seeing the house with your parents tomorrow?"

Letting out a deep breath to steady my emotions, I nodded. "It looks nice from the pictures that Mom showed me online. Hopefully a new place will help us start over."

"It's kind of ironic how you have to move back home in order to start over." Linh leaned her head against my shoulder, even though she had to hunch her back to reach me. "I'm glad to have you guys here again. I've missed you."

My cheek pressed against the top of her head. The strands that escaped her bun tickled my nose, making me forget about my problems for a minute. "I'm excited to be home, too. Hopefully Aunt Sarah feels the same way."

"Oh, she definitely does. The other day at dinner, she started to say something bad about your dad, but then she stopped herself and changed the subject. Twice."

I let out a low whistle. "I guess miracles can happen."

"I know, right?" She chewed on her lower lip. "What are you going to do about Ryan?"

"I know I have to talk to him, and I will." I swallowed at the lump in my throat that appeared every time I thought about Ryan. My heartbreak may be Ian's fault, but Ryan didn't do anything wrong. And just the thought of hurting him made me feel worse, if that was even possible. "It's the right thing to do, but right now, I just—I don't know if I can just yet."

"Then don't." Suddenly straightening up, Linh grabbed both of my hands and dragged me off the bed. "Come on. We're going to watch some TV in the living room until you're so tired that you won't even have the energy to cry anymore."

"I don't know. I don't want to watch a rom-com or one of those Hallmark movies . . ."

"Who said we're going to watch those? We're going to watch an entire season of *Law & Order* until your little love life will seem like minor first-world problems compared to what they're dealing with."

Weird as her plan was, it did sound kind of nice. If there was anything to get my mind off my sad love life, it would be criminal trials and murders. Especially when Linh tossed in an unopened package of Girl Scout Thin Mints that she was saving for a Super Special Emergency.

Heartbreak definitely qualified on that list.

We were barely through the theme song of the first episode when Linh leaned closer to me. "So, I have to ask just this once: Do they kiss the same?"

I dropped the half-eaten Thin Mint onto my lap. "Linh!"

"What? It's not every day that I could ask someone this. You're the only person I know who's dated brothers. Not to mention *twins*." She made a face like she smelled something bad. "Was it weird? It had to be weird. I mean, they have the same face. The same lips. You're basically kissing the same guy."

My left eyebrow rose. "I thought we were supposed to be getting my mind off Ian?"

Nodding, she snuggled into her blanket. "You're right. I'll ask at another time when the pain isn't as fresh."

If that would ever happen.

With a sigh, I pulled my own blanket up to my shoulders and curled up against the arm of the couch. There was a dead girl in the park and the police were gathering up the suspects, but I couldn't concentrate on anything but Linh's question.

It should have been weird, but it wasn't. Maybe because I stopped thinking of them as twins a long time ago. To me, they were two different people. Ryan was the perfect guy in practically every way.

But I didn't need perfect. I just wanted someone who understood me. Who made me want to take risks and be something more. Do more with my life. And that was Ian, without counting his kiss. Ian's kisses were like something in the movies, where music played in the background and flower petals fell in slow motion and time practically stopped until it was only the two of us. Like we were the only ones who mattered.

Or at least that's how I felt.

Moving slowly so Linh wouldn't notice, I used the edge of my blanket to dab at the fresh tears that suddenly slid down my cheeks again.

Even if my little love life *was* a minor first-world problem, it still sucked.

33

It was four o'clock as I sat in the middle of the sidewalk, staring up at the house that could be ours. I'd already been here for over twenty minutes and the longer I sat here the more I could almost imagine living here. And it was . . . nice.

Actually, it was better than nice. The house was super cute and pretty, like it was cut out from a magazine.

It was recently renovated so everything looked bright and fresh. A modern cottage with a big garage on the side. It was a one-and-a-half-story gray brick house with dark gray, almost bluish, window siding and shingles. But the columns and windows were bright white, with white grids to contrast with the darker, moodier colors. And there was a cute little bay window right in the front where I could see a window seat inside the primary bedroom.

Obviously, all those years of Mom drilling HGTV into my head were finally working.

I'd studied the listing online a couple of times, but it was different in person. The most important thing was that it felt real, like I could actually imagine us living here. I could see myself reading on the porch while Mom complained about weeding all the flower beds. And then me pretending to help so she would stop nagging me. I could even see Dad pulling into the garage with his car, hands full of groceries so Linh and I could test out the new menu for her lunch boxes. And by Linh and I, I really mean her cooking with me tasting her food.

Leaning back onto the palm of my hands, I squinted at the dormer window by the left side of the roof that Mom said would be my room. It was a little hard to see, since the sun was shining right at me from behind the house. Not to mention, my eyes were still a little puffy from crying the night before. But I could make out the pretty wood shutters framing the window.

Yeah, I *really* could see us being happy here. Jubilant. Ecstatic. Content. And for the first time in days, I felt almost happy.

The porch was wide and had rosebushes that started winding up the columns like in a fairy tale. I could take my prom pictures there. Preferable with a date who looked like Darren Criss and was taller than Ian. And I'd post our pictures all over social media so Ian would HAVE to see it.

Take that, Ian. Who needs you?

Mom's car pulled up.

Excited to go inside, I jumped to my feet and came over to her. My hands pushed against the sides of my jeans to get the dust off. "Hey, so are you ready to check it out? Where's Dad?"

She paused in getting out of the car. "So, honey . . ."

Oh no. This didn't sound good. None of Mom's *So, honey*... sentences ever ended up well. "What happened?"

Shutting the car door, she leaned against the side and crossed her arms. "It turns out that the owners accepted an offer this morning. The listing agent told me that they still wanted to have an open house and house showings, but as of noon, it's officially pending."

My heart dropped and I couldn't help frowning. "Well, that's kind of rude. Why didn't the agent tell you before about the offer? Didn't they know for at least a day or two already?"

Mom rolled her eyes. "Don't even get me started on that. She should have had the courtesy to let me know as soon as possible since I contacted her about this house over a week ago. But not everyone is an upstanding Realtor like your mom."

"I guess." A disturbing thought occurred to me. "Wait, so I've been sitting here staring at someone else's house for nearly twenty minutes? Oh my God, are they home?"

My head whipped back to look at the house in case the homeowners were watching us. I half expected to see the curtains or blinds twitch.

"No, no one's here." She laughed into her hand. "But who told you to be so early?"

"I was excited."

At my words, her face softened and she wrapped an arm around my shoulders. "I was, too. It's such a nice house."

Now that I knew the house wasn't going to be ours, I turned away. "It's okay. The gray paint's a little too gloomy for me. And what's with the color of the front door?"

"You mean . . . blue?"

"*Bright* blue." Wrinkling my nose like that was a dirty word, I waved my hand in the air like it didn't matter. "It doesn't go with the color scheme at all."

Mom laughed. "Now that you mention it, you're right. Plus, I'm not sure I like the idea of having the master bedroom in the front like that. All the neighbors could see right into the room."

"They would see *everything*." I looped an arm around Mom's waist and gave her a half hug. "It is too bad, though. I was looking forward to getting our own house."

Her hand came down to pat my wrist. "Well, we may not be able to get this house, but how would you feel about living next to Aunt Sarah and Linh?"

Confused, I glanced over at her. "Huh?"

"The Millers next door? They're planning to retire and are moving into a smaller condo so they can travel. And they asked me to be their Realtor." A bright smile crossed her face. "If we want their house, then I could get the paperwork drawn up next week. I offered to waive the Realtor fees if they let us have first dibs. That's a deal they can't refuse."

I spent so long imagining a life for us at *this* house, that to suddenly imagine living in *another* house two seconds later was a total mental whiplash. "You're serious? Isn't their house kind of old?"

Grimacing a bit, Mom nodded. "Yeah, it is a bit outdated. The bathrooms are covered in a weird mint-green tile, and there's no dishwasher in the kitchen.

Plus, there's carpet and popcorn ceilings *everywhere*. But think of how nice it would be to be next door to our family. We could have a door connecting our backyards."

"Oh, I once saw a fence that had a portion lift up so it turned into a make-shift picnic table. That would be really awesome. How long do you think the renovations will take?"

"I think we could probably get everything done in six or seven months. Although we'll have to stay with Aunt Sarah and Linh for a while. Even I know that we can't afford to stay in the hotel that long." She gave me a wistful little grin.

At the mention of living with Aunt Sarah for over half a year, my excitement faded a bit. "What about Dad? Do you think he'll be okay with living with them?"

"Who do you think convinced the Millers that condo living was the way to go?" The expression on her face was so bright that she was practically glowing with happiness. "He said that as long as we're happy, he doesn't mind taking a few insults here and there. Besides, after what happened, I think Aunt Sarah will be on her best behavior. For a month or two, at least."

Thinking of Aunt Sarah's confession, I shook my head. "I think she might surprise you."

"I hope so." Letting go of me, Mom turned toward the car. "Do you want to go check out the Millers' house? Dad's over there waiting for us."

I was already opening the passenger door. "Of course!"

A few seconds later, as I was snapping my seat belt on, I got a text from Kathy.

KATHY: Do you know what's going on with Ian?

Not sure how much she knew—although knowing Kathy, I suspected she probably knew almost everything—I still hesitated before I responded.

NINA: What do you mean?

KATHY: He was all gloomy when he came home from the grocery store yesterday. I asked him if he saw you, but he said no and went upstairs.

KATHY: And then this morning, he went back to Dad's before anyone woke up.

NINA: Wait, what?

KATHY: Yeah, he left without telling anyone. Even though he was supposed to stay the entire summer. And he won't pick up any of our phone calls. Do you think you could try calling him?

KATHY: Nina?

KATHY: Hello???

KATHY: Nina?

A hand touched me and shook me out of my daze. I blinked and looked up at Mom's concerned face. "Sorry, what?"

"I was asking if you wanted to pick up some takeout on the way home." She reached out and stroked my bangs off my face. "Are you okay? You've been staring at your phone for the past few minutes."

That was because I was still trying to wrap my head around the fact that Ian *literally* ran away right after we kissed. That he did the only thing I've always been afraid of. He made me care for him, depend on him, love him, and then left me behind.

Smothering the curse that immediately sprang to my lips, I shook my head and tucked my phone away. "It's nothing. I'm fine."

And this time I meant it. I *was* fine. Ian left and there was nothing I could do about it now. I had my own things to work on, my own family to lean on, and my own life to look forward to. And I could do it all with a broken heart.

34

Even though there was no chance of Ian and me getting together—because he ran away from me like a total jerk—I still needed to talk to Ryan and tell him the truth. I owed him that much at least.

Gah, this was going to totally suck.

"Hey, I didn't know you were stopping by. Do you want to come in?" Ryan asked, his hand was already pushing the door wider for me.

Awkwardly tucking my hair behind my ears, I shook my head. "Uh, no, thanks. I was wondering . . . could we talk? Out here?"

He let out a low whistle. "Uh-oh, that doesn't sound good. Should I be sitting down for this?"

I let out a weak laugh at his joke even though my stomach was churning like a blender with nerves. "It's not a bad thing. I mean, I guess it kind of is, but when you really think about it and give it some time, it's not."

"Yeah, that definitely doesn't sound good."

Ryan pulled the door shut and came out onto the porch. I moved back as he swung himself to sit on the balcony railing in one fluid swoop like he had done it a thousand times. Which he probably had. I knew better than to attempt it though. Knowing me, I'd hobble up and down awkwardly a couple of times or flop backward into the bushes.

Instead, I leaned against the column next to him and let out a deep breath. "So, I was thinking—"

Before I could finish though, the front door swung open and Kathy came bouncing out. "Nina! I thought I heard your voice. Linh told me that you're moving here! Is that true?" I barely had time to nod before she barreled forward with more questions. "That's so awesome! And you're going to renovate a house? When are you starting? Can I help you?"

As I decided which question to answer first, Ryan crossed his arms. "How are *you* supposed to help with renovating a house?"

She put both hands on her hips and glared at her brother. "I know how to smash things. It doesn't look that hard. Plus, it looks like so much fun on TV."

"Watching something on TV doesn't mean you can do it."

Spotting the looks on their faces, I knew that an argument was about to break out. Funny how I'd only known the Nguyens for a few short weeks, but I could recognize their looks and personalities. They were such a vital part of my life now. My heart ached when I thought about how much I would miss each of them. Especially Kathy, with her overflowing energy. Sure, we could probably still keep in touch, but it wouldn't be the same. Not to mention it would be super awkward, depending on how hurt Ryan would be. Plus, I knew I would be dying to ask her about Ian all the time.

Yeah, it would probably be better to stay away for good, no matter how sad it made me.

"I don't know if and when we'll start renovating, but I promise to call you when that happens," I lied.

Kathy let out a triumphant cheer and gave me two thumbs up as she backed through the front doorway. "I knew I always liked you. Come over and play Pictionary again. I promise I won't get mad this time. At least not *that* mad."

"Is that what you wanted to tell me?" Ryan asked, interrupting my thoughts. "That your family is moving to Austin?"

"Actually, no. I mean, we are moving here, but that isn't what I wanted to tell you. I—"

The front door popped open again, and this time it was a pretty lady who looked like she was in her mid to late thirties. Her short black hair was cut in a cute bob that framed her round face. I knew she was Ryan's aunt from phở a few weeks ago, but I had no idea which one. She held a small covered plate in one hand, and I could smell oil and meat.

"Hey, Ryan, I heard you were out here with Nina." She motioned me closer to her. "Can you help me with something?"

Even though I knew she was talking to me, I couldn't help pointing at myself as I glanced over at Ryan. "Me?"

"Yes, you. Come here a second."

Shuffling forward a few feet, I stopped as she whipped the napkin off and shoved a plate of eggrolls at me. "Try one."

This was super weird. I shot Ryan another look, but he shrugged. Since there was nothing else to do, I picked up an eggroll. It was still piping hot, so I carefully bit into it and sucked in a deep breath as I held the piece between my teeth before chewing it.

His aunt kept watching me expectantly so I quickly took another few bites until the eggroll was gone, burning my tongue a bit in the process. "It's really good. Thanks."

"That's it?"

Ryan took one and popped the whole thing into his mouth despite the fact that it was steaming hot. "It's okay, Aunt Lily. Doesn't taste like Bá's eggrolls though."

Her face fell. "It's not. I have to make eggrolls for the twins' book club party, but Bá's not home and I can't get the filling right no matter how hard I try. I tried to call her, but she doesn't know the exact recipe. She tosses stuff in and smells it to make sure it's right. I was hoping that Nina could help me figure out how to fix it with her golden tongue."

How did she know about my golden tongue? Linh. It could only have been from her. Yet when and how did she talk to Aunt Lily? And who else did she talk to in this family?

Maybe distancing myself from them wouldn't be as easy as I'd hoped.

Grabbing another eggroll, my fingers tested out the outer shell and I took tiny bites, making sure to chew it thoroughly.

"Okay, I think that it's a little bit dry. Maybe you can add more veggies like carrots or napa cabbage. But then you don't want it to be a veggie eggroll." I bit into it again and again until it was gone. There was only an oily film left on my fingers. Ryan handed me a napkin. "Maybe you can add some shrimp. My cousin did that with her wontons before to keep the filling moist. And it could use a bit more salt."

With a thoughtful expression on her face, Aunt Lily chewed on her thumbnail. "That's not the way Bá makes it. 'Course if she were here then I wouldn't be in this mess. It does sound good. How did your cousin's wontons turn out?"

"Oh, they were horrible." I laughed. "Turns out she doesn't know how to make wonton wrappers, so they were really tough yet somehow still fell apart. But the filling was delicious."

With a laugh, she nodded. "I'll make a small batch to see how it turns out. Thanks, Nina!"

"No problem."

"Looks like I'm not the only one who people depend on around here. I think I'm starting to feel a bit left out," said Ryan shaking his head. He half turned toward the steps. "Maybe we should go before someone else needs your help with something."

I knew he was teasing, but I nodded. Some privacy would be nice. "Good idea—"

The front door opened—again—and this time Ollie came strolling out. "Hey, I was looking for—"

Ryan let out a groan and shoved his hands into his pockets. "Let me guess. You were looking for Nina."

I automatically took a step toward Ollie.

He looked confused and shoved at his glasses perched on his nose. "Uh, no.

I was looking for you. I mean, it's nice to see you again, Nina. But I need Ryan to help me move some of the cars around. I have to go to the store, but I'm blocked in."

Oh. That's embarrassing.

We both flushed. Ryan took his hands out and reached for the keys Ollie was holding. "Oh. Yeah, I'll help. Which one do you need?"

His eyes sparkled. "The one all the way on the inside."

Letting out a heavy sigh, Ryan nodded. "I knew I spoke too soon. Come on. Sorry, Nina, this might take a while."

"It's okay."

As they walked down to the end of the driveway, Ryan shoved at Ollie who punched his shoulder in return. They were both laughing though, like beating each other up was the funniest thing in the world.

Boys.

There was a knock on the window behind me and I turned my head.

Two identical twin girls in matching jumpsuits waved at me from the window. Their faces were plastered against the glass. One had long, waist-length, deep-black hair that was clipped to one side, while the other one had a short bob exactly like Aunt Lily's. These must be the twins that she was talking about.

Between them was a tiny little girl who was half their size and twirling in dizzy circles. She looked like she was around four, while the other two were probably about eight.

I gave them an awkward wave, wondering how many people were in the house. It wasn't the weekend yet, and there were at least six cars crammed into the driveway. I remembered how cars were parked all the way down the street on Sunday for phở. I had assumed some house was having a party or brunch or something. At the time, I didn't know that the house was Ryan's and this was normal for them.

Ollie and Ryan systematically moved all the cars up and down the street until the blue Accord that was tucked on the inside was on the outside. All the other cars moved up a space.

Finally, Ryan came back up to the house, but he stopped short when he saw the twins still waving from the window. "Do you want to go somewhere so we won't be interrupted anymore?"

Torn between wanting privacy but not wanting to be in the car that would remind me of Ian—his voice, the way he kissed, how he held on to me—I shook my head. "It's a nice day. Maybe we could just sit on the trunk or something instead?"

"Okay."

After a lot of finger-pointing to make the girls leave the window, Ryan reached out to take my hand, but I pretended to be busy tying my hair up. If he noticed that I was acting weird, he didn't say anything. He hopped onto the back trunk and sat down. The car sunk down a bit with his weight and I climbed up beside him. My hands gripped at the smooth surface of the car.

Ryan leaned back, balancing his weight on his palms. "So, what's up?"

I blurt out the words before it was too late. "I don't think we should date anymore." I inwardly cringed as my carefully crafted speech was reduced to one insensitive sentence. Tactless. Heartless.

"Oh, okay." He slowly straightened and angled his body until he was facing me. "Hmm, do you mind if I ask why?"

I struggled with the decision to tell him everything or give him a simple answer. Would it be better to keep it short? Or would the entire truth make it hurt less?

Ryan blinked at me expectedly. "Nina?"

Remembering how hurt he was that Liv didn't tell him the truth, I caved and told him everything.

And I mean everything. From the hike where I met Ian, to the stalking at the gym and laundromat, to the day we met and how I accidentally saved his life. And the more I talked, the easier it was to keep going. So I did. I talked about the day I came for phở and found out they were twins, and how I ended up falling for Ian. But I still stressed how much Ryan meant to me and the struggle I went through.

The only thing I left out was the kiss that Ian and I had. That was the only secret I kept. Not for me, but for Ian. I didn't want Ryan to be mad at his brother. Especially when Ian had already chosen him over me.

Ryan was super quiet the entire time as he stared down the length of the driveway. And still. His face was so frozen that I didn't know if he was mad or confused. I wanted to reach out and touch him, but I didn't want to make things worse if he was mad. So I sat beside him and wrung my hands together until they were red.

After I was done and my throat was dry from all the talking, a full minute passed before he spoke. His voice was low and careful like he was trying to find the right words, in contrast to my blurting everything out. "For a second, I thought you were joking because that story is too crazy to be real."

I gave him a weak smile. "Unfortunately, it's not."

"Well, this kind of sucks."

Finally, he looked up at me and, even though his voice was light, I could see a pang of hurt in his normally happy eyes, and my stomach twisted with guilt. "I can't say I wasn't expecting something like this. I felt like we were drifting apart for the last week or two, but I never thought it was because of . . . Ian."

"It's not because of Ian." I rushed to say so he wouldn't misunderstand. My hand reached out to his elbow. "I mean, I *do* like him, but my feelings for him and my feelings for you are two completely different things. I think even if Ian wasn't around—even if I didn't meet him first and it was just you and me—it still wouldn't have worked out between us. No matter how much I would have wanted it to." Funny how I said these exact words to Ian just the other day. I could only hope that Ryan could understand me better than Ian did.

The next words I said were vitally important. Not only for Ryan and me, but also for him and Ian. "I like you a lot, but I realized that it wasn't enough or in the right way. And that it wouldn't be fair for either of us to continue dating. With or without Ian in the picture. I mean, obviously given the choice, I would definitely choose you if I could. Your brother is so *annoying*."

At that, he reluctantly laughed. "You really do know him. But I guess you can't force things that aren't there, right? Or deny things that are."

"Right."

With a sigh, Ryan laid back on top of the car; his hands stacked behind his head as he stared up at the sky. I fidgeted back and forth for a bit since I didn't know what to do. He tugged on my sleeve and nodded at the space next to him. Hesitating, I laid back next to Ryan.

How did he look so comfortable when the car was so hot and uncomfortable? But I'd put up with anything if it made things better.

"I like you, Nina."

Uh-oh. Maybe things weren't getting better after all.

My mouth opened to apologize again, but he held up his hand to stop me. "I really like you. But to be honest, I don't think I like you like *that* either. Don't get me wrong, you're really fun and nice. And you've helped me figure out a lot of things. Things I wouldn't have the courage to do." His face turned a little sad. "I was really hoping we could be more, but I think I was pushing things because I was lonely. I haven't dated anyone since Liv, and it was nice to have someone by my side again."

Turning around, I smiled at him. "I'll always be in your corner. And you helped me too. I have a lot of family problems, and you took my mind off everything."

He puffed out his chest a bit. "I'm glad I could be of service."

"I know it's too soon, but do you think maybe we could be friends later?"

"No."

My heart sunk before Ryan carefully tucked a strand of hair behind my ear. Like he'd done so many times before. But not in a flirty way. It was almost brotherly now. "Ha! Just kidding. We'll always be friends. Even if you *meant* to find Ian, you still found *me* and saved my life. And we became friends. That's something that won't ever change." He wrapped an arm around my shoulder and sighed. "Plus, my family is already in love with you. I don't think you'll be able to escape them even if you wanted to."

I laughed as a wave of relief rushed over me. His arm still fit around me perfectly like we were two puzzle pieces, but it was a different puzzle now. And as hurt as I was by Ian's disappearance, I knew I would have been equally sad if Ryan vanished from my life, too. "Good, because I do like them. Honestly. And you."

"Speaking of liking my family," he casually said as his mouth twisted into a crooked half smile. "You and Ian, huh? I should have known something was up when we were making gio. Even Bá realized it before I did."

My happy mood immediately vanished. I stared at the pitch-blue sky. There weren't even any clouds to distract myself. "Uh, no, there's no Ian and me."

He looked surprised. "Not at all? Why?"

"It just . . . didn't work out. Or couldn't work out."

With a frown, Ryan crossed his arms across his chest and stared at me. His head cocked to the left. "Is it because of me? Did that idiot choose me over you?"

"No!" I blurted out, not wanting him to know the truth. I didn't deny that Ian wasn't an idiot though.

Ryan gave a look, and I shook my head. "I told you. It's not. Ian doesn't even want to try. It's like he's scared to give it a chance. And I can't exactly force the guy."

"I mean, you could. But it's up to you."

I was dying to ask him how, but I didn't think I would like the answer.

Besides, I was done chasing after Ian. Even Prince Charming didn't have to work this hard to marry Cinderella.

Instead, my hand patted his shoulder as I pushed myself upright. "Have I told you how awesome you are?"

"Not yet, but I'm still waiting."

I laughed. "Well, you are amazing. And if you feel lonely or ever need me for anything, let me know."

With a smirk, he sat up, too. The sun shone behind his head, and the expression on his face turned mischievous. My heart twisted because for a split second he looked exactly like Ian. "I'm sure I'll think of something."

35

RYAN: So I thought of something.

NINA: Of what?

RYAN: Of something that I need. In order for me to forgive you.

NINA: I thought you already forgave me. We hugged and everything . . .

RYAN: Yeah, I changed my mind. That was too easy for you.

RYAN: If you REALLY want me to forgive you, then you have to meet me on the hiking path at Flint Rock Loop at 10:00. Close to where you met Ian the first time.

NINA: But why?

RYAN: I'm curious about the place. It's been a while since I've been there.

RYAN: It's the least you can do after you fell in love with my twin WHILE we were still dating. You owe me this much.

NINA: . . .

NINA: I'll be there at ten.

Squinting against the beaming sunlight, I glanced around the now familiar hiking trail and wondered why Ryan wanted me to come here. At the exact spot where I met Ian just weeks ago. Maybe this was some kind of weird punishment, although I knew that Ryan was too nice to do something like that.

Not too nice to coerce me to come here, though.

Moving over to the rock overlooking the stream, I glanced down at the seat. A smile crossed my face as I remembered how gently Ian took care of my cut. And how horrified we both were when I stood up and he saw the wet spot on the rock.

Then he left and I thought I would never see him again. Like now.

I rubbed my eyes and straightened up. No, no more tears. I promised Linh that I wouldn't cry anymore and damn it, I was going to keep that promise at least for today. And hopefully the day after that, until it didn't ache to think of Ian anymore.

One day at a time. I could do that.

As a branch snapped, I looked up and saw him. Like my mind had conjured him up. Again.

Ian.

Standing there in the sunlight with the giant book bag like the first time I saw him. And judging by his wrinkled forehead, he was just as confused and surprised to see me as I was.

I should be mad at him for leaving. Should turn away and ignore him like he did to me the other night. It was my turn to leave him behind for once. But I couldn't move. All I could do was stare at him as though I hadn't seen him in months rather than just a few days.

He looked tired and there were bags under his eyes. His dark hair was even messier than usual and some strands were plastered to his forehead. But he was still so handsome.

Damn it.

Wanting to run over to his side, I forced myself to stand still and scowled at him. "Why are you here?"

With wide eyes, Ian glanced around like he was looking for help or a way to escape from me. Again. "I—what are you doing here?"

"I don't need to answer your questions anymore," I announced with crossed arms. "I already told Ryan everything, and unlike you, he's understanding. And he didn't give me a guilt trip for having the courage to admit my real feelings. In fact, he even asked me to meet him here as a truce."

Ian was already starting to turn away during my rant when he suddenly jerked back to stare at me. "Wait, *Ryan* told you to come here? My Ryan?"

"No, Ryan Reynolds." The sarcasm made my voice bitter.

A flash of a boyish smile crossed his face, and I automatically smiled back for a split second before remembering that I was still pissed at him. I was determined to stand my ground, but man, it was super hard when he flashed that dimple at me.

"Seriously, my brother asked you to come here?"

I let out a heavy sigh. "Yes, that's what I just said. Why?"

Tugging on the strap of his book bag with one hand, Ian finally took a step toward me. "Because *Ryan* called me last night and told me to come here this morning. He said that our family was hiking today and it was crucial that I meet them on this path."

My mouth flopped open and closed again. "He *Parent Trapped* us? But why?"

Ian chewed on his lower lip. "I think—I think he wanted us to meet up. That this is his way of letting us know that he's okay with this. With *us*."

I know what he was saying made sense, but I couldn't wrap my brain around the fact that Ryan did all this. Although it did kind of feel like Kathy had a hand in this, too. Probably a lot.

But what now?

My heart squeezed painfully. The biggest obstacle to us being together was Ryan, and he was basically giving us his blessing on a silver platter. Metaphorically speaking. But if that was the case, then why didn't Ian look any happier? His face was blank as he studied his phone. It was hard to tell how he was feeling, if he was feeling anything.

Maybe this still didn't change anything.

Even as my heart sunk, I forced myself to turn away. My phone buzzed in my pocket, but I refused to look. It was probably Kathy or Ryan checking to see if their plan worked. They apparently forgot what a colossal idiot their brother was. Gigantic. Monstrous. Astronomical.

Whatever. I was done taking the first step. If he wanted to just forget everything, then I could—

"Yo, Nina." His voice was such a perfect imitation of Rocky's lazy drawl that I stopped in my tracks. "I think you have a text."

I jerked around to look at him, but he just gave me a half smile and nodded. Plus, the look in his eyes were so warm that my whole body tingled. With my breath caught in my throat, I dug for my phone.

IAN: Yes, I believe in love at first sight. It happened right here in this very spot. As soon as I saw you standing there on the path, with your head turned away, trying to look nonchalant while blood was dripping down your knee, I was lost. And I haven't been able to find my way back since.

IAN: My heart broke once. When you asked me if I was in love with anyone now. It took every ounce of willpower for me to not instantly grab you into my arms and kiss you again after you got out of the car. To tell you how much you meant to me and how much it tore me apart to walk away.

IAN: My favorite place in the world used to be on this hiking path. Still is. For a lot of reasons. But the most important one is because of you. Because I'm right here with you. This is where we met and this is where I'm about to kiss you in ten seconds and never let go.

My vision was blurry now, but I could still see that Ian had turned around. That he moved forward until he was right in front of me. He lifted my face with his hands. His palms cupped the sides of my cheeks, and he wiped away a few tears that escaped with his thumbs. And then he did exactly what he promised in the text.

He kissed me.

His arms wrapped around my shoulders, looping down my waist, as he pulled me closer. This time he was the one who couldn't stop moving as he stroked my face, my hair, the length of my arms. Tracing a burning path all around my body. And all I could do was hold on to his arms and kiss him back with all the love and longing that I felt.

When we finally stopped to breath, Ian kissed the top of my forehead and hugged me. "Can we start over?"

My face was squished against his shoulder, but I didn't mind. He smelled so good. "Like completely over? A new meet cute and everything?"

"I don't know. I kind of like the way we met." He leaned back and grinned down at me. "Being the hero makes me seem really good."

Raising an eyebrow, I scoffed. "And that's exactly why we need a redo."

He used the tip of his index finger to push my eyebrow back down again. "But if you really want to redo the meet cute, this is kind of the perfect place to do that."

Forcing myself to take a step back even though all I wanted to do was go back into his arms, I held out my hand. "Hi, I'm Nina. Still short for Nina. First, I'm allergic to dogs and don't know anything about superheroes. Especially not Spider-Man. And I used to have some unresolved daddy issues until an awesome guy helped me resolve them recently."

Ian snickered but reached out to grasp my hand like we were at a job interview. "My name's Ian. I have a twin brother, although I'm the more handsome twin. I'm horrible at playing piano and I like to save cute damsels in distress who help me figure out how much of an ass I am. And yet somehow she loves me anyway."

"This cute damsel of yours sounds pretty smart."

His eyes twinkled at me. "Not nearly as much as your awesome guy."

I shrugged innocently. "He's not too bad. He sucks at laser tag though."

"Ouch, that really hurts." He tugged me toward the big rock by the tree and sat down. With his arm anchored around my shoulders, I leaned my head against him and let out a soft sigh of happiness.

His fingers played with a couple strands of my hair. "Now I kind of wish I didn't live so far away. It'll suck not being able to see each other every day when school starts."

Hearing him make plans for us made my stomach flutter. I shrugged and tried to play it cool as I reached out to hold his other hand. "We still have another month and a half until that happens. And we could just see how it goes."

"Yeah, and I'll come back each weekend." He nudged the tip of my nose with his. "Maybe I'll even visit in the middle of the week if you're nice. For you, I'll brave the shitty Austin traffic any day of the week." He hesitated and frowned. "Okay, maybe not game day traffic, but I swear, *any* other day and time. So now that we got the introductions out of the way, can we go back to the kissing part?"

Letting out a deep breath, I shrugged. "I guess we could. There's no point in putting it off."

His eyebrow rose. "Don't force yourself if it's too much trouble."

By now my cheeks were hurting from smiling so hard. "Eh, I think I can suffer a bit. Since I'm such a nice person."

"Suffer, my ass."

He started to tug me in for another kiss, but I pulled away. With a serious expression, I chewed on my lower lip. "But first, can you do me a favor?"

"Anything."

This time I couldn't keep the grin off my face. "Can you say 'Yo, Nina,' again?"

His laughter seemed to echo through the trees. "Out of everything I just said, all the promises and declarations, you just want to hear the Rocky quote again?"

"Of course. You know, Rocky only calls Adrian that."

His smile was as slow as his words. "Because she's the love of his life."

My heart soared when he said the word *love*, and I couldn't help tugging his head down for another deep kiss.

This time when our lips touched though, it was different. It wasn't explosive or desperate like the first time. It wasn't even sweet and melting like the other ones. This kiss was long and lingering. Full of promises and relief. And the minty freshness on Ian's breath was addicting. I couldn't get enough.

As though he read my mind, his hand drifted up toward the back of my neck. His fingers sunk into my hair as he pulled me even closer. Not that he needed to. His touch made me want to sink even more into him. Like butter on toast. A snowball on a hot day. All I wanted to do was wrap my hands into his hair and stroke his shoulders and neck and never let go.

And what made the kiss even more delicious was the fact that we didn't have to. We could stay like this forever if we wanted to.

Well, maybe not forever, but pretty close to it.

Finally, Ian let out a deep, shuddering breath as his arms tightened around my waist. "You know what? I'll be here for game day. Hell, I'll come running back anytime you want as long as you kiss me like that every time."

"Deal." I happily wrapped my arms around his neck. "I told you I don't play fair."

His hand lifted to my face and slowly stroked the side, from the top curve of my cheek down to my chin. And then back up my neck to my earlobe. Like he couldn't stop touching me. "Oh, I've noticed. Guess it's a good thing, then."

"What is?"

Ian bent down until his lips were covering mine again. Just barely. I could feel his smile curve against my mouth, teasing me. My eyes fluttered closed and I shivered. "That I'm not going to play fair either. I'm in this to win."

"Me too." I tilted my head back so I could give him a slow wink. "It's a good thing that we're such an awesome team."

"Oh, definitely. We're the best."

ACKNOWLEDGMENTS

It feels so surreal every time I sit down to write an acknowledgments page because I cannot believe I'm at that point. How what had been this tiny little idea in my head is actually going to be a full-fledged novel in my hands. My very own book that I can stare at lovingly all day like Gollum in *The Lord of the Rings*. In a very non-creepy way.

. . . my precious.

But of course, none of this would ever be possible if it weren't for certain wonderful people in my life.

First and foremost, thank you to my editor, Jennifer Thompson, for helping me make *Just Another Meet Cute* more than I could have ever imagined it to be. I thought my book was good, and then you made it great. Not to toot my own horn, I'm just being honest. To my copy editor and proofreader, Beka Wallin and Emily Heddleson, for catching all my comma mistakes and inaccuracies and helping me learn that em dashes—annoying as they are—are still my nemesis. My eternal gratitude for the entire team at Scholastic, including Stephanie Yang, Nicko Tumamak, Janell Harris, and Victoria Velez for helping to make my dream come true.

A special thank-you for Natascha Morris and Sarah Fisk: Working with both of you has been amazing. Thank you for believing in me, and I hope I'll always have you in my corner for the rest of my writing journey. Guacamole for everyone!

To my wonderful writing partners, Shayda and Rachel. I wouldn't have been able to get this far without your support, so thank you for always being there.

This book in particular wouldn't have certain loveable chaotic characters if it weren't for my entire family. To all the Nguyens, Trans, Woos, Hoangs, etc. Thank you for *unknowingly* helping me with all the inspiration for this book. Maybe someday we'll be able to play Pictionary again.

To my mom and dad, thank you for raising me, loving me, and supporting me my entire life. I miss you every day.

And lastly, to the love of my life . . . Darren Criss.

(Okay, that was only to see if my husband noticed. Most likely he didn't, but I suppose it's only right for me to thank Darren anyway.)

To the other love of my life, my husband, Quynh. Thank you so much for being here for me. For taking me to Barnes and Noble and sitting patiently by the magazine section while I make laps around the store. For only raising an eyebrow when you see me looking at celebrity pictures for "research." For telling everyone to buy my book when you still have no idea what I write.

I love you, Khoi and Harper—more than you know. I'm so glad I stopped for an avocado smoothie all those years ago because my life changed that day I met you.

ABOUT THE AUTHOR

Photo Credit: Thuc Anh Nguyen

Jenn P. Nguyen is the author of two young adult books, *The Way to Game the Walk of Shame* and *Fake It Till You Break It*. She has a degree in business administration from the University of New Orleans and still lives in the city with her husband. Jenn spends her days reading, dreaming up YA romances, and binge-watching Korean dramas all in the name of "research."